Jayne's Endeavour

THE JOY SERIES

Jayne's Endeavour

LAUREN COMPTON

LONG GULLY PRESS

To my sisters, Johanna and Caitlin—
I'm grateful for all the fun memories we
make together.

And for Jessica, my sister-in-law and friend.

Sisters are truly a blessing. I love you all!

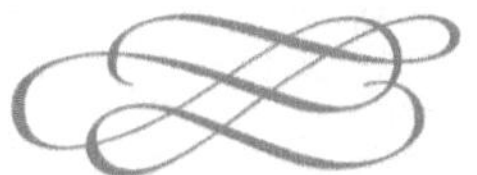

CONTENTS

A Note from the Author

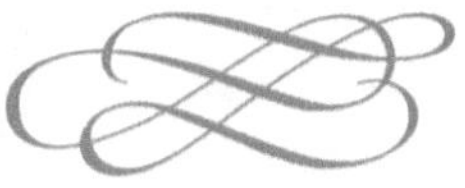

Dear Friend,

I'm so glad you're ready to start a reading adventure. But before you begin, let's take a moment to prepare for the journey! After all, I think we'd all agree that it's important to be careful what we allow into our hearts and minds. God's Word says:

Keep your heart with all diligence; for out of it are the issues of life.
Proverbs 4:23

God's Word is our best guide for knowing what is good for us. You and I need to measure everything we read (and write) against God's standards, including *Jayne's Endeavour*!

My earnest prayer is that you would grow in your faith and have the strength to obey and trust your heavenly Father. No matter what happens, delight in God and always follow Him.

May your faith in our heavenly Father be strengthened!

~ *Lauren Compton*

DELIGHT THYSELF ALSO IN THE
LORD: AND HE SHALL GIVE THEE
THE DESIRES OF THINE HEART.
COMMIT THY WAY UNTO THE
LORD; TRUST ALSO IN HIM; AND
HE SHALL BRING IT TO PASS.

PSALM 37:4-5

1

ONLY A STRANGER

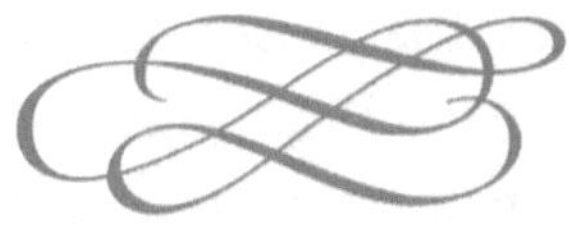

August 1872, Buninyong, Australia

A knock sounded on the door, shattering Jayne's daydream. She stopped scrubbing a moment to stretch her back. "Come in." She wiped soapy hands across her apron, then pushed at the wisps of damp brown hair that strayed around her forehead.

Jed stepped through the door and shut it firmly behind him. With big strides he moved to the fire and held out his work-roughened hands. "I just ran into a man outside who's looking for work."

Jayne's head jerked up in surprise as she studied her father's trusted friend. What was a man doing at their place in search of a job? Surely Jed didn't think they should hire him. At the same time, compassion for the stranger welled up inside of her. "Does he have a family? A home? Where does he come from?"

"Reckon he's about as homeless as a man just off the ship

from Ireland would be." Jed grinned and shook his head. "He's keen. I know that much. Said he was willing to do just about anything. Only wants a low wage. I told him he'd have to talk to you."

Jayne shook the water off her hands and walked over to the door, hoping to catch a glimpse of the stranger. She scanned the open ground around their two-room house but spotted no one. Unwilling to give up, she stared at the stand of gum trees between the house and stable. Her gaze bored into the trunks as if by looking hard enough she would be able to see through them.

A gust of cold wind hit her in the face, making her eyes close and forcing her to retreat. Jayne turned back to Jed. "I wish Daddy—" Biting her lip, she paused and changed the subject. "So the man is from Ireland." The word rolled off her tongue, sending memories, some foggy and others more distinct, flooding through her mind.

She had been just seven years old when she left Ireland on a ship destined for Australia. She could well recall packing up their few belongings, ready to stow them on board. Tucked among the items was a small plank of wood. "To help pass the time," Daddy had said, his eyes twinkling.

For days on end, it had sat there, just a boring plank. Jayne amused herself trying to work out what Daddy would turn it into, but she struggled to see past the plain surface to what it could become. Finally she asked Mam about it.

"Daddy will turn it into something beautiful." Mam smiled at her little daughter. "Wait patiently like a good lass, and you will see soon enough."

As the days grew long and the voyage hard to bear, Daddy picked up the wood and began to carve. Jayne loved to listen to the sound of his knife and watch his hands skilfully move this way and that. It reminded her of home, and the hours she'd lain awake listening to the scrape of Daddy's carpenter tools far into the night.

When she tried to peek over his shoulder at the carving, Daddy shooed her away and said, "It's a surprise. You must not look now. Wait and see. When we get to Australia, then I will show you."

True to his word, one day shortly after they docked at Port Phillip, Daddy called Jayne and her two younger sisters. They found him standing over a crate near the side of the ship, Mam proudly by his side. Something extended from the top of the crate, covered by a piece of cloth Mam had brought from Ireland.

At first, Jayne just stared at the fabric, not knowing what lay beneath it. Then realisation dawned, and she bounced up and down with excitement.

"God has graciously brought us safely to this new land," Daddy said. "Our voyage is over, but our adventure is just begin-ning. If God so blesses us, one day we will have a farm of our own. This plaque will remind us of our long voyage and God's goodness to us. It will stand on our farm as a reminder to the generations to come. We are all responsible to tell them the story of God's faithfulness." He looked at his two oldest daughters in turn and waited for them to nod. With a flourish, he lifted the cloth. Then with power and excitement radiating through his face and voice, he proclaimed the name carved into the plaque: "Auchenblae—our new home."

While Olivia and Yvonne pressed close to her sides, Jayne traced the word with her finger. How beautiful the plaque was with its elegant lettering and the happy scene that flowed across it. She wondered if their new home would be just as cosy as the hut her father had carved. Would it have trees and birds like the ones that surrounded the etched home? How very glad she felt that their voyage was over, and adventures lay ahead.

Jed spoke, breaking Jayne's reverie. "There's all those trees that still need clearing to meet the land-selection requirements. Reckon it's more than I can get done on my own in a hurry. I could do with a man on the other end of the saw."

Jayne nodded, pondering his words. Perhaps this man was the answer to her prayers. "Do you think he is of the honest and hard-working type?"

"Yep, if looks are anything to go by." Jed ran a hand over his greying beard. "The farm's yours. You need to meet him and decide for yourself."

It took a moment for Jayne to nod in agreement. She felt certain of Jed's judgment, but as he said, the farm belonged to her and her sisters. As the oldest, the responsibility rested on her shoulders. But at eighteen, how could she possibly make all the right decisions? If they lost the farm, it would be her fault.

"The man's waiting at the stable to see you. If you think he's decent-like and you can come to some agreement, he can stay in my hut. Reckon there's room enough for two."

As Jed left to go about his work, Jayne turned to the dish she'd been scrubbing, then paused. It would have to wait. As she untied her apron, she thought of what it would mean for them to have more help around the place. For one thing, she might be able to stay on top of the dishes. She sighed. Things always needed doing faster than she and her sisters could manage. In the past they'd been able to keep up with the daily tasks, but that was before— Jayne shook her head and let the thought drift away.

Instead, she let her mind wander to the man who awaited her. What would he say when he realised his potential employer was a young woman? Would he scorn her attempts to meet the land board requirements? What if she didn't ask the right questions? As doubts continued to creep into her mind, the sound of heavy footsteps approaching the door made her heartbeat quicken. Could it be that the man had come looking for her? Jayne's body tensed as a mixture of anticipation and fear filled her. What would she say to him?

"Jayne?"

Her body sagged with relief at the sound of Jed's voice. She stepped forward and pulled at the door. As it opened, cold wind blasted through the doorway, cutting through her sturdy dress. Jayne shivered, glad for the distraction.

Hands in his pockets as he huddled against the wind, Jed stood before her. "You'll do just fine out there. It's in your blood." His already wrinkled face creased further as he flashed her an encouraging smile. "Reids never give up easily."

Jayne exhaled, trying to release some of the nervous tension that filled her body. "Thank you"—she tried again to make herself relax—"if only I could remember." For the hundredth time, she noted God's provision in her father asking Jed to live with them after he'd been laid off from his job as a station hand.

She returned inside just long enough to grab her woollen cloak from the bedroom. As she stepped into the cold air, she slipped it around her shoulders. Already Jed was nowhere in sight. While trying to avoid the puddles, she patted her hair as she walked, but it rebelled against her touch like a stubborn child. As soon as she managed to get one piece back in place, another strand sprang out in defiance. She let her hand fall to her side. How could she face this man and do the many other things required of her when she couldn't even manage her own hair?

The sharp smell of wet eucalyptus trees stung her nostrils. As Jayne inhaled, filling her lungs with the scented morning air, she wondered when her sisters would return from checking on the sheep. She could picture Olivia and Yvonne strolling along, arm in arm, while Yvonne chattered non-stop about the wildlife around them. Despite her carefree nature, fourteen-year-old Yvonne was fast growing up. Circumstances had a way of making one's outlook change, and the events of the last months had matured both of her sisters from girls into young women. Seeing the change both pleased and saddened her. What kind of future lay ahead for them? The thoughts slipped from her mind as she reached the edge of the trees and glimpsed the stable.

Lifting her eyes to the sky, she prayed for courage before looking back at the familiar building. In the short time they'd been in Buninyong, the stable had grown to be her place of refuge in the winter months. Some of her fondest memories were of helping to clean harnesses and saddles inside those walls with Daddy. She could nearly smell the leather now, all fresh and clean.

Jayne took a step out into the open and glanced at the stable again, realising that once more no one was in sight. Was the man supposed to be waiting inside or outside? Surely in this weather, inside the stable would be more sensible. Making no effort to hurry, she headed for the door. Just as her fingers closed on its handle, she withdrew them and clutched her cloak.

You're a Reid. You can't give up. You must not give in. Without allowing herself more time to worry, Jayne pulled open the door. One hand flew to her heart as she spotted the stranger. Before she realised what was happening, a cry leapt from her mouth.

The tall, dark-haired man spun around. "Morning, miss." He nodded in her direction, a questioning expression crossing his face as he studied her.

She closed her eyes for a moment, trying to gain her composure as dozens of emotions rushed through her mind. Forcing herself to speak, she said in a trembling voice, "I'm Jayne. Jayne

Reid." A shuddering breath sent a tremor through her body. "Owner of Auchenblae." She grimaced. Even to her, the shocked cry and ragged gasp had sounded strange. Not to mention how ridiculous it sounded that she, a young woman, was the owner of this farm. Would he think her incapable?

After another moment's silence, the stranger answered her introduction with an easy smile. "Name's Cass."

His words, and the manner in which he spoke them, made Jayne relax slightly. In a more controlled voice, she asked, "Are you experienced with the cross-cut saw?"

"No, miss. I'm afraid not. But I'm a quick learner, willing to give almost anything a shot." His mouth spread in a grin as he relaxed against a beam.

Jayne's shoulders loosened. Jed was right. Cass did seem eager for a job. She studied the ground, unable to meet Cass's gaze. "I see. Well . . ." Something niggled in her mind. What was it? She forced herself to look into the man's face. His eyes searched hers. Struggling not to look away, Jayne tried to push aside her jitters. "What was it that brought you to Australia?" she said, asking the first question that came to her mind.

An uneasy look crossed the man's face but vanished almost as soon as Jayne noticed it. When he made no move to reply, she filled in the gap for him. "Tales of derring-do and fortune for the taking, perhaps?" Her prompting only caused further awkwardness as he shifted from one foot to the other. Jayne wanted to clutch her head in her hands. One moment he oozed confidence, and the next he seemed uneasy. Her brain was working overtime in its efforts to assess his character.

Finally he said, "Personal matter, miss." He paused and ran a hand over his head. "But I assure you it wasn't gold that brought me to this country."

When he said nothing more, Jayne gave a slow nod. A moment ago, he had seemed so friendly and relaxed, but now? Each word had been carefully weighed. Jayne eyed him. Perhaps he was a private man and didn't like telling much about himself to strangers. She decided to let it pass, though she questioned her wisdom.

Jayne drew in a deep breath of resolve. "If you will apply yourself and are willing to put in a full day of labour, it seems that you can be of use to us. My father selected this piece of crown land in the hope of securing a good future. But the land board dictates that within three years the entire property be fenced, a tenth of the land cultivated, and substantial other improvements made. We have a lot of land that still needs clearing before we can plough and plant it. If we fail to meet any of these requirements, we'll lose everything and be left with no home." Jayne stopped, fearing she might have said too much about their personal situation. Trying to act confident, she went on. "Your job, sir, will be to help us reach these goals."

Grinning, Cass nodded. "I've never been afraid of hard work."

"If that's the case, you'll do well," Jayne said and named a low wage. It was not much, she knew, but it did include a room and meals. Besides, it was all they could afford. If the man wasn't happy, then he would just have to find work elsewhere. As for themselves, if he refused, they would be no worse off than they already were.

Far from looking displeased, Cass sported a satisfied look. Jayne couldn't help but wonder if he looked too satisfied. Surely he could've done better elsewhere. Jayne knew it was partly sympathy that drove her decision. Perhaps she had been unwise. Inwardly she shrugged. If hiring him meant being able to keep her parents' land selection, it would be worth the risk. Locking eyes with him, she said, "You'll be staying out back with Jed. His hut is a few minutes' walk through the trees"—she pointed to a spot opposite the door she had entered—"in that direction."

Cass nodded. "I'm much obliged."

Before either of them were able to make further comment, Jed entered through the large stock door behind Cass. "How's it going in here?" he asked, looking at Jayne.

She gave him a small smile. "I believe you've got yourself a sawing partner."

Jed nodded his approval. Then he turned to Cass and slapped him on the back. "Good on you, mate." He gave Cass a firm handshake.

With the men's attention elsewhere for a moment, Jayne took the opportunity to study their new employee. He was a well-built and strong looking man—just right for the hard work that would be required of him. From his appearance, she guessed he must be only a bit younger than her father, about forty perhaps. Her gaze took in his dark wavy hair. Seeing it brought back her earlier feelings, and suddenly, all she wanted was to be away from the men. Hurriedly, she excused herself and walked outside with a throbbing heart.

All around her the sounds of the bush filled the air, but Jayne paid them little mind. Mechanically, she placed one foot in front of the other, focusing only on putting distance between herself and the stable.

Feeling tears threatening, Jayne began to hurry. She stumbled a few times over fallen branches, but still she didn't stop. She needed to be where no one would see her crying. Only once she reached a thick cluster of gums did she allow herself to rest.

Panting, Jayne stood there a moment. At first she wiped away the tears that splashed down her cheeks, mingling with the mud and leaves at her feet, but it was no use. She leaned her forehead against the trunk of a tree and let her emotions tumble out like waterfalls. Sob after sob wrenched her body with scarcely time to catch her breath between each one.

When they finally subsided, Jayne had no idea how much time had elapsed. Exhausted, she sank down to the leaf-strewn ground beneath the tree. Her back sagged against the support of its trunk, while the cold seeped into her body.

Jayne tilted her head back and looked up. To her aching heart, the trees seemed to offer a sense of strength in their branches that stretched far above her head. *Strength.* Jayne lingered over the word, tossing it about in her mind. She felt that all her weaknesses and doubts were swirling about, crowding in on her. Yes, if ever she, Jayne Elizabeth Reid, needed strength, it was now. She needed strength to not only face whatever the future held, but also the scars that the past had left on her.

The five months since she'd knelt by her parents' coffins seemed like five days and yet somehow like five years all at the same time. The sorrow was still fresh and new, yet it felt like ages since she'd seen her parents.

At any moment she half expected to hear Daddy whistling a tune on his way back to the house or Mam breaking into song, singing one of the hymns that had never been far from her lips. Gail. That was what Daddy had called Mam— like the songbird, the nightingale.

When she had entered the stable to meet Cass, she thought it was her tall, strong, dark-haired Daddy standing there, waiting to greet her. In his place though, she found a stranger, only a stranger.

Another wave of emotions burst forth, and Jayne rocked forward on her knees. "Oh! Daddy, Mammy, why, why did you leave me? The burden is too much to bear." Her words ended in another sob.

Then as if Mam was sitting right there with her, Jayne recalled her loving voice. *Of course you cannot bear this burden, Jayne. It is far too great, far too heavy a burden to bear alone. Give your burden to Jesus, my lass. Let Him bear it for you.* Jayne murmured the words silently to herself, then buried her face in her hands.

On that sorrowful night, she never dreamed how much she would need to recall Mam's soft words of wisdom. How many times had she played them through her mind over the past five months? Sometimes when she lay in bed at night, Jayne wondered if somehow Mam had been aware that the fever would claim her life only a few weeks after it claimed Daddy's. How Mam's death had shocked her. Always, Mam seemed so strong, able to cope with anything. And Daddy—Jayne shook her head as salty tears flowed down her cheeks and onto her lap.

In her anguish, Jayne spoke aloud. "Jesus, Mam was right." She rocked back and forth, her head in her hands. "I can't bear this alone." She sobbed. "Please Lord, give me wisdom. Show me if I'm doing the right thing."

As Jayne spoke, her thoughts came in a rush. Should she go back to Ireland? Surely the relatives she now knew only by name would take them in or at least give them a fresh start. But as quickly as the thoughts had come, the reply shot back quicker and with such force that it startled her. No! Dad and Mam worked so hard to create a new life here. So much energy and life had been poured into the dream of this farm. Her parents had grown to love the Australian bush and the wildness of the country. No, she must not throw it all away. She could not, and she would not. This was home now.

Jayne leaned back against the tree trunk and gazed up

between the branches to the grey sky above. It reminded her of the storm-tossed sea that carried her family between the continents. How quickly eleven years had passed since the voyage, until her homeland remained a blur of childish memories. But there was one encounter on the day they'd embarked from Ireland that was forever ingrained in her mind and heart.

As they prepared to set sail for Australia, she'd somehow lost hold of her mother's hand amid the bustling crowds at the dock. Terrified, seven-year-old Jayne called out for her mother, trying to see through the legs and skirts around her.

After long minutes of searching and crying, Jayne caught a glimpse of the glistening sea. It called her closer and closer. When she spied the flapping sails and tall masts of a ship as it bobbed up and down on the waves, she began to picture herself as a sailor's wife, adventuring the far seas and finding hidden treasures. As her imagination drifted, so did her little legs, until she had wandered to the edge of the wharf and could look down into the depths of the ocean. Enthralled by the soothing sounds of the waves as they crashed against the wooden pillars, she leaned against a low railing and started to grow sleepy. Suddenly, her peaceful dreaming was shattered by a growl from behind her. Jerking around, she spotted the largest dog she'd ever seen—its black head almost level with her own. Teeth bared, the mongrel charged, knocking Jayne onto her back by the edge of the wharf.

Whimpering, Jayne pressed herself against the planks as the dog's panting echoed in her ears, drowning out every other noise. Its teeth loomed closer and closer. Terror rendered her limbs powerless. Even if she survived those teeth, what if the dog knocked her into the dark sea below? What lurked in the water's depths?

Jayne's entire body felt frozen. Just as she was preparing to feel the sharpness of teeth in her flesh, a larger shadow loomed above the dog. It was her daddy. Towering above the dog, he looked fiercer and taller than a warrior. With his strong carpenter's hands, he swung her to his chest.

Relief made Jayne's body limp as she listened to the beating of her father's heart. She was safe. She could rest fully in her father's love and his ability to protect her from anything that would harm her. No matter what lay ahead here or in the new land that awaited them, she had no reason for fear.

Jayne's thoughts drifted from the faraway scene back to her present trials. What about Olivia and Yvonne? Was she being unfair to them? How could she raise and protect her sisters all by herself? Would her decision to stay at Auchenblae put them through unnecessary hardship and danger? The silence that followed her questions seemed to make them reverberate in the bushland around her.

Back to Jayne's mind rushed the words of a middle-aged woman from a few weeks ago. "You'll only cause your sisters more grief and hardship with your foolish notions. A girl, a young girl, running a farm. Hmph!" Mrs. Sterling's eyes had flashed. "What would your poor parents think? They'd roll in their graves if they knew what you were up to. I say you would do well to listen to your elders, Jayne Reid."

Once again Jayne wished she had never become acquainted with the meddling woman her mother had met at a charity afternoon tea. She had tried to explain to Mrs. Sterling on several occasions that it was not as if she were running the farm all by herself. Jed was always ready to help and offer much-needed advice. Besides, she thought her parents would whole-heartedly approve, and that she would bring them honour, not shame, by keeping their hopes and dreams alive.

As for Mrs. Sterling's accusation of only a young girl running a farm—Jayne clenched her teeth. She was no longer a girl but a woman. Yet this time Mrs. Sterling's words had cut deep, touching on the very thing that worried Jayne most—her sisters.

A flock of cockatoos flew across the sky, piercing her thoughts with their harsh cries. Jayne breathed in a lungful of the crisp winter air, then exhaled. Their cries seemed to represent all the cries of her heart. What if Mrs. Sterling had been right? Was she being selfish? The thought filled Jayne with horror.

As if in answer to her questions, a snatch of music drifted to Jayne on the breeze. It came to her faintly at first, then grew stronger until Jayne recognised the singer's voice. It was Yvonne. Her two sisters must be walking nearby. She pressed herself closer to the tree trunk, hoping she wouldn't be discovered in the state she was in.

She squeezed her eyes shut and focused on the words, trying to figure out what the song was. After a moment, Jayne realised that the tune was familiar, but she didn't recognise the words. Her youngest sister seemed to be making them up as she went. Only one phrase held importance to Jayne. It seemed to be crying out to her.

God is our source of joy even 'midst the darkest of times.

2
A Neighbour's Concern

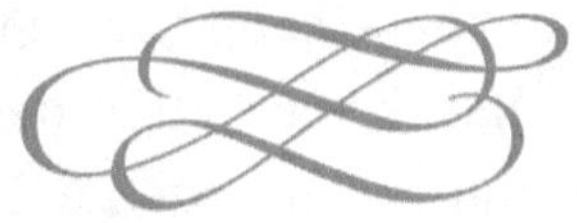

Jayne slung her father's saddle onto Betsie's broad chestnut back and ran a hand over the leather, still feeling torn between her desire to ride Wattle and the sensibleness of choosing Betsie. Her father's horse was energetic. Betsie was reliable, unlikely to baulk no matter how many times a rabbit darted in front of her.

She adjusted the saddle's position, then scratched Betsie's forehead. Despite her quandary over which horse to ride, she couldn't help but feel a fondness for the faithful mare. As she tightened the girth, Jayne breathed in the stable's mingled aroma of horses, leather, and fresh hay—the rich smell of memories.

As much as she wished that Mrs. O'Donnell was in full health, she was glad for an excuse to make the trip to their nearest neighbour. Though there was a handful of other neighbours scattered around them in various directions, the

O'Donnells were the ones who had gone out of their way to make the Reids feel welcome from the very start. Perhaps it was their shared faith that made the difference.

Until her parent's deaths, it hadn't been uncommon for Mr. O'Donnell to pop by on his way back from town to discuss the best methods of tree felling, fencing, or the many other tasks that land selection demanded. And how well Jayne remembered the afternoons when the day's work had been accomplished faster than normal, and Mam would hitch up the cart and take them to visit with Mrs. O'Donnell. They'd never gone visiting empty-handed but always came back richer than when they'd left.

How she longed for those happy visits to resume. Maybe once Mrs. O'Donnell's health was better, they could gather up some sewing projects and spend a productive afternoon with their neighbour once more. Yet Jayne didn't know if she'd be able to face the visits—not without her mam there too.

Jayne led Betsie outside and stopped to check the girth strap. Already it hung two inches below Betsie's belly. Grimacing, Jayne tightened it again. Ahead a twig snapped. Then Jayne's ears caught the scuffle of footsteps sliding through wet leaves. A couple more seconds of waiting revealed the source. Walking towards her came Olivia—a small calico sack in one hand and a billycan swinging from the other. Behind her followed Yvonne, who skipped along with a dainty step.

"All ready?" Olivia asked. She flipped one of her light brown plaits over her shoulder and held out the billy. "If you're not careful, you'll end up having a bath in beef tea. Why don't you just take the cart?"

Jayne shrugged. "I haven't been riding for ages." She walked Betsie in a circle, then halted a couple of feet from her youngest sister. While Yvonne stroked the star beneath Bestie's forelock,

Jayne slid her hand into the warm gap between Betsie and the girth strap. Her fingers tingled, glad for a haven from the cold. As she tightened the strap one more notch, the leather creaked, then settled into place. With both hands she leaned her weight into the stirrup. When the saddle stayed put, she began searching for somewhere to mount.

Olivia pointed out a fallen tree. When the threesome reached the log, Yvonne plonked down on one end of it and tilted her blond head up towards Jayne. "I wish we were all going. We used to have such fun."

Without answering, Jayne leapt onto the log beside her sister. Her feet slipped on the moss-covered wood. Scrambling for balance, she wavered and threw her arms out to keep from falling. Olivia tried to steady her but had both hands already full. Clutching for something to stop her fall, Jayne managed to find Olivia's shoulder in time to avoid landing headfirst in a prickly bush.

As Jayne released her grip on her shoulder, Olivia laughed. "You nearly got a wash in beef tea sooner than I expected."

Jayne shook her head and planted her feet firmly on the log. Then she turned to answer Yvonne. Her younger sister's eyes were full of amusement, and Jayne felt a smile pulling at her own lips. Then she sobered. "I know we did. But the three of us would tire Mrs. O'Donnell too much." She placed her foot in the stirrup and gathered her skirts in one hand. As she positioned her other hand on the saddle and sunk her weight into the stirrup, the saddle fell sideways. A cry of alarm flew from her lips as she tried to yank her foot from the stirrup to avoid being flung to the ground.

As the stirrup loosened its hold, Betsie sidestepped towards her. Jayne tilted backwards. At the last possible second, she righted herself and landed feet first in the mud. Brown spots flew upwards, splattering the underside of her petticoat.

"On second thought, it might be a mud bath you'll get." Olivia shook her head at Jayne, but a smile danced on her lips.

Jayne laughed half-heartedly as she righted the saddle. "Perhaps you were right about taking the cart." She let out her breath and leaned her head against the saddle to calm her racing heart. After retightening the girth and making certain the saddle was not going to slip again, Jayne remounted. With a feeling of satisfaction, she looked down at Olivia. "Hopefully I'll reach the O'Donnell's in one piece." Then she locked eyes with Yvonne. "When I get back, I'll tell you all about the visit. Maybe next time we'll all be able to go."

Yvonne nodded, her face taking on a wistful expression. "Almost like old times."

Still smiling, Olivia passed the billy up to Jayne. Then she reached up to attach the sack to the saddle. "Are you sure you'll manage all right?" she asked.

Jayne nodded, eyeing the cloth Olivia had wound around the billy to keep the lid from falling off. "Don't worry. I'll take it slow on the way and make up for it coming back."

Reins in one hand and billy perched precariously on her lap with the other, Jayne called goodbye and set off at a steady walk. Once she reached the road that connected Auchenblae with the O'Donnell farm, she felt grateful for her decision to ride Betsie. The road was so full of potholes from the recent heavy rains that travel in their cart would have been uncomfortable at best. She certainly wouldn't have arrived resembling anything that looked respectable.

Just then Betsie stumbled and lost her footing on the slippery ground. Jayne lurched forward, causing the billy to tilt. As she yanked on the reins, beef tea seeped through the fabric onto her leg, while Betsie slid farther towards a water-filled ditch. Jayne leaned backwards and did her best to grip the billy. The moment Betsie stopped her sliding and stood upright, Jayne inspected the circle of wetness on her dress. The patch was dark and cold. Keeping a firm grasp on the reins, she worked to tighten the billy cloth. Then shivering, she forced herself to ride even more slowly.

Jayne was relieved when the O'Donnell's house finally came into view. She walked Betsie up to the small bark hut, then stared at the billy in her hand. The wind buffeted her as she waited in the hope Mr. O'Donnell would emerge from one of the out-buildings. But aside from the clucking of chooks, everything was silent. Jayne contemplated her next move, but only two options presented themselves. The first was to wait for help to arrive. The second was to somehow dismount with the billy in hand. Neither appeared very satisfactory.

Jayne slipped her feet out of the stirrups and tried to throw her leg over the saddle while keeping the billy in front of her. But she soon saw that this would only succeed in spilling whatever was left of its contents. Having no other option, she manoeuvred her body until she sat facing out. From this position the ground looked much farther away. Clutching the billy in both hands while the reins sat unattended, she prepared to descend. With her back to the saddle, she slid downwards slowly but quickly gained momentum. As her feet hit the earth, she heard a sickening rip and turned to find her dress caught on the stirrup.

A warm flush spread on her face. Jayne placed the billy on the ground and freed her dress with as much dignity as she could muster. A three-inch tear stared back at her. To make matters worse, from the knee down her dress was splattered in mud. Jayne groaned. At eighteen she ought to be old enough to stop getting into this sort of a mess. With a shake of her head, she stooped to retrieve the billy from its spot on the ground. It still felt full. At least something had arrived unharmed. She consoled herself with this fact before noticing the mud that oozed around the billy's sides—more mess. Even with her eyes closed in frustration, all she saw was mud.

With the billy held far from her dress, Jayne managed to tie Betsy loosely to the hitching post with one hand. Then she squelched to where Olivia had tied the sack. With numb fingers, she unfastened the knotted calico and tugged it free. Once the sack was firmly in her grip, she headed for refuge from the mud and wetness.

Jayne tapped softly at the hut's door, not wanting to wake Mrs. O'Donnell if she slept. No welcoming call or movement came from inside, so Jayne pushed open the door and tiptoed in. A glow from the fire illuminated the sleeping form of her friend. Even though Jayne longed to hear how the O'Donnells fared, the sight filled her heart with gladness. There would be time to exchange news later. For now the warmth and rest would do her friend good.

The sound of raspy breathing accompanied Jayne's steps to the centre of the room. With one hand she upended the sack on the table. The plum pudding rolled out and landed with a thump. Her eyes flew to Mrs. O'Donnell, but to her relief, the woman slept on without so much as a flicker of the eyelids.

Even the coarse cloth that still concealed it couldn't mask the pudding's richness, and Jayne's stomach growled as she sniffed the air. A fat sliver after her ride in the cold would certainly help to allay her hunger. Still eyeing the pudding, she set the billy on the table. As Jayne unwound the billy's cloth, the sound of a moan brought her head up.

Mrs. O'Donnell's eyes fluttered, and she stirred in her chair.

In a moment she was staring back at Jayne. "My dear, you should have woken me," she said without so much as a how-do-you-do. "But never mind that now. I've been hoping you would come for days." Mrs. O'Donnell clutched her chest and coughed.

Jayne opened her mouth to ask if she'd been feeling worse, but Mrs. O'Donnell cut her off.

"I would've come myself if Evan hadn't insisted I stay indoors. I have been feeling rather poorly, but still, I think he ought to have let me go due to the circumstances." She wheezed and pushed herself up straighter. "Never mind. You're here now, and that's what matters."

"I hope the wet weather hasn't made your cough worse," Jayne said, trying to work out what circumstances Mrs. O'Donnell was referring to. The cloth she had finished unwinding dropped to the table.

"Never mind my health." Mrs. O'Donnell dismissed Jayne's query with a wave of her hand. "It's you I'm worried about, dear."

Jayne bit her lip, wondering if Mrs. O'Donnell's concern had anything to do with keeping Daddy's land selection.

"That new farmhand of yours, what's his name? Cassidy or Casey? Oh, never mind. Something is wrong. That's the only matter of importance." Mrs. O'Donnell paused, seeming to notice the confusion on Jayne's face. "Oh dear, I'm afraid I'm getting you all muddled up. Let me start from the beginning." Another coughing fit delayed the flow of her words. When it ended, she adjusted her shawl and settled back in her rocker. "After visiting at your place late last week, Mrs. Arthur dropped in to see how I was faring. That's when she told me about your new farm hand. What did you say his name is, dear?"

"Cass, but—"

"Ah, that's right. I remember now," Mrs. O'Donnell said, still trying to catch her breath. "As I was saying, Mrs. Arthur told me all about your new farmhand, Casey." A smile brightened her face. "You know how she can talk."

"Yes, I mean no—but what does this have to do with your concern for me?" Jayne's confused gaze dropped to her skirt. Upon being reminded of its tattered appearance, she stepped farther behind the table.

"That's just it." Mrs. O'Donnell's face lost its brightness as she hurried on. "A few days before Mrs. Arthur's visit, my husband was heading to town when a stranger hailed him from behind and said all friendly-like, 'Excuse me, sir. I'm looking for a man by the name of Brian Reid. I'd be obliged if you could point me to his farm.'"

A pang of grief struck Jayne as she wondered what man could have been seeking her father. Didn't he know Daddy was dead and had been for many months? Surely Mrs. O'Donnell didn't think the man that spoke to her husband was the same person they'd hired. It couldn't be. Cass hadn't said a word about her father. And how could he have known who they were? He certainly didn't act like he knew anything about them.

Mrs. O'Donnell placed a hand on her chest as her words were interrupted by more coughing. When she could speak again, she said, "My husband informed Casey the farm was only a wee distance away, but he wouldn't be a-findin' Mr. Reid there now."

As tears filled Jayne's eyes and slipped down her cheeks, heavy boots stamped on the boards placed outside the door. A moment later the door grated on its hinges, and Mr. O'Donnell stepped inside. His eyes took in Jayne's strained face. "Afternoon," he said as he gave her a kind smile. Placing his hat on a hook by the door, he turned to his wife. "Ye aren't filling the lassie's head with nonsense, are ye?"

Mrs. O'Donnell looked down and tugged at the quilt on her lap without answering. Then she nodded.

A slight frown creased Mr. O'Donnell's forehead. "I wouldn't have sent the man to their house if I hadn't thought he was decent-like. Stop worryin' the lassie."

Mrs. O'Donnell stared into the fire and said in a small voice, "I was only concerned for the lassies, living all alone like they do. Something doesn't seem right. What if—" Her chest rising and falling with effort, she met her husband's eyes.

"Now, Aileen." His voice softened. "I know ye are worried, but Jed be a wise man. He'll keep an eye on things."

"I'm grateful for your concern, Mrs. O'Donnell," Jayne said, finding the courage to speak up. Despite the calmness of her voice, a sense of dread nestled in the pit of her stomach. Had she made some sort of terrible mistake when she hired Cass? She pushed the thought away, forcing herself to look only at the facts. "But so far Cass has been a great help. He—" Her voice wavered. "He applies himself to every task we give him. On top of that, if he sees something that needs doing, he goes right ahead and does it. I really can't fault him." She swallowed. "Besides, we need the help right now, or we'll never make it in time. Cass seems like an answer to our prayers."

Mr. O'Donnell nodded. "Ye lassies have taken on a mighty big task. I'm right pleased Cass is helping some with the burden."

Despite his reassuring words, Jayne still couldn't help fearing the implications of Mrs. O'Donnell's tale. Perhaps it wasn't true. Maybe her friend had dreamt it up. She had been very ill. But then, hadn't Mr. O'Donnell just confirmed the story? Jayne shook her head to clear her confusion.

"Aren't you a dear!" Mrs. O'Donnell's voice sounded breathy as her eyes fastened on the food items in front of Jayne. "I've always been able to count on the Reids to show compassion to us. First your dear mother"—her eyes glistened—"and now you lassies. May God bless you." Mrs. O'Donnell grasped her stomach as a cough racked her small frame. Gasping for breath, she lurched to the edge of her chair.

Jayne rushed to Mrs. O'Donnell's side and rubbed her back. When the coughing fit subsided, Mrs. O'Donnell slumped against her chair, still struggling for breath. Jayne eyed her with concern. The woman's hunched body and drawn face made her appear frail and old. Earlier she had seemed so relaxed as she rested by the fire. Now Jayne feared that any sign of well-being had been a mirage.

With this worry came a new concern. It was August, and the bitterness of winter was not yet over. If the temperature continued to drop like it had the past few days, they might even have snow before the week was over. With Mr. O'Donnell working outside, the fire could easily burn out, leaving the room chilly. How would Mrs. O'Donnell's body fare in frigid weather?

"My bones are aching. Must mean the weather is going to turn foul again." Mrs. O'Donnell interrupted Jayne's musings, rubbing her knee as she spoke. "You'll excuse the dirty floor won't you, Jayne dear? I'm afraid this sickness has knocked the wind out of me." She broke off as another fit of coughing accented her words. Her body doubled over, and she drew a wheezing breath. "Don't mind me. Once this dreadful cough starts, it scarcely sees fit to let me be." As if to prove that she was right, another spasm wracked her body. When it subsided, Mrs. O'Donnell sagged against the arm of her chair, too exhausted to say anything more.

Jayne knelt beside Mrs. O'Donnell's chair, ignoring the cold that seeped into her bones and the discomfort of the roughly planked floor. Her hand moved in rhythmic circles over Mrs.

O'Donnell's back. All the while talking pleasantly of Olivia and Yvonne, she tucked the intricately made quilt more snugly around the older woman's legs.

"Talk to them," Mam had said, referring to the sick and elderly she loved so. "Tell them of pleasant times. It is of more worth than the most expensive treatment."

Mam had been right. Time and time again, Jayne watched as Mam drew people out of their misery and self-pity by talking to them of cheery things.

As Jayne continued to talk, Mr. O'Donnell placed a log on the fire, sending sparks flying. The added fuel served as a welcome defence against the cold that threatened the room.

When she could think of nothing else to say, Jayne lapsed into silence. Lifting her head, she listened. Wind howled around the small hut. She knew it must be late but made no move to leave. Instead, she moved silently to the other side of Mrs. O'Donnell. Before crouching down again, she stretched her arm, trying to relieve the ache that gripped it. At least on this side, she was closer to the fire. Heat stretched out its fingers to drive away the chill settling into her bones. A blast of wind made the roof creak. As if in defiance to the stormy weather, the fire crackled and popped. Jayne shivered. Despite the dancing flames, the little hut still seemed too cold.

Pushing aside her own thoughts and discomforts, Jayne continued to talk, this time about spring with its lush paddocks full of grass for the stock and lanes edged with wildflowers. As she chattered, she realised with surprise that the ache in her own heart didn't seem quite as bad. A spark kindled within her at the thought of spring and its newness. Deep down she knew things would never be the same again, but she couldn't help hoping that maybe with the coming of spring everything would be all right.

Mrs. O'Donnell shifted in her chair, and Jayne realised she'd been so deep in thought that she'd stopped talking. Mrs. O'Donnell's wheezing was less pronounced, but each breath still came only with painful effort.

Jayne watched Mr. O'Donnell reach for the billy and dip a pannikin into the tea. As if sensing her gaze, he looked up. "Ye best head on home. The weather be growin' chillier by the minute."

Jayne bit her lip, then nodded in agreement. A far-off rumble of thunder filled the air as she looked back at Mrs. O'Donnell. The woman's eyes lay closed, and she appeared to have drifted into a restful sleep.

"Don't ye worry none," Mr. O'Donnell said. "I'll see to it that she drinks a steaming cup of this mix when she wakes. 'Spect it'll do her a world of good. Appreciate yer kindness to her." He set the pannikin on the table and looked at Jayne closely. "Now, don't ye go worrin' about what Aileen done said. If I hadn't thought the man to be deservin' of trust, I wouldn't have pointed him to yer farm." He waited for her to nod, then without another word, he picked up the sack that lay on the table and started for the door.

Jayne placed a hand on Mrs. O'Donnell's forehead, trying to ease the worry that filled her heart. The coolness beneath her fingers offered Jayne a sliver of comfort. Her eyes lingered once more on Mrs. O'Donnell's relaxed face before she turned to follow Mr. O'Donnell to the door.

The wind wailed as Mr. O'Donnell pulled the door open just wide enough for Jayne to step out. Then he too ventured into the bitter cold. Once the door was firmly shut, Mr. O'Donnell turned towards her. "I'm a mite worried about her, Jayne," he said, not heeding his own words of a few minutes ago. "She's been sick-like before, but this time she just isn't bouncin' back like she used to. I'm doing all I can for her . . ." He ran a hand over his head. When he stopped speaking, their eyes locked.

The worry in his face brought back her own feeling of helplessness as she stood by the bed of her ailing parents, and Jayne jerked her gaze away. Her muscles tensed as she tried to hide her shaking, but it was no use. She risked another look at Mr. O'Donnell. This physically strong man, used to providing for himself and his wife, now looked to her for help. What could she say? Unable to stand his desperation, she blurted out the first thing that came to her mind. "We'll be praying for Mrs. O'Donnell." Jayne paused and for the slightest moment touched his arm. "For you both." Such simple words. Why had they been such a struggle?

His eyes lost their hopeless look, and he nodded. "Thank ye." Motioning to the stable behind the house, he said, "I put yer horse in the end stall. It looked a bit poorly standing out in the cold, all wet."

An image of Betsie standing huddled against the stormy weather flashed through her mind, and immediately, Jayne felt guilty and embarrassed. Her preoccupation with Mrs. O'Donnell had made her forget to think about the well-being of her mount.

Mr. O'Donnell strode towards the stable, and in a few moments he returned, leading Betsie behind him. He looked out at the gathering clouds and wind and shook his head. "Don't like the look of the weather none. I wouldn't spare yer horse. I'd go with ye, but I don't much like the thought of leavin' Aileen more than I have to while she's so poorly." He handed the reins to Jayne and with a nod turned towards the house. The door shut behind him with a thud, leaving Jayne alone.

Jayne shivered and pulled her cloak closer as she turned to

retighten Betsie's girth. As she bent her head, icy wind whipped Betsie's mane across her eyes and mouth. The lash of wiry hair left her face stinging. Ignoring the discomfort, Jayne tugged on the reins. "Come on, girl. Looks like it's just you and me."

Dodging between puddles and the muddiest spots, Jayne picked her way towards the road. Partway there, her feet sank into ankle-deep mud. The suction pulled at her boots as she struggled to free herself. Balancing herself against Betsie's neck, she managed to pull one foot free. The mud squelched as her second boot came unstuck. She edged around the mud until she came to firmer ground.

Upon reaching the road, Jayne began her hunt for a makeshift mounting block. As she trudged on without finding anything, she hunched her shoulders against the wind. Finally, a few yards off the road, Jayne spotted what she was after. She manoeuvred Betsie until she stood parallel to the fallen log. From beneath her dirty skirts, two mud-clumped boots appeared. With a sigh Jayne wiped them as best as she could on the grass and prepared to mount. Her heart leapt with gratitude as she noticed that the saddle felt dry. How thoughtful Mr. O' Donnell was.

Once seated, Jayne paused to pull her scarf over her mouth and nose. Then she urged Betsie into an energetic trot. A glance at the horizon told her that more rain was on the way. Clouds continued to gather in dark masses, looming ominously above the treetops as the sky blackened. Following Mr. O'Donnell's advice, she prodded her horse into a canter.

Halfway home the skies opened, and torrents of rain poured down upon her. Jayne fought to maintain her grip on the slippery reins as she peered ahead, but the gathering darkness and rain distorted everything more than a couple of feet away. Raindrops splattered on her face, forcing her eyes to narrow to tiny slits.

Right above her head, two birds squawked and flew to cover.

Betsie championed on, head bent to one side, her only protest to shake her neck and slow to a trot. Though it probably wasn't possible to get any wetter than she already was, Jayne tucked her head to her chest, finally succumbing to her desire to avoid the oncoming rain. From this position she tried to fix her eyes on the road beneath Betsie's hooves. At least the constant blur of mud and water assured her they were still moving forward.

Jayne allowed Betsie to pick her own way up the trail that led past the house to the stable. The rain still fell in torrents but seemed to have lessened. Through the trees, she could just make out the glow of a lantern shining through the window. Rather than bolstering her spirits, it only caused her heart to sink lower as her longing for the warmth of a fire intensified.

Seeming to share Jayne's feelings, Betsie nodded her head and broke into a trot again as they passed the house. As the stable came into view a low nicker erupted from deep within Betsie's chest. Without waiting for a command, she slid to a stop right in front of the double door.

Jayne's fingers were so numb that only her eyes told her that she still held the reins. She slid stiffly to the ground and leaned against Betsie, allowing the horse's warmth to seep into her body. The comforting sensation only lasted a moment before Betsie nudged Jayne with her nose, nearly walking right over her in her eagerness to get inside.

"All right, girl." Jayne sighed, fumbling with the heavy door until she managed to throw it open. As she stepped inside, her foot caught on the uneven ground, and she stumbled forward, just managing to catch herself before she tumbled over.

Once she was inside the stable, the freezing wind no longer buffeted her. Everything was quiet for a moment. Then a dull thump echoed through the building, followed by a scuffling noise, and once again, all fell silent. In the darkness Mrs. O'Donnell's tale haunted her. Trying to push down her fear, she scrambled to find the lantern. As she fumbled along the planks with her fingers, she hit the lantern, and pain shot through her hand. The next moment her fingers curled around a wire handle.

Twice Jayne tried to light the lantern's candle. Both times the wind blew it out. As she began to try again, two dark figures plunged into the stable.

3

The Verse

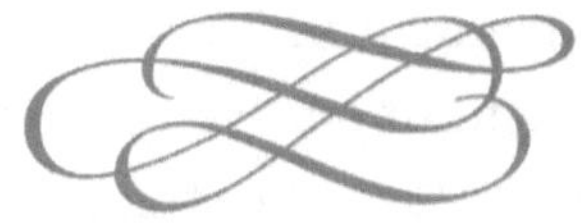

Jayne froze.

Then one of the figures reached out and thrust its arms around her, and she heard Yvonne's muffled voice saying, "You're home."

"What happened?" asked Olivia, concern filling her voice. She took the lantern from Jayne, and a moment later the three were illuminated by its glow.

Jayne barely heard Olivia's question. The warm light and the presence of her sisters made her feel safe, and she nearly forgot her discomfort. Shadows danced along the stable walls, and the lantern light revealed white puffs of air coming from her sisters' mouths.

Olivia leaned closer and peered at Jayne's face. "Never mind what happened. It's freezing out here, and you're wet through." She stamped her feet against the cold. "You two go inside. I'll see to Betsie."

Jayne started to protest, but Olivia took the reins out of her hand. "I've already seen to the other animals. Go."

Jayne smiled her consent with numb lips and ran a hand over Betsie's tangled mane. As she stood immobile, Yvonne grasped her arm and pulled her out into the night. The rain had lessened to a drizzle, but wind lashed at the sisters with more ferocity than before. Heads bowed, they stumbled along side by side, fighting the wind as it pushed their long skirts against their legs, making movement difficult. Overhead, the tree canopy raged and twisted, the branches threatening to snap at any moment.

Jayne tried to murmur a prayer for safety. Despite her instinct to flee, the weight of her wet garments hung like lead around her, and she didn't have the strength to keep going. She stopped. The house seemed so far away.

Positioning herself in front of Jayne, Yvonne tugged her sister forward, dragging her along. Jayne tried to protest, but the words disappeared into the storm. When at last they reached the comfort of their home, Jayne had no fight left. She let her younger sister propel her towards the bedroom.

"Let's get you out of that dress and into something warmer." Already Yvonne's fingers moved down the line of buttons. She pulled the wet dress over Jayne's head and surveyed her sister's petticoats with dismay. "I thought so, wet through." She laid a dry work dress on the bed. "There now, you can get into this."

Still feeling dazed, Jayne turned to the bed. Beneath her hands the clean dress felt soft and warm, and she wanted only to be enfolded in its warmth. She had brought the garment partway to her body before she realised that she still had wet clothes on. Panting with the effort, Jayne rid herself of the drenched petticoats. As she watched, the dirt floor beneath the clothes turned to mud. Just as she struggled into her dress, Yvonne bustled in.

"Come," Yvonne said, "I have a chair in front of the fire for you." She paused to look Jayne over from head to toe, then nodded in apparent satisfaction. "We don't want you getting sick. I'd have to do all your chores." Her eyes danced as she guided Jayne through the doorway with gentle firmness.

Jayne found herself before a rocking chair in front of the crackling fire. A gentle tug and push sent her down into the wooden seat. Shaking from head to toe, and teeth chattering with cold, Jayne felt a prickly blanket being placed around her shoulders. Through a haze of sleepiness, she watched her sister retrieve a hairbrush.

Yvonne undid Jayne's braid, and began to run the brush through her sister's matted hair. Jayne felt her muscles relax. Despite her best efforts, her eyes started to shut. Her head slumped forward, and the brush caught in her hair tugging it at the roots. Her senses reawakened, Jayne sniffed deeply. "Something smells good." She motioned to the pot hanging near the edge of the fire. "Is it Colcannon?"

A relieved sigh followed Jayne's question. "Good. You're speaking again." Yvonne's hands lay motionless against Jayne's shoulders. "I was so worried that you were sick."

Jayne twisted to look her sister in the face. "Oh Vonnie, I didn't mean to concern you." The traces of fear in her sister's eyes made her cringe. "I'll be all right."

Yvonne nodded and ran the brush through Jayne's hair once more before stopping. "There, I'll leave it to dry while I see to our food." She fluttered about the room in a soothing rhythm. "Would you like a cup of tea?" she asked. Without waiting for Jayne to reply, she lifted a pannikin from its hook. The sound of pouring liquid filled the house, giving the room a cosy feeling.

Jayne's eyelids felt heavy, but she managed a smile. Mam had trained her sister well.

Yvonne handed her the cup. "Drink up."

With a bang the door flew open, and Olivia rushed inside. "Brrr! Sure is cold out there." She tossed her damp shawl on a chair and huddled next to Jayne. Rubbing her hands up and down her arms, she shivered again. "I don't envy you having to ride out in that."

Yvonne got a long-handled spoon from the wall and dished up big dollops of the cabbage and mashed potato dish. Next to the mounds, she added some carrots and broad beans from their garden. Jayne watched the steam rising from the plates, then pushed herself to her feet. As heavy rain bucketed down again, she glanced up at the ceiling. "Sure is wintery, and don't I know it." She pictured Jed huddled inside his small hut with Cass as they ate their evening meal. She hoped they were managing to keep warm.

Jayne walked to the wash bucket in the corner of the room and gazed at her reflection in the water's still surface. With a shake of her head, she poked her hands into the water's depths, shattering the forlorn image. The cold bit into her fingers, and she quickly pulled them back out. Then, seeing that her hands were still covered with mud, she plunged them back into the water and scrubbed until her red fingers felt numb and sore.

As Olivia took her place by the wash bucket, Jayne walked back to the fire and rubbed her hands together. The fire erupted into a series of hisses as droplets flew into the flames. Once feeling had started to return to her hands, Jayne pulled her chair over to the table and sank down as Yvonne pushed a plate of steaming food in front of her. A growl from her stomach let everyone know how hungry she felt.

With a smile, Yvonne sat down beside Jayne. Her hand slipped over Jayne's fingers as Olivia took a seat opposite them. Together the three sisters bowed their heads, and Jayne began to pray. "Thank You, Lord, for providing us with hot food and a warm house. Be with those who don't have these blessings and make us grateful. Thank You also for bringing us safely together again. Please watch over Mr. and Mrs. O'Donnell, and give them strength for whatever the days may bring."

Jayne's fervent amen was echoed around the table, and as if on cue, Olivia and Yvonne turned eager eyes upon her. Jayne smiled and waited for her sisters to pepper her with questions. Her fork was only halfway to her mouth when the barrage began.

"Mrs. O'Donnell still isn't well?" Olivia's face tightened with concern.

Jayne shook her head. Around mouthfuls, she filled in her sisters on all that had transpired since she left them. When she came to the part where she spattered her dress with mud, their eyes filled with sympathy, but Jayne was not fooled.

Olivia's mouth was the first to twitch at the corners. Then all traces of sympathy vanished, and she began laughing unashamedly. In a moment Yvonne was laughing along with her.

Jayne threw up her hands in mock dismay, then joined in good-naturedly. She still felt annoyed that she'd managed to damage her dress again, but at least she could laugh about it now. Since she was little, her mam had continually cautioned her to look before she leapt, and leaping was exactly what had gotten her into this mess. Jayne sobered. Maybe next time she leapt into something, it would have much graver ramifications than a torn and muddied dress. She determined to ask God for help.

The mood in the room changed, and her sisters fell silent as Jayne told of Mrs. O'Donnell's uncontrollable cough. Turning to Yvonne, she said, "I didn't manage it today, but if the weather gets better in the next couple of days, you should ride over and tidy up the hut for them. I doubt Mrs. O'Donnell has gotten much of anything done of late, and there's probably a great many things that need doing. Besides, the company alone will do her good."

Yvonne nodded, her eyes sparkling. "I hope the weather clears soon."

"We should make Mrs. O'Donnell some of the cough syrup Mam always made for us," Olivia said. "One of us can make it tomorrow if we have the right ingredients. Then it'll be ready whenever Yvonne goes." She looked at Jayne for approval.

Before she could respond, a loud tapping sounded on the door. Jayne rose to her feet and asked, "Who else would be out on a night like this?" Olivia and Yvonne hurried to clear the table as she yanked at the door. She needn't have pulled so hard, for the wind thrust the door from her grasp and flung it against the wall with a thud that shook the house.

Another blast of wind shot through the open doorway, blowing Jed in with it. Arms straining, he grasped the door and forced it shut. He sagged against the doorframe. "Phew! That's some weather." Straightening up, he patted his trouser pocket and grinned. "Thought you might like a bit of music to brighten your night."

Gladness filled Jayne's heart. But before she could say anything, Yvonne hurried over with a cry of welcome. Jed chuckled when he found himself suddenly caught in a hug. As he disentangled himself and moved towards the fire, he tugged Yvonne's plait with a playful grin.

"You're just in time for dessert," Olivia said, eyes dancing. "You must've waited outside till we finished our vegetables."

Jed grinned. "Not tonight. It's too cold for an old man like me to be standing around." Wind battered the tin roof as he moved nearer the fire and rubbed his arms.

"Oh! Don't say that. You're not old." Yvonne's face clouded over at the thought.

"Compared to a girl of fourteen I am," Jed said, chuckling as he saw the pout on her face. He took a big gulp of the tea she handed him. "Ah, that's better." Nodding his thanks, he pulled out his harmonica. Then he rubbed its well-worn surface and put it to his lips. After a few experimental puffs, the real music began, the melody bouncing around the wooden walls and joining the harmony of the crackling fire. As the last note faded, another tune sprang forth, and it seemed to Jayne that Jed's whole body was part of the music.

With the scraping of wood against wood, Olivia pulled out a chair and sat down with a pile of mending in her lap. Just the thought of being seated brought a flood of exhaustion over Jayne's body, and she realised that her legs were trembling. Clutching at the back of Olivia's chair, she hoped no one would notice. But the music held everyone's attention, enabling Jayne to collapse heavily into her own chair. With relief she let her body soak up the warmth and the music like a healing salve.

While the girls hummed along, Jed played tune after tune. Finally he pocketed his harmonica. As he reached for the large Bible on the carved shelf above the fire, he said, "Perhaps it's time for that pudding you mentioned." He looked at Yvonne and winked. "The thought's making my mouth water, so as I can barely stand it."

Jayne knew she should get up and help her sisters serve the

dessert, but she couldn't seem to get her body to cooperate. As she struggled to rise, Olivia spotted her and motioned for her to stay seated.

Jed opened the Bible and thumbed through its pages. Then he cleared his throat and began reading aloud. "Let God arise, let His enemies be scattered . . ."

Jayne leaned back and closed her eyes. Listening to the Bible was something she had enjoyed for as long as she could remember. Every day Daddy had read to them in his deep voice. But now Jayne often found that she was the one doing the reading.

Jed paused to accept the bowl he was offered, then read on. "A father to the fatherless, and a judge of the widows is God in His holy habitation."

Jayne leaned forward, her own pudding forgotten. She strained to glimpse the chapter number. It was Psalm 68. Fixing her gaze on the wall, she tried to concentrate on the rest of the passage. But over and over her mind replayed the words. *A father to the fatherless.* Just what did it mean? And what were its implications for her?

Olivia nudged her, and Jayne glanced up to see that Jed had finished reading and was studying her.

"Cass will be disappointed he missed this pudding." Jed took another mouthful. "Maybe I should ask him to come next time?"

Jayne nodded, stumbling over her words. "Of course. If you think so. Anybody is welcome at the Reids' table." She poked at her untouched pudding with her spoon. "Mam would've been sure to ask him already."

"That she would've. I can hear her saying it now. 'A hundred thousand welcomes!' " There was a catch in his voice as he said, "You're becoming more like her by the day."

Jayne's head jerked up. More than anything she longed to copy Mam's example of godliness, but it seemed far beyond her reach.

Jed met her eyes and smiled. "Cass was pretty beat tonight, anyway." He chuckled. "Already asleep when I left. Reckon he's working a mite harder than he's used to." He paused. "Thought he would've been used to hard work. Him a working-class Irishman." He grinned and ran a hand over his beard. "Maybe they don't work 'em as hard in Ireland."

"Maybe it was the journey," Jayne said, missing the teasing in Jed's voice. "I was young when I made that same voyage, but old enough to remember it was tough. Days and nights with no break from the tossing of the sea." She stopped, remembering the feeling of being trapped onboard. "And the seasickness." Jayne groaned as she recalled its effect on herself and the people around her. "If you weren't strong it would kill you, apart from God's mercy, of course."

Jed nodded soberly, but as he put the harmonica to his lips again, his eyes twinkled. He played one of the girls' favourites, this time both feet tapping away to the lively rhythm.

Feeling she ought not to put it off any longer, Jayne slipped into her bedroom to retrieve a pile of mending. As she sat back down, Yvonne started singing in a clear, high voice, so like Mam's. A tear slipped down Jayne's cheek, catching her off guard. She swiped it away before anyone could have a chance to spot it. Refusing to dwell on her sorrow, she blended her own voice with Yvonne's.

Olivia joined in on the chorus, and what Jayne saw in her sister's face replaced her sadness with a smile. Looking happy and carefree, Olivia grew more and more animated as she sang. Even though Olivia was having fun, the depth and maturity Jayne saw in her sister's gaze made her eyes mist over. She looked away quickly and shook her head. Her tears came far too readily these days.

Jayne focused on Yvonne instead. Dear, dear Vonnie. The sight of her sitting there, blonde plait neatly over one shoulder and a dimpled smile on her face, was enough to make anybody's heart melt. Jayne thought for the second time that day that perhaps everything would work out all right.

4

A Second Warning

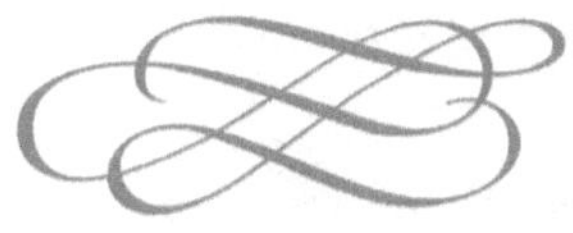

Jayne sat up in bed, and immediately the cold air sent chills running up and down her body. She lay back down again, pulling the covers around herself and savouring every piece of warmth they offered.

But five minutes later, knowing she shouldn't stay in bed any longer, Jayne pulled her blankets back and jumped to the floor. Cold nipped at her feet while, fingers flying, she pulled on her clothes. Then she went to stoke the fire back to a merry crackle. As she finished, she heard her sisters begin to stir. Further rousing them with a cheery "good morning," she donned her warm cloak and headed out to milk Checkers, buckets in hand.

All around her fog swirled, blanketing the day with dampness. She shuddered as branches poked their fingers towards her through the mist. When she arrived at the stable, Jayne set one of her pails down to unlatch the small door and heard Jed's voice hailing her. They exchanged morning greetings, then walked together towards Checkers's stall.

As Jayne paused to scratch Checkers on the face, Jed grabbed an armful of hay from the far end of the stable. He dumped it in Checkers's trough, then stepped aside, brushing off his clothes as he went. After a heartfelt moo that made Jayne laugh, the cow started munching. Jayne fetched the milking stool off the wall, and soon streams of milk spattered into the bucket, making a merry rhythm that filled the morning silence.

Jed lingered, leaning both arms on the top railing of the stall as he watched.

Her hands moving rhythmically, Jayne smiled up at him. "Thank you for the music last night."

Jed nodded and rubbed his arms. "Sure is chilly this morning. Might snow."

"If the weather doesn't get too bad, I thought I'd take Betsie and go to town a day early. We need to get the ingredients for some cough mixture for Mrs. O'Donnell." Jayne steadied the milking bucket as Checkers shifted. "No sense in making her wait any longer than necessary. Her health will only get harder to fix. I'm hoping to go this afternoon after we get some cleaning done."

Jed stuck his hands in his pockets and fixed a serious gaze on her. "Mind you don't leave it too late with the weather so threatening. We don't want a repeat of yesterday, or it's you who'll be needing that mixture."

Jayne nodded, knowing they both saw the same image in their minds—that of first Daddy, then Mammy lying sick in bed. "Maybe I should go before lunch. Hopefully any rain will hold off until I get back."

Jayne poked her head into the bedroom where Yvonne was intent on re-plaiting her hair. "Would you mind going over the list I wrote one more time?" she asked. "I don't want to buy anything we don't need." Barely listening for Yvonne's reply, Jayne dashed out of the house to find Olivia.

Jayne fell into step with her sister as Olivia entered the stand of trees between the house and stable. Thick mud covered the path ahead. With a small leap, Jayne dodged a particularly slushy spot, throwing her arms out for balance. As she landed, her feet slipped, leaving two long streaks in the mud. Olivia gasped, but Jayne regained her balance and flashed her sister a grin. When they came to a wide puddle a few steps later, Jayne stepped over it more carefully.

Olivia gave her a sidelong glance and nodded in approval. "I've got my eye on you. Else you'll have your good dress ruined before we've even made it to the stable, let alone the store."

When Jayne reached the next puddle, she stopped and waited for Olivia to look. Then she deliberately lifted her hem high above the puddle's edge. Head held erect, Jayne stepped around it in the most lady-like fashion she could muster. Her display of manners was rewarded with a laugh. Grinning, Jayne covered the remaining ground with less dignity.

On entering the stable, Jayne went straight to the stall where Betsie stood. She admired the mare's mud-free coat, feeling pleased with herself for remembering to brush it earlier. As she led Betsie from the stall, Jayne glanced down. "That's odd."

"What is?"

"This floor. It looks a lot cleaner than I remember it being a few hours ago. I'm sure there was scattered hay and manure on it. Not to mention the hair from Betsie's coat."

Olivia bent down and peered at the ground. "Either someone else swept it, or you're imagining things. But it wasn't me, if that's what you're wondering."

Jayne inspected the dirt floor closely. "Nope. It's definitely been swept. I can see the broom marks. If it wasn't you or me, then I wonder who it was. Cass and Jed have been in the paddock cutting trees most of the morning, and Yvonne has been inside cleaning." She shrugged. "I suppose it doesn't really matter. It's just odd, that's all."

"Maybe you did it and forgot," Olivia said. "You've done it so many times that you could do it in your sleep." She looked down at the floor again and ran her foot over it. "We'd better get going if we're to be back before the weather grows worse."

Shaking her head in wonder, Jayne led Betsie to where the cart stood. Together the girls backed Betsie between the shafts and did up the harnesses. Jayne waited for Olivia to climb into the cart and take the reins, before jumping up beside her.

Branches whipped at the cart's sides as they rolled and bumped towards the house. At a loud call from Jayne, Yvonne appeared almost instantly, both her hair and dress immaculate. As Yvonne stepped up into the cart, Jayne rubbed the uneven surface of the reins. The feeling of the leather between her fingers reminded her of a time shortly after Daddy purchased his first horse and saddle. He'd swung her up in front of him and took her riding. Yvonne had been too frightened to bounce along so high up. Olivia had been somewhat better. Only Jayne shared her father's delight as she placed her own little hands on the reins behind Daddy's.

Jayne could not stop herself from smiling as the first shops appeared. Carriages, some expensive and some more plain like their own cart, dotted the streets. A couple of horses tied in front of the drapery store stamped and nickered, shifting their feet and stretching their heads down to the ground. A little boy with a scarf streaming behind him ran across the street in front of them, calling to someone Jayne could not see.

As she directed Betsie towards the general store, Jayne suddenly got the feeling someone was watching her, and she stiffened. After casting a look over her shoulder, she glanced at Olivia to see if she had noticed anything, but her sister appeared to be absorbed in gazing at a shop's display. Trying to shake her uneasiness, Jayne fixed her attention on a woman who was swaying down the footpath wearing an elaborate dress with a large bustle.

As they neared Mrs. Young's Hotel, loud voices drew Jayne's attention towards it, and she locked eyes with a silent observer who leaned against the wall of the hotel, his hands in his pockets. As the stocky man with a thick moustache nodded at her and continued to stare, Jayne looked away, pretending not to have noticed.

Jayne guided Betsie to the opposite side of the intersection and brought her to a halt in front of Brydon and Hedrick's general store. As she rose from her seat, Jayne couldn't resist looking over to where the man had been. Her gaze lingered just long enough to confirm that the sandy-haired man was still there. Worse still, he hadn't stopped staring. Jayne gave Yvonne a push, urging her to get down, then quickly jumped to the ground herself.

Chattering as they walked, Olivia and Yvonne started towards the door of the shop, but Olivia hesitated and looked back. Jayne motioned for them to go ahead without her. The sooner she got her sisters away from the staring stranger the better.

As Jayne approached the hitching post, she pivoted unobtrusively until she could see the man out of the corner of her eye. To her dismay, he had moved down the street to lean against the bank building—directly opposite the general store. Perhaps the man had only wanted to stretch his legs a little. Still, his rudeness left her feeling indignant and unsettled.

Jayne's fingers felt clumsy as she hurried to finish looping the reins around the pole. A puff of smoke rose from the cigar in the man's mouth and hovered about his head, making him appear sinister. His brazen staring continued. Jayne finished securing Betsie and turned away from the street and the middle-aged man's hardened face. Though her pulse raced, she lifted her chin.

A bell tinkled above her as she pushed open the door and stepped inside the shop. The warmth of the store and the familiar smells made her breathe a sigh of relief. Walking slowly so she could scan the floor to ceiling shelves, Jayne approached the counter.

"Why, hello, Miss Reid. What can I do for you today?" Mr. Hedrick asked, resting his arms on the counter.

Jayne smiled at the friendly storekeeper, who had a neatly-trimmed moustache and brown hair that was greying at the temples, and returned his greeting. "That man out there. I haven't seen him around before." She pointed down the narrow store to the window. "Do you know who he is?"

Mr. Hedrick peered towards the window, then came around his counter and led the way to the front of the store. When he reached the window, his eyes followed the direction of Jayne's pointing finger, and he said, "That's Mr. Thomas Lamberton. He's been in here on more than one occasion, buying spirits and wine. From what I hear, he made his fortune on the Victorian goldfields." Mr. Hedrick looked back at Jayne. "What interest do you have in the man?"

Jayne hesitated.

Mr. Hedrick smiled and waited with a look of patient interest.

Jayne drew a deep breath. "Well, you see, I noticed him just now . . . staring." Her gaze dropped to the ground. "His behaviour made me feel ill at ease. I just wondered—"

Mr. Hedrick nodded and looked out the window again. "I think I understand. He has gotten himself a bit of a reputation around town. As far as I know he's only been here a few weeks, though. How do I put it?" It was Mr. Hedrick's turn to stop and consider his words. He shook his head. "It's the way in which he goes about talking to people that leaves a bit to be desired. He tends to conduct himself with a rather arrogant air." He placed his hands on his hips. "He's not caused any trouble here though."

Mr. Hedrick straightened his vest and moved back to the counter. "Now then, can I get you anything?" He stepped aside as a shop assistant moved past him, arms laden with brown packages.

Jayne nodded and looked around for Yvonne. Her sister stood in the middle of the store near the display of ribbons, lace, and other sewing notions, fingering some cream-coloured lace.

Yvonne's head turned towards the counter as if she sensed Jayne's gaze. With a smile, she walked towards the back of the shop. "Here's our list, Mr. Hedrick." Yvonne held out a small piece of paper.

Mr. Hedrick acknowledged Yvonne with a nod. "I'll fill it myself." He ran a hand over his clean-shaven cheek as he glanced down at the paper. Then he turned his gaze back to Yvonne. "Have you been looking after Jed? I haven't seen him around lately."

"He's well, thank you." Yvonne's face lit up. "I'll tell him you asked."

Mr. Hedrick smiled. "Be sure to tell him to call in next time he comes this way."

Yvonne nodded. "I will."

Mr. Hedrick watched Yvonne move away to continue perusing the ribbons and lace with Olivia. Then instead of turning to the shelves behind him, he leaned across the counter towards Jayne. "I just remembered something that may concern you. When your hired man was in town the other day, Mr. Lamberton singled him out."

"You mean Cass?" Jayne asked.

Mr. Hedrick nodded. "They met across the road there, in front of the bank." He pointed out the window, and Jayne realised that Mr. Lamberton was now nowhere to be seen.

"I could see the whole thing from where I was helping a customer," Mr. Hedrick continued, "but I'm afraid I couldn't hear what passed between them. Now, I don't know for sure, but it looked like Mr. Lamberton knew your hired man."

Jayne doubted that was possible but kept silent, not wanting to be rude. Besides what would Cass, or anyone else, want with someone who seemed so obnoxious?

"You see, Lamberton walked straight up to Cass and gave him a hearty slap on the back. It looked as if they might have been waiting for each other." Mr. Hedrick shrugged. "I guess I shouldn't speculate. What I do know is that after conversing for a little while, Mr. Lamberton got aggravated. Then Cass started shaking his head fiercely, and they parted ways."

"I wonder what it was all about," Jayne said, as her mind began going over all kinds of scenarios.

"Afraid I don't know. It's just that the character of one who keeps company with Lamberton might be rather doubtful. I felt I ought to warn you."

Jayne continued to gaze at the spot in front of the bank. This wasn't the only time someone had voiced some sort of doubt about Cass's character. First it was Mrs. O'Donnell and now this story. Jayne bit her lip, realising that was all it was—a story. She had no way of knowing what the circumstances between Mr. Lamberton and Cass had been.

As she turned back to Mr. Hedrick, he picked up their list from where it lay on the counter. "Only a few things today," he said, looking at Jayne kindly. "How are you faring?"

Mr. Hedrick's compassion brought sudden tears to Jayne's eyes. She said only, "Has not God promised to provide for all our needs?"

Mr. Hedrick's eyes glistened as he nodded and turned to measure linseeds for the girls' cough mixture.

5
Unsettled Feelings

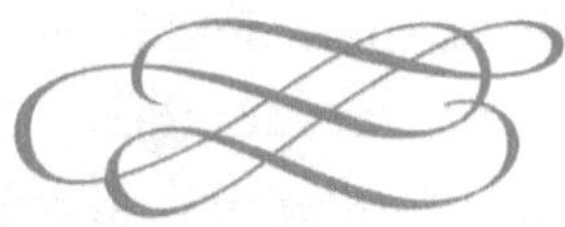

Jayne half sat up and rubbed her face with both hands. She had tossed and turned all night, trying to escape a staring Lamberton in her dreams—dreams so clear that she could still picture them now. No matter how far she had run down twisting country lanes, she could not escape from Lamberton's cold, unblinking eyes. He was always standing a few yards away—staring. Expelling her breath slowly, she gazed up at the ceiling and shoved back her covers, trying to push the man out of her thoughts.

Somewhere outside a magpie warbled. Jayne rolled over and peered across the room at her sleeping sisters. At least they seemed to have had a peaceful night. She brushed at her hazy eyes and climbed out of bed, her one thought to get away from this place of nightmares. Reaching beneath her bed, she found what she desired. Then she slipped her shawl off its hook and tiptoed out of the room.

The fat diary in her hand was more than just a book to Jayne.

Though one of her most precious possessions, it was scuffed and worn around the edges. The damage was not from lack of care but from constant use and the many times she had carried it outside. Often things seemed to make more sense when she could put them down on paper, and these pages were an outlet for her deepest thoughts and emotions. A feeling of gratitude swelled in her heart as she remembered how many times God had used the act of writing to help her through a trial.

Moving carefully in the darkness, Jayne made her way to the kitchen table and set her diary where it would be safe. She shivered. Only a few glowing coals remained from last night's fire, but if she hurried, perhaps she would be able to drive the chill from the room before her sisters got up.

She fumbled around, hoping to find a few small pieces of wood in the crate by the fireplace. Her hands came back empty. Jayne groaned and pulled her shawl tighter. Somehow they must have forgotten to check the wood last night.

Resigning herself to an early morning trip outside, she slipped her boots on and headed for the door. In the darkened sky, a few lone stars twinkled at her through the clouds. Smiling, Jayne threw back her head and took a moment to enjoy the morning sky, suddenly glad the wood had run out.

When she arrived at the shelter tacked behind the house, she noted the outline of a sizeable woodpile with relief. There would be no need to make the trek to their larger, unsplit pile at the stable. Reaching inside the shelter, Jayne discovered that some of the wood felt damp to her touch. She tossed the pieces aside and continued to run her hand over the rough surfaces. Finally, she managed to locate what she was after.

Returning to the fire, she knelt to arrange the small chunks of wood over the coals. As she leaned over and blew on the embers, they came alive, flashing and dancing in pretty patterns. Satisfied, Jayne headed back outside to the woodpile to fetch a few larger logs. As she piled them into her arms, a nearby magpie warbled. From farther back, another one joined in.

She turned towards the sound, and started, sure she had seen a large movement beneath the trees. As she peered more intently into the darkness, adrenaline made her tighten her hold on the wood. Straining to catch another movement, Jayne waited. A minute dragged by, but still she saw nothing. The wood grew heavier in her arms, and her inactivity made the cold seem worse. With a shrug, she moved on. No doubt it had just been a kangaroo.

Once inside, she added a log to the fire. By now, there were a few small flames, giving the fireplace a sense of warmth. She lit a candle and placed the holder carefully on the floor. With pen in hand and a pot of ink nearby, she sat cross-legged beside the candle, cradling her diary in her lap. When she'd made herself as comfortable as she could, she began to wish she had her quilt to snuggle up in. Instead, she shuffled backwards until her back rested against the fireplace stones.

While the fire started to crackle, Jayne poured her heart out to God in the pages of her diary. A log burst into flames and drove some of the chill from the room as she asked for strength and wisdom to meet the challenges of the day.

Jayne set her open diary beside her to let the ink finish drying and reached for another log to place on the fire. The warmth of the growing flames encircled her body. She flexed her cramped hand and turned to stare into the flames. In this position she prayed and mused over the day until a soft sound made her head lift.

"You're up early," Olivia said, her voice soft and a bit croaky.

She too clasped a shawl over her nightgown and crowded as close to the fire as she could without catching her hem alight. "Couldn't you sleep?"

Jayne hesitated before shaking her head. Olivia knew her well, and it would be pointless to hide anything from her. She was getting ready to reveal the cause of her unrest, when Yvonne chose that moment to emerge from the bedroom.

Yvonne squinted at them through sleepy eyes and shuffled to the table, where she sat with her elbow propped on the table and her head resting on her hand. A blank look settled on her face as she stared at a spot somewhere above Jayne's head.

Jayne smiled. The only time her youngest sister ever looked rumpled was when she first got up. Her hair always managed to escape its plait, sticking out here and there at funny angles. Jayne got up and gave her a hug.

As Jayne dressed, she continued to make plans. After tending to the animals with Olivia and eating breakfast, she would start simmering the cough mixture. Then there was the baking to do. If the three of them worked hard in the morning, they could get a good portion of the chores done before Yvonne headed off to the O'Donnells'. Then there might be time for a walk to her favourite hollow of trees. She finished re-plaiting her hair, then coiled it near the base of her neck in readiness for the day's work.

When she stepped outside a moment later with milk buckets in hand, the sun had begun to peek its head over the horizon, illuminating the farm in brilliant gold as its rays pierced the fog. Jayne's breath showed in fluffy, white puffs as she breathed in the crisp air. It felt wonderful to be alive. She hovered by the door to admire the beauty of the morning for a moment longer. As the sunlight continued to brighten, Olivia stepped out and stood by her side. Together they lingered in awed silence, drinking in God's handiwork.

"It's beautiful, isn't it?" Olivia said.

Feeling that words were inadequate to describe what lay around her, Jayne nodded. Both girls started walking at the same time, as if the beauty propelled them forward. Jayne could barely keep the skip from her step as they wound their way down the frosty path to where their tasks awaited them. Overhead, birds flew from tree to tree, chirping and calling to each other as they searched for food. Their urging was too much for Jayne to resist. She lifted her voice in praise right along with them.

They reached the stable all too soon and set right to work. Olivia scooped up some grain for Checkers, who stood waiting patiently in her stall, while from a nearby pen her calf mooed. Olivia went to the calf, and in a few moments had coaxed it in to playing with her.

As Jayne sat down on the milking stool, a wave of tiredness hit her, and the beauty of the morning seemed far away. "Olivia," she said in a sober tone that made her sister stop her frolicking.

Olivia walked to where they could see each other and waited, but Jayne remained silent, her hands automatically going about their job.

Olivia stepped closer. "What is it?"

"Probably nothing."

Olivia placed a hand on her hip and raised her eyebrows.

A sheepish grin spread across Jayne's face. As milk streamed into the bucket, she started explaining the cause of her restless night. To her own ears the tale of the staring stranger sounded foolish, like she was making a big story out of nothing. In truth, she probably was.

Olivia stood listening, her face expressionless until Jayne finished. Then with a frown she moved closer and leaned on the railing. "I doubt it was anything sinister. We don't know Mr. Lamberton, so it's not likely he knows us." She blew out her breath, making a white cloud in front of her.

For a while there was silence, aside from the cow's munching and the noise of the milk hitting the sides of the bucket. Finally, Olivia straightened up. "He couldn't know that our parents aren't here, could he?" Even before she had finished speaking, Olivia shook her head, dismissing her own words.

Jayne, however, clamped her hands tightly around Checkers's teats. Olivia always tended to look at the bright side of life. The little bit of doubt in her words spoke volumes, making Jayne feel more miserable than before. She had hoped that Olivia would laugh the situation off.

As Checkers tried to sidestep, Jayne realised that she still gripped the cow's teats. She let go and gave Checkers a pat, wondering about the wisdom of having shared her thoughts with Olivia. She hadn't meant to scare her sister, but perhaps the desire to share her worries had been selfish. All she seemed to have done was cause her sister unneeded concern over a problem that was only in her head. On the other hand, they could not afford to keep secrets from each other.

It had always seemed to help when she shared her burden with Mam or Daddy. Why did everything have to be so complicated now?

Jayne resisted stamping her foot in frustration. "You're right," she said to Olivia. "We should just forget the whole thing. We don't know him, and he doesn't know us. It's that simple." But it didn't feel simple. Jayne couldn't help but sigh.

Olivia nodded. "It's probably nothing." Without another

word, she left the stable to continue her chores.

Jayne was left with her own thoughts to keep her company—thoughts about what the future might hold. She could not help wishing that they had fled out the door with Olivia.

The house smelled of scrambled eggs when Jayne walked in half an hour later. The aroma caused her mouth to water and her stomach to growl noisily. She washed up and went about setting the table. As she set the last plate down, Olivia came in with a bucket of water and added it to the pot hanging over the fire. A second later Yvonne announced that the food was ready.

The three sat down and gave thanks for the day and the hot meal before them. Then Jayne scooped up a large serving of eggs for herself and passed the pot to Yvonne, who was seated across from her at the rough wooden table.

"Should we bake extra for the O'Donnells today?" asked Yvonne as she served herself.

Jayne nodded. Most weeks Mam had made extra for one person or another and wrapped it in a clean cloth to take with them to church. There was no reason Jayne could see to stop this custom now. God would continue to provide for their needs, just as He always had. A barely audible sigh escaped her lips. She took another mouthful and tried to shake aside her many worries by figuring out how many loaves they would need.

Because tomorrow was Sunday, they would be making double the normal quantity of Irish soda bread. Their baking load had also increased since Jed had moved onto the property. It would take some time to get it all baked. As Jayne added up the final quantity of loaves in her head, she realised she had forgotten all about Cass. Despite herself, she smiled. Jed had declared that Cass had a heartier appetite than a calf who hadn't been fed for a week.

There was also the butter waiting to be churned. At least the jobs were inside near the fire. Jayne pushed her chair back and helped Olivia stack the plates and cooking pots on one end of the table. The clatter of tin echoed through the little home as Yvonne fetched the washing-up tub from its hook on the wall.

Impatiently, Jayne stepped over to check the water, which hadn't had long to heat. Her fingertips broke the water's smooth surface, but it was still only lukewarm. She shrugged. She needed the pot in order to start on the medicine, and time was wasting. With the help of a cast iron arm that protruded from the fireplace wall, she deftly swung the pot in an arc over the hearth, then heaved it onto the table for her sister.

While Jayne set about measuring linseed into the now empty pot, Yvonne soaped up the dishwater. Across the table from Yvonne, Olivia got out a pan and measured out brown flour and salt. As Jayne finished with the linseed and began slicing sticky, black liquorice for the cough syrup, Yvonne started humming. The sound filled the small house with its sweetness, chasing away some of the gloom that lurked in the corners of the home and hearts of the girls, always threatening to dampen their spirits at the least invitation.

Jayne studied Olivia as her sister bent over the table, intent on preparing the first batch of soda bread. All of them had grown up making and eating this staple, and Olivia was no exception. Since they were old enough to crawl, they had clambered around Mam while she prepared the dough. In fact, as soon as they were old enough to stand on a chair beside her, Mam taught each one of them how to make the simple yet filling bread. Jayne wiped at the corner of her eye. It was funny how the simplest of things were filled with so many memories. Through blurry eyes she continued to watch as Olivia mixed the ingredients together. When her sister went to fetch the soured buttermilk, Jayne went back to her own task.

As soon as she finished chopping the last piece of liquorice, she dumped it all into the pot, glad to have the strong aniseed aroma farther away from her nose. Then Jayne placed the pot on the hook, poured water over the mix, and swung it over the fire to simmer while she prepared the last ingredient.

The smell of the brown sugar candy was as tantalising as it had been at the shop yesterday. Jayne tipped the golden lumps into a bowl and started pounding. Each time she thumped the rough stone down, lumps of the lolly flew around the bowl. As another piece slid away without even chipping, Jayne bit her lip in frustration. For the second time that day, she fought the urge to stamp her foot.

Yvonne's humming stopped, and Jayne looked up from her pounding, thinking Yvonne must have noticed her agitation. But her youngest sister stood staring at the wall, a puzzled look on her face. "What colour were Mam's eyes?"

"Blue," Jayne said, her voice catching at her sister's vulnerableness.

Yvonne nodded and resumed her scrubbing. "I just wanted to make sure. Do you ever forget those things?"

Jayne opened her mouth, but her voice seemed stuck in her throat. Yvonne was already humming again—this time one of Mam's favourite tunes. Jayne looked over at Olivia, who had stopped to listen to the exchange. Their eyes met briefly, each mirroring the other's pain.

Jayne bent her head and continued trying to smash the lollies into pieces. She pounded more vigorously than before, as if to crush up her feelings along with the lollies. Then she caught Olivia watching her.

Her hand stopped, and her eyes slid shut as she tried to get a grip on her composure. After a prayer for help, she returned to her task, ignoring the temptation to eat a piece of the hard-boiled lolly. But when Yvonne passed, Jayne slipped her a small chunk. Her youngest sister's eyes lit up with delight at the unexpected treat. Jayne smiled, feeling sure that Vonnie's delight was more of a treat to her than if she had eaten the lolly herself.

Glad of the opportunity to escape the house for a moment, Jayne walked out to the vegetable patch for some carrots. She swung open the gate and surveyed the area where they had planted carrots earlier in the year, but the rows, spotted here and there with delicate green foliage, appeared alarmingly empty. With a growing feeling of dismay, she spun around to make sure she was in the right spot. Her stomach twisted as the action confirmed that she was. It could only mean that their supply was dwindling faster than she had anticipated.

Scolding herself for not watching the garden more carefully, Jayne bent down, grasped a handful of velvety carrot tops, and yanked. They pulled free of the ground more easily than she expected, and her arms flailed as she struggled to keep her balance, sending a shower of loose dirt from the carrots over her hair and dress. Once she had her footing, she brushed the dirt from her eyes and inspected the slim carrots. Perhaps they just hadn't grown as large as last season. That might explain the lack of produce left in the ground.

Just before she left the garden with her apron bulging with lumps, Jayne looked back over the rows of carrots and made a mental note to plant some more as soon as possible. Perhaps she would be able to start clearing a section of the garden today.

Either way, it would be a while before the new crop was ready to eat. In the meantime their task was to make the carrots last as long as possible. She shook her head and sighed.

The morning passed by swiftly as the girls worked side by side. By the time it was necessary to deliver the stew and bread to Jed's hut, they had baked multiple loaves, churned the butter, and completed the cough syrup for Mrs. O'Donnell.

Straight after dinner, Jayne left the table to hitch up Betsie for Yvonne. Then she led the buggy up to the house and held Betsie while her sister climbed up. Yvonne accepted the stoneware jug of cough syrup and the bundles of bread and stew with pleasure written all over her face.

The usually laid-back mare seemed eager to be off. While some days Betsie could certainly do with a large dose of Vonnie's spark, today Yvonne's enthusiasm seemed to have rubbed off on her. Jayne ran a hand over Betsie's rump, then smiled at her sister. "Make sure you're back before dark."

Jayne waved until Yvonne had disappeared around the bend. Even after the noise of the cart had faded away, she stayed staring into the distance. Finally, she roused herself with a shake and turned to go back to her chores.

Jayne pushed back her hair and sighed wearily. The last batch of bread was cooking, and Olivia had gone off to check on their flock, which was beginning to drop lambs.

By the amount of light coming through the window, it looked to be nearing three-thirty. A glance at the clock told her she was correct. The day was nearly over, but her work was not. She dragged her feet as she walked over to the water buckets, thinking about Jed and Cass. By now both men were probably getting ready to ride to a meeting in Buninyong. She could picture them splashing water on their faces and hair despite the cold, as Daddy had when he went to town.

Jayne stooped to pick up the buckets, knowing she couldn't put off refilling them any longer. She felt like complaining, but there was no one to listen. In her head she could hear Mam's familiar words. *Everything goes easier when you're armed with a smile.* Grudgingly, Jayne tried to make use of Mam's advice, but her mouth refused to cooperate. Her frustration mounting, she sighed. The sooner she started, the sooner the tiresome task would be completed. At least until the next time it was necessary to tote water.

She hadn't gone more than a few steps out the door before two familiar horses trotted into sight. As they passed the house, Jed waved, and Cass lifted his hat. Then both horses and riders vanished from view.

The sight of Jed's friendly grin helped her step lighten a bit, but the well still seemed farther away than usual. Not a sound broke the silence of the afternoon, and Jayne's tired mind distorted the stillness, making the atmosphere seem eerie.

She hooked her bucket to the well rope and lowered it down until it hit the water with a thud that seemed unnaturally loud. Jayne looked around uneasily, then began turning the well's handle in the opposite direction. The rope tensed as the now heavy bucket climbed back up. Jayne leaned over and watched its ascent. Finally she lifted the bucket to the ground, hooked the second bucket to the rope, and the task started all over again. Then came the tedious journey back to the house. Her feet felt heavy as she thought of the several long trips that awaited her.

Jayne walked back from the well with her second load, lost

in thought. A lone bird called mournfully through the silence. She watched it for a moment; then it flew away, leaving her all alone again.

As she rounded the corner of the house, her feet stopped moving. Despite the silence, Jayne had failed to hear the noise of carriage wheels coming up the drive. Nor had she heard the jingle of harnesses. Yet sure enough, there stood an expensive-looking carriage.

Without looking at Jayne, the driver leapt to the ground and started towards the house, looking it up and down as if it were of great interest to him. Her curiosity aroused, Jayne started forward to find out who the man was.

6

$\mathcal{T}$HE $\mathcal{T}$HREAT

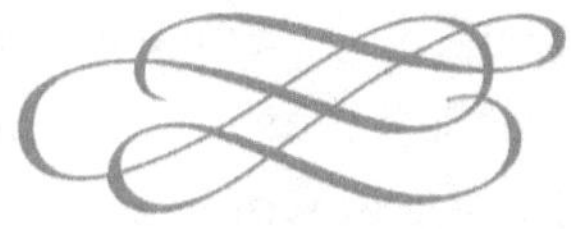

"Small house," the man with a bowler hat was saying to himself, seeming oblivious to Jayne's presence as he peered at the surroundings. "Any stable? Ah well. I can build one soon enough."

Jayne froze. Why was this man talking as if he owned their farm?

The man laughed to himself, as if he had said something funny, unnerving Jayne even further. Was that his plan? Turning, he looked Jayne full in the face for the first time since his arrival. "Forgive me," he said, his tone exaggerated. "Where are my manners?"

As Jayne took a step backwards, he laughed again. "Allow me to introduce myself, madam." He bowed low with a flourish of his hat, revealing sandy-coloured hair. "Mr. Thomas Lamberton at your service."

Jayne stared, unable to find her voice as one of her buckets clattered to the ground. The source of her nightmare stood before her. No longer was there a blanket to hide behind. Nor a way of escape.

"And you're Miss Jayne Reid." He tilted his hat back and looked her up and down. "No need to introduce yourself. I already know all about you and your two lovely sisters." He grinned arrogantly, his words mocking her.

At the mention of her sisters, Jayne felt her stomach flip. How did he know about them? What else was he privy to? Already he seemed to know too much. How she wished that Jed had not ridden to town, for she had no idea what to do.

She clenched her hands and drew a deep breath to calm herself. She must be strong. "Sir." Despite her best efforts the word resembled a croak. Her nails bit into her palms as she tried again. "Sir, I have much to do. If you would please state the purpose of your visit . . ." Her voice trailed off. Actually, as much as she wished to make sense of the situation, she dreaded his reply.

Mr. Lamberton paced in a small circle, looking all around. "Yes," he said, without as much as a glance in her direction, "this suits fine." As he moved, he tapped a coiled whip against his trouser leg.

Looking at his horses as they edged around skittishly, Jayne felt sure Mr. Lamberton had no need of the whip. She wondered if he held it only to intimidate her.

As Lamberton continued tapping and pacing, his face took on a pleased look. At last he ceased his deliberations and turned to Jayne. "Let's get down to business."

"Business?" Jayne stammered. "What do you mean?"

Lamberton roared with laughter as if she had said something witty. Then struggling to suppress his amusement, he shook his head with an air of sympathy. "Let's be open with one another. We both know your dear parents are dead. There's no way a girl like you can manage all this." He gestured at the house and land with a sweep of his large hand. "You'll never be able to meet the land board requirements by the time your lease is up. You'll be a failure."

Jayne stiffened. She had heard those words before. Had Mrs. Sterling sent him here? As soon as the thought entered her mind, she chided herself. She had no right to suspect Mrs. Sterling of such a thing without proof. Yet how had he known that three young girls were holding this selection?

Lamberton leaned forward. "Find a place in town near your friends and live the life of a young girl. A life of safety and comfort. Allow me to take this responsibility off your hands." He smiled as he finished speaking, but his words seemed edged with threats.

A shiver ran down her back. Even if she wanted to do as Lamberton suggested—which she certainly didn't—she had no means of buying another house. All that her parents had possessed was invested in this piece of land. If they lost it, her and her sisters would be left with nothing.

"Well?" Mr. Lamberton began tapping his whip again. "I'm sure the land board will see the sense in my proposal, even if you do not."

"Proposal?" Jayne sucked in her breath. Surely this must all be a misunderstanding. "I'm afraid you must be mistaken, Mr. Lamberton. I know of no proposal, and I have no desire to know yours. I'm afraid I must ask you to leave at once."

Mr. Lamberton dismissed her words with a swipe of his whip. "Do try to be reasonable. Under the circumstances, I'm sure the land board will see that it's best for you to hand over your lease to me." A cruel smile slid over his face. "They're too busy to waste time on the likes of you. You'll never fulfil their requirements in time."

"Let me make something clear," Jayne said, her voice soft and clear. "My parents selected this land in the hopes of securing a strong future for their family. I have every intention of meeting every requirement imposed by the land board"—she straightened her back, which ached from tension—"and with God's help I shall."

Mr. Lamberton tensed, losing the last shreds of his genial facade. "Let *me* make things clear." He struck his whip against his boot. "We could have done this the easy way, but now you have forced my hand. The land board *will* see that I, Thomas Lamberton, can do a better job than you and your measly sisters will ever be capable of."

Lamberton stood so close to her that Jayne felt the warmth of his breath on her cheeks, and she flinched as he scoffed in her face. Never in her life had a man made her feel so small and worthless. Through the fog of her distress, a portion of Scripture entered her mind. *The Lord is on my side; I will not fear: what can man do unto me?*

"Now that we understand each other"—Lamberton took a step backwards, as if deciding his efforts to intimidate her had gone far enough—"we can come to an agreement on how to approach the land board. That is, if you can manage to speak civilly."

Jayne stared at him, too shaken to think of any response.

Mr. Lamberton smiled. "Or perhaps you intend to force me to go myself and persuade them to see things in the right light?"

Jayne stiffened. Would he really go to the land board? And if he did, would they side with him? Were they able to deem her unfit for holding the lease? After all, it had been her parents, not herself or her sisters, who had been given the right to the land selection.

When she said nothing, Mr. Lamberton took a few steps towards her. Jayne cringed but refused to lower her gaze. In Jesus she would be strong.

Despite the chill in the air, Mr. Lamberton's neck turned a dark red. "You, you—" The hand holding his whip clenched so tightly his knuckles turned white, and his arm shook as he pointed the whip at Jayne's chest. Then he drew a deep breath. Abruptly he turned on his heel and strode towards the waiting carriage. As he began to climb up, he missed his footing and dropped backwards, leaving a deep imprint in the ground. As he brushed mud from the seat of his trousers, his entire body shook with rage. He leapt to the seat and turned enraged eyes on Jayne. "You haven't seen the last of me." With violent movements, he cracked his whip above the poor horses' backs again and again, sending the carriage careening through the trees, while screeching birds flew from their treetop perches.

Jayne stood alone in the clearing, her heart thumping. It all seemed like a bad dream. She looked around. All that remained to tell of the man's visit were deep marks in the mud.

The birds fluttered back to their roosts and all fell still. In the silence that followed, Jayne wondered to what lengths Mr. Lamberton would go in order to obtain their farm. Her shoulders sagged, and she started to tremble. Gradually she became aware of a cold sensation in her leg, and she looked down, noticing for the first time that one side of her skirts clung to her in a wet, soggy mess. She stared at the dark patch, then pulled at the fabric, trying to get rid of the discomfort.

Still holding the wet material out to the side, Jayne took a few steps forward. Suddenly her shin connected with something and sent it rattling along the ground. She cried out in pain. As she did, all the memories came flooding back—the dropped bucket, her fear, and the unfinished task of fetching the water. She stooped to retrieve the spinning bucket and tried to locate the second one. It was not until she had turned in a full circle that she spotted it standing upright, contents still intact.

A movement near the trees caught her eye, and a familiar figure stepped through a gap in the trees—Olivia. Waving, she called to Jayne, her face aglow from her romp in the paddock. The sight released Jayne's grip on her emotions, and silent tears coursed down her cheeks.

Olivia ran the last few feet to where her sister stood, concern written all over her face. "What's happened? What's the matter?" she asked. "Yvonne. Is she all right?"

Jayne nodded. "Everyone's fine." She set the buckets down and wiped her eyes.

Without a word, Olivia picked up the water buckets and turned towards the house. Jayne trailed along behind. Once they got inside, Olivia turned to her sister with one hand on her hip. "Now, sit down and tell me what the matter is."

Wiping her eyes again, Jayne sat down as bidden. Though she tried to stop the flow, tears continued to trickle down her cheeks. The words felt trapped in her throat.

"Jayne, what's wrong?" Care filled Olivia's eyes as she crouched down before her older sister. "Please tell me. I want to help, but I don't know what's going on."

Through her own blurry vision, Jayne saw tears forming in her sister's eyes. Jayne sniffed and nodded. "It was horrible, so horrible. I didn't know what he would do." She covered her face with her hands. "What if he comes back?"

Olivia rocked back on her heels, her eyes wide. "What if who comes back?"

"That man I saw the other day. The one I told you about.

I was collecting water and all of a sudden he appeared from nowhere. I didn't even hear the carriage. He was just there."

"Well, what did he want?" Olivia stood up and put her arm around Jayne's shoulders. "I know it's been hard lately, but you need to calm down. If we go letting little things get on top of us, it'll just make everything so much harder. He might have come here by mistake."

Jayne shook her head. "You don't understand." She jumped to her feet and began pacing. "He didn't come here by accident. He knew all about us. Our names. Even about our parents. He wants to take their home and their dreams away from us."

Olivia gasped. "We don't have the money for the rent, but it's not due yet. We still have time. Surely he can't do anything."

"I know, I know." Jayne groaned. "He was so angry. I felt so frightened that I couldn't think." She slumped back down into her chair and buried her face in her hands.

The door flew open. Jayne yanked her hands from her face and leapt from her seat. Olivia placed a restraining hand on her arm. "It's just Yvonne."

Jayne turned away from the door, trying to erase any tell-tale signs of unrest from her face. When she turned back, Yvonne was bouncing around the hut, telling stories of her visit with Mrs. O'Donnell.

"It's been the best day we've had for such a long time, don't you think?" Yvonne looked at Jayne expectantly.

Jayne's heart sank. What could she say? She smiled half-heartedly, wishing there was some way to escape the question. She couldn't pretend nothing was wrong when her whole world felt like a mess. But her sister seemed not to notice her lack of response.

As Yvonne helped Olivia ready the evening meal, she fairly

danced about, chattering of her visit, Betsie, the weather, and a million other things until Jayne could stand it no longer. Not even stopping for her cloak, she went to the door, pausing only when Olivia called something after her. Not bothering to learn what it was, she murmured an excuse, then slipped out the door. At last she was free.

Looking over her shoulder at every noise, Jayne headed straight for the stable. Her hope was to find Jed's horse inside eating hay. If it was, she'd locate Jed and tell him everything. An audible sigh escaped her lips when no horse greeted her. She went over to the stall where they milked, leaned her head on her arms, and burst into tears. Nothing made sense anymore.

Her tears continued until the thought of Jed and Cass finding her in such a state made her look around as if they were already watching. Sniffling and choking back her tears, she searched for something to occupy herself with. Her eyes fell upon the broom that lay against the wall. Though the floor was already tidy, she began to sweep.

Off in the distance a cow mooed. Jayne whacked herself on the forehead. She hadn't done the evening chores. That was what Olivia had said as she left, something about the chores.

By the time she had completed her tasks, Jayne was shivering all over. As she hurried away from the henhouse, the noise of chooks shifting on their perches sounded behind her. Darkness had almost settled over the bush.

Intending to check the stable again to see if Jed was back, Jayne quickened her steps. But when she reached the garden, she hesitated. Everything was so full of shadows and stillness. Feeling impatient at her silliness, she stamped her foot. What could a little bit of darkness do to anybody?

In a nearby tree, a bird squabbled and flapped, trying to get settled for the night. Jayne jumped and clutched at her chest, heart thumping. The distance to the stable seemed to double, and dark shapes loomed everywhere. She cast a look over her shoulder to where she could see the glow of light from the house. Its security seemed far away.

She turned fully as something moving appeared on the track that led past the house. The figure was coming towards her. A scream rose in her throat. In the next moment, a horse whinnied. Jayne tilted her head back and breathed with relief. Jed had returned. She would know Spark's whinny anywhere. Breaking into a run, she called out Jed's name.

Jed pulled Spark to a stop in front of her and leaned forward in his saddle. "What's up? You're out late."

Just then, another horse trotted up alongside Jed, and Jayne's heart sank. She had forgotten all about Cass. As he peered down at her from atop Wattle, Jayne looked away. For all she knew, it was he that had betrayed them to Lamberton.

Jed jumped to the ground. "What's going on?" he asked again.

Jayne tried to motion towards Cass without being obvious. The shadowy figure belonging to Cass seemed to grow more rigid as Jed nodded and lowered his voice. "I'll be in just as soon as I can."

Jayne heard him talking to Cass, but she didn't pay any attention. With a sigh she trudged back towards the house, feeling as if she had no place to go. She didn't feel like facing her youngest sister again. Nor did she feel like being out in the dark with who knows who about.

The sound of crunching footsteps made Jayne spin around to find Jed grinning at her, while in the distance, Cass led the horses away.

The moon rose in the sky, casting eerie light over their faces as they walked to the house in silence. Just knowing that Jed would listen to her story made Jayne feel better.

When they reached the house, relief washed over Olivia's features. A pang of regret touched Jayne as she watched Yvonne take in her tearstained face. Her youngest sister would have to be told everything.

Jayne sat down in the chair Jed pulled up for her and stared into the flames. The room fell silent for a moment as Jed leaned against the mantelshelf, waiting. Olivia laid a hand on Jayne's shoulder. "Tell him," she said, her eyes encouraging. "Go from the start."

Jayne's words came in a muddle as she relayed her first sighting of Mr. Lamberton at the general store. But at least they were out. She went on to tell of Mr. Lamberton's visit—from the moment she saw his carriage on their property to the last crack of his whip.

As Jayne painted the final scene, she glanced at Yvonne, who still stood in the same place as when they first entered, her eyes wide and her face pale. How she wished Yvonne had been spared this extra worry.

A popping noise from the fire pulled her attention back towards Jed, who ran a hand over his face and looked at the ground.

"I felt so small, so weak and inadequate." Jayne's throat ached from unshed tears. "How am I meant to be all that I need to be?" She wanted to go on, to ask Jed how she was supposed to help her sisters to be strong when she herself was so weak. But she just couldn't do it.

For a long moment Jed said nothing as his jaw muscles tensed and relaxed. Then he looked Jayne straight in the eyes and said hoarsely, "I'm sorry I wasn't here to help. So sorry. I could've prevented you so much grief." He shook his head and banged his fist on his knee, muttering something Jayne couldn't make out.

Alarmed, Jayne glanced at Olivia, who shrugged in puzzlement. As Jayne looked back at Jed, he fixed his eyes on her again. They were wild, but wild with what? Was it anger or perhaps grief?

"I was married once."

Jayne could do nothing but stare at him. Her family had known Jed since coming to Australia eleven years before. Not once had he ever mentioned a wife.

"She needed help too, but I wasn't there. She was pregnant. I was called away suddenly on important business. I didn't have a choice. I had to go, or I'd lose my job. I wouldn't have had anything to support my wife and child. She depended on me, but I wasn't there, Jayne." He ran a hand over his head and repeated his words. "I'm so sorry I wasn't there to help."

Jayne didn't feel sure whether he was referring to the past or present. What did you say when someone revealed a long-kept secret? No words could ever be enough. "Jed."

He waved his hand. "I shouldn't burden you with my life scars. It's all in the past now." He pulled at his beard. "Gone. Just as the seasons pass away."

After a long moment, he stood up. "On Monday I'll ride into town and do some asking around, see what there is to know about the man." He looked at Jayne, then Olivia, and last of all Yvonne. "I told your father I would watch out for his girls. While God gives me breath, I intend to keep my promise."

He walked over to Yvonne and tousled her hair. "I'll keep an eye on things. Don't you worry none."

Jayne felt relieved to hear the normal tone back in Jed's

voice. He motioned for her to walk to the door with him, and she stepped outside into the darkness, wrapping her arms around herself to shield her body from the bitter cold. Night sounds rustled. Jayne couldn't help glancing behind Jed to check the shadows.

"I don't like the sound of the man at all." Jed grasped Jayne's shoulder as if to convey the sincerity of his words. "If you need me for anything, I'll do all in my power to be there for you."

"I know you will, Jed." Jayne looked at the ground, wondering if she should say anything more about what he had revealed. Jed would risk his life to help any of them. So why did she hesitate now, when a few reassuring words might help him? She looked up to meet his gaze, fighting the desire to look away again. "It wasn't your fault all those years ago."

Jed shook his head. "I don't blame myself, not anymore. Time and grace heals the ache, but the questions don't ever disappear."

As Jed walked away into the night, Jayne wondered what his wife's name was and how long ago it had happened. Funny how her own problems didn't seem as bad when she focused on something besides herself.

Later that night, when her sisters slept, Jayne pulled out her diary, longing to turn her mass of thoughts into words on a page. For a long time she sat deep in thought, pondering over the day's events, diary in hand. It seemed like a week since she had sent Yvonne on her way with the cough mixture. As she began to write, her thoughts came faster than her pen could move. Somewhere along the way, they turned into a prayer.

When her pen stopped moving, her eyes felt drawn to the shelf above the fire, and her gaze fell on the plaque Daddy had made for Mam. She went over to it and traced the words with her finger.

CHRIST IS THE HEAD
of this house,
THE UNSEEN GUEST
at every meal,
THE SILENT LISTENER
to every conversation.

She went back to her diary and copied the words on the page. Christ was indeed present, and He was Lord over all. After the ink dried, she laid her hand across the page as if to grasp the words.

7
Mam's Story

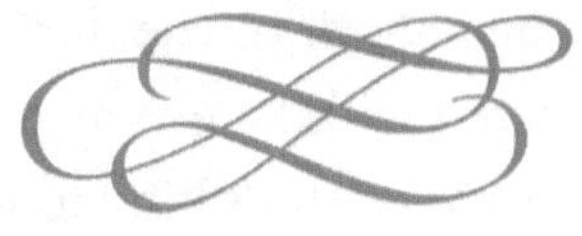

Jayne's eyes flicked open. Suddenly alert, she lay for a moment peering into the darkness. What was it that she had heard? She rolled onto her side and listened. The sound came again. This time Jayne felt sure she knew what it was. As the noise continued, she pulled back her quilts and stepped reluctantly into the coldness of the room.

She crept over to the bed shared by her sisters and placed a hand on the closest form. "What's the matter, Vonnie?" She kept her voice low, trying to spare Olivia's sleep. As Yvonne buried her face into the pillow and refused to answer, Jayne felt sure she already knew the cause of her sister's crying. That horrible man. She felt a surge of anger towards Lamberton for bringing more trouble upon them.

Beneath her touch, Yvonne's body trembled. A sharp pain lingered in Jayne's heart, but no matter how much she longed to fix the situation, she couldn't. She was unable to ever make her parents come back. She knelt and stroked her sister's hair, turning her sense of helplessness into a silent prayer. As she begged God to put an end to the heartache, she fought against the tightness in her throat, determined not to give way to her emotions.

Still struggling, she placed an arm around Yvonne's shoulders and gave her a loving squeeze. "Tell me what's wrong." The subdued tone in her voice only added to the loneliness of the night.

Yvonne's head moved almost imperceptibly. "I miss Mammy and Daddy"—her voice trembled—"so much." A loud sob cut off any other words.

Olivia moaned, and the bed creaked as she half sat up and propped her head on her hand. In the darkness, she fumbled around until she connected with Jayne's arm.

The understanding in her sister's kind touch filled Jayne with gratitude. It communicated more than a hundred words ever could. They were all suffering. More than ever, Jayne wanted to take away both her sisters' pain. So intense was her desire that she didn't think she could bear it.

"They wanted us to be joyful." Yvonne's breath came in gasps. "I don't feel like I'm doing a very good job." The noise of her crying filled the room again.

"Yes, you are." Jayne hugged her youngest sister. "I know it's hard." Her own words ended in a little sob as she covered her face with her hands. Gone was her resolve to always be strong for her sisters.

Whimpering, Yvonne reached out and clung to Jayne's hand. "I'm so scared." Her grip tightened. "What if that horrible man comes back? We'll have nowhere to go. Even with you and Olivia here, I feel so alone." As the storm within erupted, Yvonne buried her head beneath her pillow and sobbed.

Jayne shivered. Cold and tired, she wished she'd never even

heard the name Lamberton. A shuddery sigh came from Olivia's side of the bed. Then the blankets rustled, and Olivia's dark shape moved against the wall to make room. Jayne rose from the freezing floor and climbed over Yvonne, doing her best not to hurt her on the way over. Snuggling between the warmth of her sisters' bodies, she pulled the quilts up to her chin.

Before Jayne could try to ease Yvonne's worries, Olivia said, "Maybe he'll never come back. Who knows? We might never see him again." The blankets tightened. "Jayne did tell him we weren't interested in handing over the lease."

"I don't know what will happen." Jayne struggled to control the waver in her voice. "But even if he does come back, God will protect us. I know He will." She wanted to tell them that Christ was sovereign, but the words seemed stuck in her throat, blocked by the threat of more tears.

When Jayne could still feel Yvonne's body trembling, she tried again. "We're doing all right. Everything will be fine." She didn't mention the fact that they had little money, or that their vegetable crop was not as good as usual.

Yvonne pulled the pillow from her head. "But what about Lam—"

"I won't let him take our property." Jayne's tone left no room for arguing. "Please don't worry about the ifs. It won't do any good." How she wished she could take her own advice to heart.

Drawing a shuddering breath, Yvonne rolled on her side to face Jayne. "Tell me about our names."

Jayne suppressed a groan. She'd known the request would come, but after all that had happened, why did it have to be tonight?

"Say it like it was Mam telling the story. I want to close my eyes and pretend it's really her."

Jayne bit her lip. Not now, she wasn't ready. She had heard the story a hundred times. But to tell it like Mam while keeping a grip on her emotions . . . Silently, she begged God to help her.

There was a movement under the blankets as Jayne felt Olivia's hand searching for her own. Clasping the offered lifeline, Jayne closed her eyes and pushed aside her growing desire to flee the room. After a deep breath, she began. "A long time ago before I was even born, my parents went through very tough times." Jayne stopped. It had always been Mam's story. It almost felt wrong to be the one telling it. But at the sound of Yvonne sniffling back tears, Jayne knew she had to go on.

"My parents were behind on their rent, and my father's health had been troubling him. For months they never knew where their next meal would come from. Desperation gripped them. If things continued how they were for much longer, they wouldn't have a home.

"My father and mother cried out to God, seeking His purpose in their suffering. God remained faithful to them and always provided for their needs just in time. It was through these trials that God showed them the joy of the Lord was their strength. They could not rely on themselves or on earthly things. Only God would never fail them. They chose to delight in Him.

"A short time later, they found out my mother was expecting. They decided if their baby was a girl, they would call her Abigail—my Father is joy—to remind their daughter of the important lessons God had taught them. All through my life they told me, 'Abigail, let the joy of the Lord be the strength of your life.'

"When I grew up and got married, I told Brian the story behind my name. He decided to carry on the legacy—a legacy of faith. We called our first daughter Jayne, meaning 'God is gracious.'" Jayne paused. Every time Mam reached this part of the story, she had smiled and taken Jayne's hand with love radiating through her eyes and touch.

Jayne swallowed and cleared her throat. All she had to do was concentrate on the next word, the next sentence. "Without realising it, we had chosen a name beginning with J, the first letter of the word that had become so important to me—joy. The name reminded me that to be strong, I needed to delight in the Lord, for God is always gracious.

"When we were having our second child, your daddy suggested that we call our new baby, whether boy or girl, a name starting with O. If God blessed us with a third child, then we could complete the special word. We decided on Olivia, symbol of peace."

A tremor ran through Olivia's body, then a shuddery breath sounded in the darkness. Jayne's voice choked, but she kept going. "A few years later, I gave birth to another precious baby girl. Your daddy, true to his word, searched for a name we liked that begun with Y. It was no easy task, but we finally found one. Our little Yvonne completed the special word—joy.

"No matter what happens in my three jewels' lives, you must turn to God and remember that your joy is in Him. In Him you can find strength and joy during every trial. God is gracious, always gracious. You must commit your way to Him." Jayne paused. Now that the end was here, it felt like she was closing the door on her parents—a final goodbye. Using every ounce of her willpower, she ended the story just as Mam always had. "You must never forget."

8

ANOTHER ISSUE

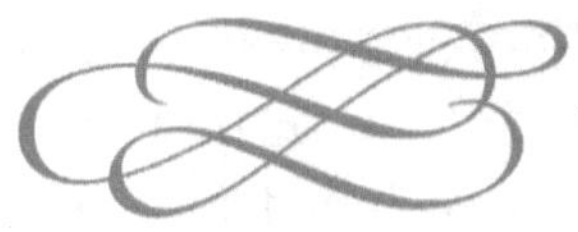

Jayne yawned as they rode to church the next morning. All around them the birds chirped, and the sun shone. Everything seemed to defy the sorrow of the night before. Even the crisp wind that toyed with her hair seemed to be inviting her to lay aside her cares. Jayne threw her head back, letting the sun warm her face. She wouldn't fight the freshness of the morning.

By the time their cart reached the church building, Jayne had the odd desire to skip up the steps to the door. A chuckle almost escaped her lips as she thought of what Mrs. Sterling would think if she saw her.

The church bell rang out in the winter air, causing Jayne to gaze up at the slate steeple as it glimmered in the sunlight. She felt Yvonne's arm link through her own and happiness swelled through her. Though refraining from skipping, Jayne allowed herself the pleasure of a light step as she ascended towards the entry.

The rustle of skirts and muffled coughs and thumps greeted

them as Jayne searched the wooden pews for Jed and Cass. As she slipped into the space beside them, Reverend Hastie approached the pulpit and looked out over the congregation with a smile.

After the final hymn, Jayne began winding her way towards the back of the building, where a group of women she recognised stood chatting together. She was partway there, when someone called her name. Before she could turn around, two hands clasped her arm.

"I've been hoping all morning that you'd come. I'd nearly given up hope, but here you are. Just spotted you this very instant," said Mrs. Arthur, gasping to catch her breath.

Jayne didn't have time to respond before she was being hurried along to a more secluded spot near the wall, wondering what she might have done to arouse the talkative woman's attention. Bracing herself, Jayne waited for Mrs. Arthur to say her piece. She didn't have to wait long.

"You know that new worker of yours? The one Mrs. O'Donnell told me about." Mrs. Arthur looked around, then leaned her stout body closer. "Tall, dark hair, Irish brogue?"

Though she wanted to roll her eyes, Jayne gave the expected nod. It wasn't as if she owned a large station with a dozen farm hands. But if she had information, this auburn-haired woman would find some way to proclaim it. Sometimes she wondered why Mam had invested so much time in Mrs. Arthur, but that was Mam—loving the hard to love.

"Well he came into the hotel when I was working yesterday, just as nice as pie and sly as a fox. And do you know what he did?" Mrs. Arthur paused for effect.

Jayne fought a grimace. Whether or not she wanted to know, she was about to be enlightened. "No, I'm quite sure I don't."

"He started asking questions about your family, that's what. Now, I know how you feel about gossip, Jayne. But in this case, I think you'd be wise to listen. This is not just mindless tales. It's straight from the horse's mouth. Thought he'd come in and get information from a prattling woman and go on his devious way. But he didn't count on me telling you." She placed her hand on her hip with an air of triumph.

The smell of the mingled perfumes in the room overwhelmed Jayne's senses, making her light-headed. She shot a glance at the nearby window which stretched high up towards the lofty ceiling. It barred the fresh air she craved. She looked beyond the crowds to the doorway, and the sight of Cass as he leaned against the doorframe made her forget her need for air. As Jayne watched, Revered Hastie walked up and shook Cass's offered hand. Both men laughed heartily. Then with a nod, Cass disappeared out the door.

In her ear, Mrs. Arthur droned on, oblivious to her lack of audience. Jayne wondered how much she had missed, as she refocused on the stream of words.

"I answered his nosey questions but kept my replies brief and to the point. I was pleased as punch with myself afterwards. Don't know what his interest was. But how it could've been honourable, I certainly can't see."

Jayne's eyes met Mrs. Arthur's, and she shrugged a little helplessly. "I don't know either, but he's a hard worker."

Mrs. Arthur raised her eyebrows. "Be that as it may, you know the old saying. Where there's smoke, there's fire."

Jayne opened her mouth, only to be interrupted.

"There are no buts about it, young woman. I'd be keeping an eye on that one. Or getting rid of him before you regret the day you hired him. I don't like to presume ill of someone, but"—she looked at Jayne meaningfully—"there are your sisters to think about, not to mention yourself. I'd hate to see you robbed of all you have left on this earth." Mrs. Arthur beckoned Jayne to come nearer, and reluctantly, she obeyed.

"He even wanted to know where your dear folks had been laid to rest. Now, if you don't call that strange, then I don't know what is. I've been wondering about it ever since. What does he—a stranger—plan to do with such information? The moment my husband arrived home, I put it to him. Said he certainly didn't know either."

Jayne shook her head wearily. "I can't imagine why he'd want that information." She felt a bit guilty over the relief she felt to see Olivia and Yvonne heading her way.

Mrs. Arthur spotted them too. She waved, then turned back to Jayne with a sigh. "Well, forewarned is forearmed. I'll be praying for you and your sisters as I always do. Just remember, you'll not find a thrush in a hawk's nest."

Jayne bade Mrs. Arthur farewell and hurried to meet her sisters. Together they walked into the sunshine and fresh air. The area surrounding the hitching posts was filled with the sounds of people laughing and talking as they mingled with each other. Jayne shook her head at the contrast between their light-heartedness and the conversation she had just experienced. Again she shook her head, then laughed when she saw Yvonne watching. "Don't mind me." She took her seat and picked up the reins, refraining from shaking her head a third time. What a strange mix of emotions.

Olivia nudged her. "Jed and Cass left a while ago."

In answer, Jayne slapped the reins across Betsie's back. No matter the cause, she ought not keep Jed's stomach waiting while she daydreamed.

When Jed knocked on the door a while later, Jayne opened it with a smile on her face. "A hundred thousand welcomes to you!"

Jed winked and nodded approvingly at Jayne, while Cass stepped up beside him.

Cass chuckled. "I see you're minding Irish hospitality. Your parents would be pleased, I'm sure." He appeared to be about to say something else, but Jayne turned away.

Once inside, Cass locked eyes with Jayne, giving her no way of escape. "I regret not having been in time to meet with your parents. My sincerest sympathy to you all."

Jayne bit her lip, then murmured the expected thanks for his condolences. Who was this man, and what did he want? She had no desire for compassion from a man she wasn't sure she could trust. Her gaze swung to Jed.

His face was sympathetic. "Why don't we eat? I'm sure Cass is hungry." He gave Cass a playful elbow.

Jayne forced a laugh. "The food is piping hot. Isn't that right, Vonnie?"

Yvonne glanced between Jayne and Cass as if sensing her older sister's tension. Then her face relaxed, and with a nod she danced over to give the stew a stir, while Olivia finished buttering the wedges of bread and pushed the plate to the middle of the table. As she watched her sisters, Jayne fought to focus on the necessary steps to take as hostess. She probably ought to offer Cass a drink, but she couldn't face speaking to him again—not yet. Once her mind had cleared of Mrs. Arthur's words everything would be fine.

Empty tin plates glared at her from the table. The stew. She would dish up the meal. As Yvonne picked up the serving spoon, Jayne opened her mouth to tell her little sister to sit down. Then she stopped. Nothing appeared to give Yvonne greater joy than serving others. After casting one last look around to see that everything was taken care of, Jayne sat down and clenched her hands in her lap.

Jed pulled out a chair and motioned for Cass to sit beside him. As the tall man took his seat, Jayne kept her eyes on her plate. At least the activity going on around her gave the appearance that nothing was amiss. She would try to do the same.

As soon as Jed gave thanks for the meal, Jayne searched for something to say, but before she had a chance to speak, Jed began questioning Cass about Ireland. At first Jayne cared only that someone else was making conversation. But as Cass talked, Jayne felt surprised at how keen she was to hear what he had to say. She watched to see if her sisters felt the same way. Both sat with their eyes fixed on Cass, every so often remembering to fork something into their mouths.

Her parents had often reinforced the fact that Australia was home now, but they had also made a point of telling stories about Ireland regularly. Jayne didn't realise how much she had missed it. She found herself joining the conversation with ease.

Jed broke a piece of bread off the wedge on his plate. "Now that you've thrilled us with tales of the fair Irish shores, what of your family? Who managed to keep you filled and out of mischief?"

Cass shook his head. "I'm sure I've already told enough to keep your minds full for hours." He took his time cutting a piece of mutton. "Distracting everyone from the good food, I am."

As Cass took to chewing his meat, silence hung about the room. Jed cleared his throat. "I thought Reverend Hastie made some good points this morning."

Jayne nodded and glanced over at Cass. He was staring at the plaque over the fireplace. Then his gaze flicked over the rest of the articles on the shelf. As Cass's eyes continued to rove around the room, Jayne's curiosity grew. Suddenly an arm bumped her, and Jayne jerked her gaze back to the table. Looking around, she realised that Olivia, Yvonne, and Jed were staring at her. Her face tingled as she noticed that Cass now stared too. She turned her head towards Olivia, hoping for some clue as to what was happening.

Olivia laughed and grinned at her. "Never mind. It appears you weren't listening anyway."

From across the table, Jed's rumbling laugh broke out. Jayne joined in, relieved that she had missed something in the conversation, rather than been caught watching Cass. As talk began to flow again, she tried to keep her attention on what was being said to avoid further embarrassment. Cass also appeared to be making an effort to join in again. Yet as Jayne watched him laugh and talk, she couldn't help noticing that his eyes continued to drift over the room. More than once Jed asked him something only to be answered by a questioning look.

When she saw Jed shoot Cass a sideways glance, the sight filled her with something akin to relief. She had begun to worry that she was just imagining things. But if Jed thought Cass's behaviour strange, then indeed it must be odd—not something contrived by her imagination. As that thought sank in, her feelings of relief vanished.

Jed's chair scraped against the ground as he stood up, and Jayne jumped

"Reckon your mind is wandering today," he said, smiling down at her.

Jayne laughed. "I'm sorry. Perhaps if I move around a bit, I'll pay better attention." She jumped up to retrieve the Bible from the shelf before Jed could move in its direction. After handing the book to Jed, she turned to Cass. "Would you like a cup of tea?"

His brown eyes were sober as he nodded, and Jayne quickly turned to ask Jed the same question. The rattle of tin cups interrupted the growing silence as Jayne set them in front of the men and filled the cups to the brim.

After Jed had finished several chapters of Scripture, he turned to Yvonne. "What song should we sing?"

Yvonne screwed up her eyes for a moment. When she opened them again, she led the group in the first verse of "Be Thou My Vision."

Jayne's heart warmed as she joined in. She could not help wondering if Yvonne had chosen it for her. The lump that frequently troubled her since the death of her parents formed in her throat. Only with effort did she manage to push it away and keep singing. The words of the second verse—*Thou my great Father, I Thy true son*—went straight to her heart. They reminded her of something else, but she couldn't think what.

As Jayne sang the last words of the hymn, she meant them with all of her being: "Heart of my own heart, whatever befall, still be my vision, O Ruler of all." Her voice trailed off, and she realised why the words of the second verse had been so familiar. They reminded her of the verse Jed had read on that cold and dreary night. What had it been? Jayne closed her eyes, trying to picture the verse in her mind. Finally she gave in with a shake of her head. When everyone left, she would look it up again.

Jed laid his hand on the Bible, then stood up. "We'd best be going. Cass might need some rest so he can keep up with me this week."

Cass winked at Yvonne. "I'm just getting warmed up. We Irish folk know how to work."

Jed laughed. "Maybe so. But I could do with a rest myself."

After the two men left, Olivia and Yvonne went outside to take advantage of the pleasant weather, while Jayne decided to try to get some rest herself. But as she sat on the edge of her bed, her mind refused to be silent, and her body felt tense. It would be useless to lie down. Yet indecision made her stay on the bed's edge a moment longer. Finally, yearning for something to keep her hands and mind busy, Jayne went to the scrap basket in the corner of the room. Pieces of fabric flew to the floor as she rummaged through the odds and ends. Near the bottom of the basket, she found a piece of material left over from making petticoats.

Gathering up the other necessary items, Jayne pulled her cloak from the bedroom wall. For though the sky was blue and the sun shone, the air still held a bitterness. With all in readiness, she went over to the volume on the table and opened it to the book of Psalms. Flipping through it, she managed to locate the verse she had been unable to remember. *A father to the fatherless, and a judge of the widows is God in His holy habitation.* She read it over until she could say it from memory.

Once outside Jayne roamed until she found a haven where she could sit undisturbed. Then she settled herself on a log and let herself relax into the day. As she threaded her needle, the chirping birds and crisp air soothed her turmoil like a salve.

When at last the cold drove her inside, Jayne tucked the needlework beneath her cloak so her sisters wouldn't notice it. Before she hid the fabric under her pillow, she looked at it once more. Letters curled across its surface in rich purple. When she had time, she would finish the verse and embroider clusters of flowers around the words.

With a lighter heart, she went to join her sisters in the main room, a smile lighting her face. Tonight was her favourite evening of the entire week. No pressing duties demanded her attention, and they could read favourite sections from God's Word as the fire blazed. Then came songs of thanksgiving and praise—as many as they could think of. When their voices grew weary of singing, they were free to chatter until only a few red coals winked at them. Tired but refreshed, the evening would leave them ready for another week of hard work.

Jayne hummed as she pushed aside the tea dishes and worked with her sisters to prepare for the evening's activities. Already she savoured the thought of warm milk with a dash of cinnamon and a little brown sugar.

As Yvonne heated the milk, Olivia pulled three chairs closer to the fire. Jayne stoked the coals, enjoying their vibrancy. Just as she threw a log onto the fire to set it ablaze, a quick rap sounded on the door. Her head twirled towards the sound. Before she could move towards it, the door opened, and Jed stuck his head in.

"Jayne," he said, "I need you to come with me."

9
NIGHT ADVENTURE

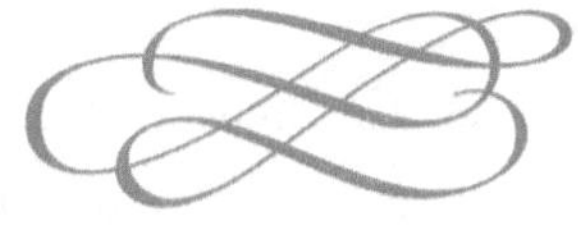

Jayne was on her feet in an instant and heading for the door, but Jed stopped her. "Get your cloak. It's a clear night, so the temperature's dropping fast."

As Jayne hurried to do as she was told, she heard the murmur of Jed's voice but could pick up no indication as to what was wrong. Maybe the lantern she'd seen dangling from his hand meant he'd been out checking the sheep one last time.

As soon as she returned, Jed stepped back into the night. Jayne followed, almost running to keep up with his long strides.

"One of the ewes is having trouble giving birth." Jed led the way through the trees, kicking aside branches that might trip her. "I noticed the ewe when I checked earlier, and the lamb's head is still hanging out. Must be stuck."

"Where's Cass?" Jayne asked.

Jed shrugged. "He went off about an hour ago. Didn't have time to try and find him. Besides, it'll be good for you to watch."

Jayne nodded and shivered simultaneously. Jed was right. It was cold, but she was glad to have the opportunity to help. Perhaps one day she would need to help a ewe by herself. She shivered again. After a mild day, the cold seemed worse than usual.

As she slipped on something round and hard, Jayne let out a cry of surprise. Jed caught her arm just in time to stop her from hitting the wet ground. When she had recovered her balance, she looked down to see what she had stepped on. At the edge of the lantern light lay a pile of carrot stubs. Jayne frowned and moved them with her toe. She wanted to examine them further, but Jed and the circle of light had already gone ahead. With an inward shrug, she ran to catch up.

As they neared the flock, the bleating of sheep broke through the darkness. Jayne peered around, trying to spot the ewe that was giving birth. All she could see was a mass of blobs until Jed pointed away from the flock to a clump of shrubs. There stood a ewe and beside it a newborn lamb. Jayne breathed a sigh of relief, silently thanking God, but Jed held up his lantern and pointed to the back of the sheep.

"Twins," he said. "See?"

Then Jayne saw what she had missed before—a tiny white head still protruded from its mother. "Oh! The poor thing. Is it still alive?"

Jed shrugged. "Maybe, maybe not. We'll have to catch the ewe before we can help the lamb at all."

A shovel hit the ground beside Jed with a thud, and Jayne shuddered, wondering how she had missed seeing the tool beforehand.

"Right then, let's try and catch her. You go around that way." He pointed behind the sheep. "We'll try and corner her." As Jed and Jayne closed in on the sheep, it took off at a run.

Jayne cringed as she saw the lamb's head jerking up and down with the ewe's every movement, but there was no other option. The ewe had to be caught, and it wasn't making things easy. The sheep trotted towards the safety of its flock as if hungry dogs were yapping at its heels. Before Jayne could dash in front of it, the ewe made a mad leap into the midst of the other sheep. She heard Jed groan.

Jayne glanced over her shoulder to see what had happened to the abandoned lamb. It was far back, still near the shrubs where they had left it. Baaing for its mother, the lamb rose to stand on wobbly legs, then plopped back to the ground. Despite the frustration she had felt a moment before, Jayne grinned.

An owl hooted as Jed stood with hands on hips, trying to work out the best way to separate the ewe from the rest of the flock. While she waited, Jayne looked up at the dark sky, where millions of stars twinkled down at her. The half-moon gave just enough light for her to make out the shapes of other sheep huddled in the distance.

Jayne looked back towards the lamb in the grass, and glimpsed another light bobbing up and down, the yellow glow drawing closer and closer. She hoped it was Cass. Perhaps he would be able to help catch the troublesome ewe. She strained to see who it was, and finally, she could just make out the form of the person who held the lantern. It was much too small to be Cass.

Another shape emerged from behind the first. This second form was taller and moved as if carrying something heavy. As they got closer, Jayne recognised her sisters. The lantern swung from Yvonne's hand, and Olivia followed with a bucket.

Once Olivia set her load on the ground, Jed began giving out orders. "Right"—he looked at Jayne—"you start walking behind the sheep and chase them towards me. Olivia, Yvonne, don't let them past you. As they come by me, I'll try to grab her." Trapped between the fence and the girls, the sheep milled in a tight mob. Jed lifted his lantern higher, trying to spot the right ewe.

Yvonne let out a cry. "I see it. Look! There it is." She jumped up and down, pointing to the ewe as it darted by her.

Jed set his lantern on the ground and made a leap for the ewe. He grabbed its fleece and held on as it struggled to run by with the rest. Pushing the sheep onto its side, he signalled for Jayne to grab hold.

She dropped onto the icy ground next to the sheep and grasped two of its legs. Watching its heavy breathing, a wave of compassion washed over her. As Jed took off his coat and rolled up his shirtsleeves, the ewe began to thrash about. For a moment Jayne thought she would lose her grip. In desperation she placed her knee over the sheep's neck. She heard Jed giving her directions, but all she could think about was not letting go. Her arms strained as her hands slipped, and just when she thought she had no hope of maintaining her grasp, the sheep calmed and lay still. Jayne slumped forward, her breath coming in gasps.

"Good job."

Jayne looked up into Jed's laughing eyes as he clapped her on the back.

Olivia brought the bucket of water forward. The ring of light from Yvonne's lantern illuminated the steam rising from the surface. Immediately, Jed began scrubbing his hands and forearms. As soon as he finished, he crouched behind the ewe.

"The front legs should come out before the head." He bent closer. "I'll have to poke around until I find 'em." He looked at Jayne. "You'd best be ready to hold her. She won't like me feeling around."

Jayne nodded and prepared herself for another struggle. As

soon as Jed started to insert his hand into the ewe, the sheep fought Jayne's hold. Olivia dropped to the ground and together they held on as the ewe continued to squirm away from the pain.

As Yvonne scrunched her nose up, Jayne couldn't help smiling. A moan erupted from the sheep, and Jayne bit her lip, her amusement fading. Yvonne dropped to her knees and patted the sheep's head. "You poor thing." Tears glistened in her eyes.

"Has to be done. Both'd die if I didn't help." Jed pulled his hand out, and the sheep stopped grunting. "Think I've found the legs. Both pointed in the wrong position." As soon as he started feeling around again, the sheep grunted. "There, one's the right way. If I could just get the other leg in place." His arm tightened and pulled.

The sheep's heart was pounding now—so hard Jayne couldn't bear to watch. She glanced over at Jed just in time to see the slight flicker of a smile. "Think I might have the other leg right. If I could just . . ." His words trailed off as he tried again.

Yvonne squatted down and draped her arm around Jayne's shoulders, leaning her head silently against her sister's. Jayne could sense her distress. Poor Vonnie. She had such a tender heart. The thought struck Jayne as if it were a new revelation. How she wanted to shield her sister from anything that would cause her pain.

Jayne leaned forward as the lamb emerged, coated in a yellowy film. After all that trouble, it slipped out so fast that she nearly missed its birth.

Jed's eyes twinkled as he looked at Yvonne. "It's a girl and still alive." He reached down to pick up the slimy new arrival and deposit it by the ewe's head. "Wouldn't be surprised if the mother doesn't want much to do with it. Let her go a minute, Jayne."

Jayne and Olivia released their hold, but their hands still

hovered at the ready. The ewe kept staring straight ahead, not once looking in the lamb's direction. The seconds grew long. A night bird swept overhead, calling as it disappeared into the treetops.

Jed tore off a handful of grass and rubbed the lamb briskly to clean off some of the film. Once he had finished, he beckoned to Olivia and Yvonne. "You two take a lamb each and carry them back to the house. Stick 'em near the fire till we get back. I'll let the ewe rest a bit longer before we take her up to the stable."

As Jed spoke, Jayne looked around for the other lamb, which had been forgotten amidst the struggles. A faint bleating came from the shrubs nearby. Olivia had already started in that direction, and she came back a moment later with a white head poking out from between the folds of her cloak.

Yvonne gingerly picked up the newest lamb and wrapped it in her cloak, talking to it softly. Jayne smiled at the picture her sisters made. "Here, do you want the lantern?"

Olivia shook her head. "It'll be too hard to carry."

"Are you sure?"

Olivia looked out at the dark shapes surrounding them. Glancing back at the friendly light of the lantern, she shifted the lamb to one arm and grasped the handle. "If it gets too difficult, I'll leave it and find it in the morning."

Jayne nodded as her two sisters began their slow march back to the house.

Jed rose to his feet and gave his hands a quick scrub in the bucket Olivia had left behind. He pointed to the ewe, which was now sitting up. "You make sure she doesn't go anywhere while I finish checking the rest of the flock." Jed strode into the blackness with the remaining lantern held high.

Jayne found herself sitting in the dark and cold with only the ewe for company. She would've been only too glad to join the lambs by the cosy fire, but she had no hope of that anytime soon. So she sat half-straddling the ewe, shivering and watching the lantern bob around the paddock. Every so often the light disappeared behind a tree. Each time it faded from view, she strained to catch another glimpse, trying to shake off the feeling of being alone in the night.

Jayne longed to stand up and walk around but didn't dare to, lest the ewe catch her unawares and dart off to join the rest of the flock. As time moved on, she let her imagination run wild. Every noise turned into the footstep of someone lurking behind her. Thoughts of Mr. Lamberton and his threat to return made her tense with every new sound. A branch snapped. Huddling low beneath her cloak, Jayne tried to make herself less noticeable. Relief flooded her heart as the lantern swung in her direction and advanced closer to the spot where she crouched. Finally, Jed stood by her side.

"Best I can tell, the rest are fine." He set the lantern with its half-burnt candle near Jayne and picked up the shovel. Puzzled, Jayne watched him dig a hole about the depth of a lamb. When Jed bent down to push something onto the shovel, realisation dawned on her.

"Why do you bother?" she asked, as she watched him bury the afterbirth.

"Guards against attracting crows and stray dogs." He threw more dirt into the hole. "Before you know it, it'll be foxes we have to guard against. Only someone with no livestock would've been daft enough to introduce 'em. Those city-bred Englishmen think only of their sporting pleasure. But it'll be no good when foxes start attacking our livelihood."

Jayne nodded. Foxes hadn't been popular with farmers in

Ireland either. Though it made her shudder to think of a fox stalking a lamb, secretly she wished she could see one. Perhaps they weren't so bad apart from that.

When Jed finished his task, he offered Jayne his hand to help her stand up. She stared at it in horror. Even in the darkness, she could make out the specks of red his quick scrub had failed to remove. When he didn't draw his hand back, Jayne laid her fingertips inside it. A moment later, when her legs buckled, she was grateful she had. If not for Jed's grasp, she would have been right back on the ground.

"Let's get you and this sheep back to some warmth. It won't be easy. She isn't going to want to leave the other sheep. But the sooner we try to get some colostrum into those young'uns, the better."

Jayne began moving forward on wooden legs, managing to shuffle into position between the ewe and the rest of the flock. The ewe took a few steps, then lunged to the side. For a moment Jayne's feet wouldn't cooperate. At the last possible instant, she leapt in front of the sheep and held out her cloak to scare it.

The ewe made a dozen more attempts to return to the flock, but each time Jayne was ready and blocked its path. At last it began to move in the right direction, and together Jayne and Jed urged the ewe homeward with voice and arms. With the stable finally in view, Jed turned to Jayne. "Go on in and sit by the fire. I'll put the ewe in a pen."

Jayne shook her head. The cold was better than a lonely walk through the dark. "I can wait a bit longer."

Once the ewe was secured, they entered the house to see that Olivia and Yvonne had pulled their chairs as close to the fire as they could without catching their dresses alight.

Stretching out his hands to the warmth, Jed nodded towards the bundles nestled in the girls' arms. "By the looks of it, you two have found yourself some friends."

Jayne leaned over and stroked the littlest lamb.

Jed chuckled. "Let's get them back to their mother before you lot decide to keep them." He retrieved his lantern from the table, then turned back to Jayne. "You can stay put if you want."

Jayne nodded. Weary and cold, she had no desire to go any-where—not even for cute lambs. While the others headed out into the cold, she sat by the fire, but tiredness soon made it too hard for her to stay upright in the chair. Glancing around the room, she searched unsuccessfully for the lantern she and her sisters shared. Maybe they had taken it. She couldn't remember, nor did she particularly care. She would have to look for it in the morning.

Feeling her way in the darkness, Jayne changed into a warm nightgown and fell into the softness of her covers. As she closed her eyes, she couldn't remember the last time her bed had felt so good.

10
MAKING ENDS MEET

"Jayne, Jayne, you'll never guess what's happened." Yvonne gasped for breath as she halted in front of Checker's stall. "The lantern we left out is missing. Nowhere to be found."

Olivia came up behind Yvonne. "We looked everywhere."

Jayne groaned and set her milk pails on the ground outside the pen. She had forgotten to ask about the lantern. "Where did you leave it?" she asked Olivia.

"It was too difficult for me to carry the lamb and the lantern last night. Halfway home we decided to leave it by a tree. We made sure we left it where we could find it, but—" She lifted her hands in a helpless shrug.

Jayne didn't like the possibilities that her mind immediately conjured up. To Yvonne it was just an exciting mystery, but to Jayne the implications seemed serious. Had someone been creeping around their property in the dark? Was it someone connected with Mr. Lamberton? Or worse still, could it have been Lamberton himself? As Jayne remembered how she had sat alone in the dark last night, a tingle ran down her spine.

Olivia watched Jayne's face closely. "What do you think happened to it?"

Jayne shrugged, unwilling to voice her thoughts. She patted Checkers as she disciplined herself to think of a more obvious solution. "You probably just forgot where you put it. Come, and we'll all look."

Olivia nodded. "Sure enough it hasn't grown legs and walked off. More than likely we just had the wrong place."

Jayne shook her head at herself. Why must she always jump to the worst possible conclusion? Still feeling frustrated, she called out to Yvonne, who was already heading out of the stable. "Wait till I put these pails inside."

Yvonne turned and grinned, bouncing up and down as if she could barely stay put.

Jayne walked towards the house as fast as she could without splashing milk over her dress. What were her sisters thinking, leaving their only lantern in the middle of nowhere? The rent on their property was due soon, and as it was, they didn't have enough money to pay it. They could not go on being so careless.

Jayne shook her head. She was being unfair. Ordinarily, it would have been safe to leave anything anywhere on their property without fear of it being stolen. She sincerely hoped Jed's enquiries in town would solve all these worries.

The three sisters searched for half an hour, being sure to check around the base of every tree and every shrub close to where Olivia and Yvonne had walked the night before. Unwilling to admit defeat, they even started looking in the branches of low-growing bushes— just in case Olivia had unknowingly hung the lantern there. Finally they gave up hope of finding it and turned homeward.

"I guess we'll just have to do without a lantern for the time being," Jayne said, feeling gloomy at the prospect. The skip disappeared from Yvonne's step, and Olivia gazed silently around her, as if hoping the lantern would suddenly appear.

They were in sight of the house when a voice called out for them to wait. Cass strolled towards them, something hanging from his hand. "I found this last night when I was out for a breath of fresh air."

Jayne felt her eyebrows shoot upwards. It was their missing lantern. Then her surprise turned to suspicion. It had been a chilly night to get a breath of fresh air.

Seeing her hesitation, Cass dropped his outstretched hand and took a step back. "I presumed it was yours."

Olivia stared at Jayne with a frown, then walked forward and took the lantern from Cass. "Thank you for being so kind as to bring it back to us." A smile lit her face as she explained how they thought someone must have stolen it.

Cass threw back his head and laughed. His eyes full of merriness, he motioned behind him. "How'd those young lambs fare through the night?"

While he stood there grinning, the picture of attentiveness, Olivia and Yvonne jumped right in to tell him all about it. Gesturing animatedly, they took turns describing how Jed had forced the mother to stand still while they helped the lambs feed. Jayne watched the group, trying not to scowl. Cass was too smooth.

When Cass met her eyes, Jayne instantly looked away. "You'll have to take me to see those wee lambs sometime," he said. With a wave, he turned to go about his day's work.

"What's the matter with you?" Olivia whispered as soon as Cass was out of hearing.

"The candle is missing." Jayne's voice was equally low. When no light dawned in Olivia's eyes, she went on. "How did the lantern get into Cass's possession, and why is the candle inside it gone?"

"You needn't be so suspicious. Not everyone is sinister, you know. It was silly of us to think the lantern was stolen in the first place. Besides, you heard Cass say he was just getting some fresh air. There's nothing strange about that, is there?" Olivia gave a little laugh. "What would Cass want with a half-burned candle anyway? It probably just fell out."

Yvonne, who had skipped ahead humming merrily, spun around and grinned. "What are you two whispering about?"

Her words put an immediate end to the conversation, but Jayne kept on turning the situation around in her head. Olivia was right. What would Cass, or anyone else for that matter, want with a candle? Even as the thought occurred to her, she wondered if perhaps someone *had* wanted the candle. Not of course for the candle itself but as a way to scare her. Could even Cass himself have had such motives?

"I've been thinking."

Jed ceased hacking away at a bush and waited for Jayne to go on.

"You know how Daddy used to do odd jobs here and there, whenever he was able?"

A look of understanding came into Jed's eyes.

"I've been thinking we, I mean Olivia, Vonnie, and I, should try to find some odd jobs we can do. The second lot of rent money is due at the end of the year." Jayne fiddled with the end of her braid. "And even with the money Daddy and Mammy put aside already"—she squeezed her eyes shut—"there isn't enough."

When Jayne opened her eyes, everything looked blurry. "If we can't pay the rent, we'll lose our farm."

Though his hands were grime-covered, Jed wrapped one arm around her shoulders and gave her a reassuring squeeze. He sighed and looked out at the vast bush that needed clearing. "I'm sorry." He stopped, swallowed, then tried again. "I'm sorry you have so much to bear, but God knows better than I do."

He blew out a puff of air. "A long time ago God taught me something, Jayne. He made me realise that He was bigger than my problems and far stronger than all my weaknesses." He brushed a hand across his face. "Are not five sparrows sold for two farthings, and not one of them is forgotten before God? But even the very hairs of your head are all numbered." He looked her full in the face with tears glistening in his eyes. "Fear not therefore: ye are of more value than many sparrows."

Jayne bent down and toyed with one of the shrubs Jed had just chopped out, hiding her face from him. For a long moment, neither said anything.

When she stood up, Jed motioned to the patch of ground he was clearing. "While I finish off here, I'll pray over what you've said. I'll let you know what I think before I head for town this afternoon." He hoisted his axe ready to resume work. "Don't you go forgetting your names." His axe connected with the base of a shrub.

Jayne smiled half-heartedly. He was right. She must not forget. But it was not as easy as she had once thought it to be.

Jayne tipped a bucketful of water into the cauldron over the outside fire. Then came another trip to the well so they could top up the washtubs Olivia had already partly filled with boiling water.

As she worked, Jayne again pondered Jed's impending visit to town and the information he might uncover about Lamberton. Would knowing more make things worse or set her mind at ease? The sting of a few boiling droplets on her face called her back to reality, and she jumped backwards.

Yvonne looked up from where she had nearly finished sorting the clothes. "Poor Jayne." Her eyes clouded with sympathy. "You ought to be more careful."

Jayne rolled up her sleeves while Olivia grated soap into one of the washtubs that rested on a wooden crate. Once she'd given the water a few stirs, Olivia picked up the washboard and scrubbed the first article back and forth along its ridges. As each item was rubbed free of dirt, Olivia tossed it into a bucket, ready for Yvonne to place it in the wash boiler.

Once the clothes had been boiled, Jayne's arms flexed as she pounded the items up and down in rinse water, not stopping until every trace of soap disappeared from the fabric. When the first batch looked satisfactory, Jayne called Yvonne. Without a word Jayne handed the stick to her sister and took her new station behind the wringer.

As water streamed from between the rollers, Jayne tried to imagine she was sitting by a creek on a hot summer day. But when she closed her eyes, all she could see was swirling water and petticoats. Instead of birds singing a sweet melody, the clunking of the handle grated in her ears.

A sharp pinch on her fingertips brought her head snapping downwards as they connected with the wood of the roller. A flush of surprise washed over her as she pulled away her throbbing fingers. Just as quickly, Jayne tossed a glance over her shoulder to see if anyone had witnessed her foolishness. Her eyes went back to her fingers. There would be a nice bruise for sure. Not wanting to admit that she had been daydreaming, she picked up another item and went back to work.

Every now and then the sun peeked out from behind a grey cloud, brightening the otherwise dull day. Despite the cold, a trickle of sweat ran down the side of Jayne's face. As she wiped it away, she noticed two spots on Olivia's cheeks that resembled the raspberry drops at the store. As if echoing Jayne's feelings of exhaustion, Yvonne stopped plunging for a moment and stretched.

Jayne walked over to the boiler and pushed the wash stick around and around, grateful for the excuse to change positions. The front of her dress and apron were damp and her back weary from the constant lifting and bending. She tried not to dwell on her discomfort but found it increasingly hard to remain cheerful as she walked back to her station by the wringer. Though she felt like moaning, the knowledge that her sisters' arms and backs were aching like her own stopped her.

Jayne tried to think of something to sing, but the only tune that came to mind was a funeral dirge. Rolling her eyes, she tried again. Upon her success, Yvonne and Olivia's voices joined hers and mingled with the melodic swishing of the water. The mood lifted, and the pile seemed to grow smaller inch by inch.

While Jayne was feeding yet another article through the wooden rollers, Jed appeared. "I've done my thinking. Reckon you and I should leave straight after lunch to put our plans to work."

Jayne's stomach did a somersault. She hadn't been expecting to look for work so soon.

The moment Jed left, Jayne turned to her sisters with an explanation, trying hard to gauge their response. Their faces registered a mixture of surprise and distress, and there was something else too. Perhaps it was a sense of fortitude that she saw in Olivia's expression and bearing. Yes, that was it—a firm resolve.

Her youngest sister seemed to be having a harder time deciding what reaction to have. Yvonne stood motionless, her chin resting against the top of the sturdy pole she'd been plunging clothes with. But her eyes followed Jayne's every move.

Jayne realised that Yvonne was watching to see what her own attitude was. As this knowledge dawned on her, she felt sobered by the amount of influence she had, and it was suddenly obvious that her tone didn't convey enthusiasm for the idea. She tried to brighten her voice. "I'll ask around for washing, ironing, mending, that sort of thing. Anything we can get to earn some money. People are bound to have things they want doing." Jayne pushed at the wisps of hair around her face. "We don't have any other choice." The moment the words exited her mouth, she wished she could drag them back inside.

Yvonne lifted her head and smiled. But her lips quivered, and the smile failed to reach her eyes like it usually did. Then her eyes slipped shut in a way that reminded Jayne of herself. When they reopened, Yvonne spoke in a clear, steady voice. "I guess mending can sort of be classed as sewing after all. Even if it isn't as lovely as making a new dress."

Jayne stared at Yvonne. When had her littlest sister begun showing such depth of maturity? Running her fingers over the rough handle of the wringer, Jayne smiled, hoping it fully conveyed the appreciation she felt.

"Now"—she clapped her hands playfully in Yvonne's direction—"why don't you heat up the leftover stew, so I can be ready when Jed wants to leave." The younger girl didn't need to be asked twice. She relinquished her hold on the sturdy stick and ran inside.

As the door banged shut behind Yvonne, Olivia lowered her hands into the murky wash-water again. "You know we'll help all we can."

All three girls were grateful for the respite provided by meal-time, but it seemed they'd only just collapsed into their seats when it was time to set to work again. Olivia and Yvonne stacked up the dirty dishes to be washed later while Jayne changed out of her wet dress in preparation for her trip to town. As she brushed and tidied up her hair, a twinge of guilt gripped her. They had left Jed and Cass's clothes until last as they were by far the dirtiest—and now the task would be left to her sisters while she was elsewhere.

The horses reached town too soon for Jayne's liking. From her seat in the cart, she watched Jed ride away on Spark, leaving her to go about the rest of her mission alone. As Betsie continued forward, Jayne tried to work out what to say. How should she go about marching up to a stranger and asking them to give her their belongings? Would they trust her?

"Excuse me, ma'am." Betsie's ears flickered as Jayne spoke aloud to nobody. "My sisters and I are struggling at the moment. And well, would you happen to have washing, or mending, or . . ." Jayne left her sentence unfinished and sucked in a deep breath. When she neared a tidy looking house, she pulled on the reins to stop—then relaxed her grip and let Betsie keep going. She looked over her shoulder to see if Jed watched from nearby. He wasn't in sight, and Jayne knew that she was just stalling. Knowing she really couldn't put it off any longer, she brought the cart to a stop in front of the next house.

All the way up the path, her mind raced as she tried to memorise what she had to say. But as she stood by the door ready to knock, the reality of what she was about to do hit her, and she cringed. In a flash, she was reminded of her father's caution not to be ashamed of any honest task. Here she stood, too prideful to knock on the door, while over and over during their first months in Australia, her father had humbled himself to provide for his family. He seldom complained; rather, he had rejoiced in God's provision.

Before her courage fled, Jayne lifted her hand and rapped at the door. When it opened, Mrs. Sterling's form filled the doorway. The middle-aged woman stood motionless as they stared at each other. Mrs. Sterling was first to recover her wits. "Well? What do you want?" She gave Jayne a hard look, making no move to invite her in.

Jayne was abundantly glad of this lack of courtesy, for she had no more desire to enter Mrs. Sterling's house than to enter a den of lions. She opened her mouth to excuse herself, but an image of her sisters scrubbing by themselves so she could find work urged her on. Feeling sick to her stomach, Jayne forced the words out. "I'm after work. Laundry work."

A smug look came over the woman's face. "I see the farm girl has become a washerwoman as well. Didn't I tell you that you wouldn't succeed? If you'd heeded my counsel, it wouldn't have come to this." Mrs. Sterling screwed her mouth up and narrowed her eyes. "How many doors do you plan to knock on like this, Jayne?"

Jayne swallowed down the angry retort that sprang to her mind and turned to walk away. As she did so, Mrs. Sterling commanded her to stop, and something in her tone made Jayne's head jerk around. "How much do you charge for this laundry work?"

The triumphant look in Mrs. Sterling's eyes set Jayne's mind whirling as she tried to figure out what the woman's scheme could be. Although she knew she ought to be grateful for any work she could get, she was unable to deny the very real feelings of bitterness that surged through her. She named a price through gritted teeth.

Mrs. Sterling's lips curled. "Good!" She spun on her heel, her skirts swishing like leaves caught in a winter wind.

The door stood ajar, allowing Jayne to view the interior of the house. Standing on tiptoes, she leaned as far inside as she could without entering, scanning the room at the end of the short passageway. As she had expected, everything was decorated to convey a false sense of social standing and wealth, much like the apparel of the woman herself. The gaudy furnishings gave the home a very unwelcoming feeling. Involuntarily, Jayne shuddered and took a step backwards.

The distant clicking of Mrs. Sterling's returning steps made Jayne brace herself. Oh, how she longed to turn her nose up in the air and say she had no need of this woman's money. She pictured herself walking calmly and daintily down the path without the dirty clothes, while Mrs. Sterling stared at her retreating figure, full of indignation. But the truth would not go away, try as Jayne might to rid herself of it. They needed the work.

As Mrs. Sterling reappeared, carrying a basket of clothing, Jayne's eyebrows shot up. Calling the clothes dirty was an understatement. She had never seen filthier clothes in her life. Not even her father's dirtiest work clothes had been this bad. Jayne worked to hide her dismay as she wondered if the woman had rubbed the clothes in a bucket of dirt and grime.

When the triumphant look in Mrs. Sterling's eyes crept over her entire face, Jayne guessed she hadn't been successful in hiding her horror.

Jayne reached for the basket, murmuring something about delivering the clean items in a timely manner. The spiteful look Mrs. Sterling shot her made the bundle feel burdensome even to her work-conditioned arms.

"As you work and break your back, remember it's not too late to heed an older and wiser woman's counsel."

Jayne tried to recall exactly what Mrs. Sterling's wise counsel had been. As she remembered it, all the woman had done was tell her what terrible decisions she was making.

Jayne stumbled a little as she walked down the path but didn't look back to see if Mrs. Sterling watched. It was not until she was driving away that the reason for the filthiness of the clothes dawned on her. Mrs. Sterling's husband worked as a shift captain in one of the local mines. Jayne looked down at the grime on her hands and felt a new reason for discouragement well up within her. How many other women in town had husbands working in the mines? Jayne knew the answer.

11
LURKING DANGER

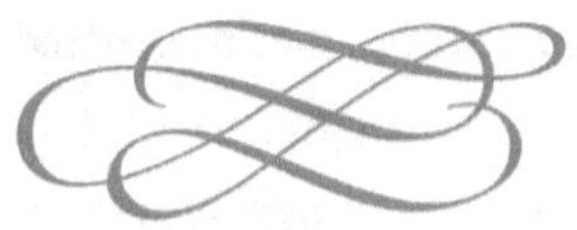

As Jayne continued her trek around town, facing house after house, she kept trying to guess what information Jed might unearth. Finally, after bidding an elderly woman goodbye, she decided that neither she nor her little cart could take any more.

The cart's contents bounced and shifted as Jayne prodded Betsie towards the agreed-upon meeting spot. Just beyond the main street, she stopped by a little picket fence, longing for a peaceful spot away from people, away from gossip, and away from questioning eyes. Trying to be as inconspicuous as possible, Jayne shrank back into her seat. She had no desire to speak to anyone else.

A horse and rider trotted into view, followed by a jolting carriage, and a child ran across the street, calling to his friend. A few spits of rain fell on Jayne's face and hands, driving her further down into her seat. Her head bowed, she soon became lost in thought as she considered her experiences of the past few hours.

At least not all her encounters had been as horrid as the one with Mrs. Sterling. Still, more people than Jayne cared to remember had sent her away curtly. Other women had been more courteous, smiling and saying, "Maybe next time." One woman had even offered her a warm drink to drive away the chill.

Jayne couldn't help smiling as she remembered one young boy who had answered the door with crumbs all over his face, saying that his mother was feeling poorly and couldn't receive visitors. His cheeky smile had warmed her all the way down to her toes.

Jayne yawned and sighed all at once as she turned to survey her load, which had been stacked at awkward angles, its contents varying from a few articles of mending to bundles of ironing. She supposed collecting it had been worth suffering through the condescending glances. If her efforts helped secure her parents' farm, it would only be a small sacrifice.

A drop of rain slapped Jayne on the cheek, but even its sting couldn't stop a smile from touching her lips as she spotted the unfinished baby quilt. Even before the tired-looking woman handed it to her, Jayne had decided to ask Yvonne to work on it. She could hardly wait to see her sister's face. At least with this, Yvonne wouldn't have to imagine that mending was the same as sewing.

A horse snorted next to her ear, and Jayne's hand flew to her chest.

A man chuckled. "Daydreaming again?"

Her heart continued to race as Jed grinned at her. He rode up alongside the cart, his eyes flicking over the baskets and bundles. "Looks like a productive trip."

Jayne clucked to Betsie and fell in beside Jed, who had already turned to begin the homeward ride. When Betsie started to lag,

Jayne forced her forward and turned to Jed with a hundred questions on her lips—but Jed was ready with a question of his own.

"Have any problems?"

Jayne's shoulders lifted in a shrug, but she knew such an answer would never satisfy Jed. "I survived. Some people were nicer than others."

Jed nodded and looked about to ask something else, but desperation sent words flying from her mouth. "What happened?"

Jed motioned ahead to the bush. "Wait till we're out of town."

Jayne sighed in frustration. She felt like she would burst if she had to wait much longer to hear what he'd found out. She wanted to plead with Jed to tell her right away, but knew his logic was sound. She entertained the idea of pushing Betsie into a canter, but again logic won out. The last thing she wanted was to act like a foolish child. Even so, her own legs would carry her faster than Betsie was moving.

The instant they reached a more secluded section of road, Jayne turned to Jed again. "What did you find out?"

A flock of pink and grey galahs chose that moment to fly across the track with a chatter of high-pitched calls. As soon as they passed, Jed replied. "Did plenty of asking around. Found out what I could, but no one knows Lamberton's history." He shrugged. "Nope, not a one. Asked at the general store, the butcher, couple of men who work at the mines, even asked at the hotel where he's staying. People have mixed feelings about the man, but that's about it."

Jed halted Spark and waited for her to catch up. "I stopped in to see Will Caffrey at the blacksmith shop as well. Way he sees things, Lamberton is real friendly-like to the people who jump when he wants them to, but at the least trouble he flies off in a rage. Caffrey seemed to think he had plenty of money to plonk around too."

"Mr. Hedrick told me Lamberton had been in buying spirits a few times."

Jed shook his head. "I'm talking big money." He cleared his throat. "He bought Widow Eddington's place."

Jayne's hand flew to her chest. "Not the Mrs. Eddington we know. She'd never have sold." Jayne searched Jed's face, clinging to the hope there was some mistake.

Jed shifted in the saddle, then returned her gaze, his eyes soft. "I heard it from a reliable source."

Jayne had known Mrs. Eddington since the first week they'd moved to Buninyong. Often she had visited the kindly woman with Mam. Gentle as she was, Mrs. Eddington had been adamant she would never sell her home, though due to its location she'd had many offers.

Jayne felt a wave of guilt. She hadn't visited Mrs. Eddington for a while. Had something happened to make her need to sell? Jayne refocused on Jed as another question rose in her mind. "What does he plan to do with it?"

Jed shrugged. "Nobody knew that either." He turned his horse to face her, and his look was long and steadying. "He's been asking questions about you and your sisters."

Jayne brought Betsie to an abrupt halt. "Why?" Her voice cracked on the word. They had more than enough to deal with already, and she couldn't take any more. Why did Lamberton have to choose to pick on them?

Anger suddenly propelled her to her feet. "Doesn't anyone know anything? Why is he in Buninyong? Where did he come from? What does he do?" Jayne's voice choked, forcing her to stop and swallow several times before she could go on. "Oh! I just wish he'd go back to wherever he came from." She slumped back into her seat.

"I'm sorry, Jayne. I'm afraid everyone just said the same thing. Turned up one day by himself. Hangs 'round town with plenty of money to spend, then disappears for a couple of days. Nobody knows where he goes or what he does." Jed's sigh broke the silence. "Nope, nobody knows a thing about him."

Jed shook his head and started riding again. "Caffrey was shoeing Lamberton's horse the other day. Said he'd never seen such a magnificent creature. He was ashamed to admit he was so taken with the horse that he told Lamberton a lot. Every time Caffrey asked a question though, Lamberton craftily dodged answering it. Caffrey didn't realise it until I questioned him this afternoon. Said he asked Lamberton where he got the horse. But Lamberton never did tell him, just launched into a tale of how agile the horse is."

Jed shook his head again. "Will's a good fellow and not easily taken in, but he disclosed information about himself and others without even realising what was happening." He sighed. "I tried to track down the man himself, but nobody seemed to know his whereabouts."

The wind picked up, swirling their words away and making further talk impossible. Jayne was left with the feeling that she was one of the people Mr. Lamberton knew much about, while she knew nothing about him. She picked up a leafy twig that had landed beside her and tossed it into a gust of wind. How she wished she'd never heard of the name Lamberton.

Though Betsie now kept a steady pace, Jayne sent the reins flicking over her back. She stared gloomily at the grey sky and found herself regretting that she had controlled her tongue when she spoke to Mrs. Sterling earlier. It would give her great satisfaction to go back and tell that odious woman not to think so highly of herself and her wisdom. She could picture herself tossing the basket of filthy clothes in front of her and proclaiming that she, Jayne Reid, was every bit as much of a lady as the finest woman in Buninyong.

Betsie must have sensed her agitation, for she sped up and closed in behind Jed's horse. Spark's tail flicked with displeasure. As Jayne worked to get Betsie back into line, she felt a twinge of remorse for her bad attitude. She was shamed even further by the kindness in Jed's face as he glanced back to see what was happening. She felt glad that Jed could not read her thoughts, until she realised God knew and saw all things. Saddened by this knowledge, she slumped into her seat.

With a discouraged heart, Jayne whispered oft-repeated words into the wind. "Let every man be swift to hear, slow to speak, slow to wrath: For the wrath of man worketh not the righteousness of God." Jayne knew she would spend her whole life working on these commands. Maybe one day she wouldn't be so hot-headed.

As Jayne drove up to the house, Olivia and Yvonne rushed outside. Before she could even come to a stop, their cheerful voices greeted her.

Smiling, Yvonne pulled herself up and peered into the cart. "Look how much you have."

Olivia grinned. "There's nearly no room left in the cart for you, Jayne. It's wonderful. The more the better." Her face showed she meant every word.

As Jayne saw her sisters' earnestness, her own irritation melted away. She knew they'd been working all day and were tired out from doing the washing. Now she'd brought them more work, and they genuinely rejoiced. She jumped to the ground and hugged them both.

Jed looped Spark's reins over a tree branch and came to

help the girls carry the sacks and baskets inside. As he entered the house, he only just managed to duck in time to avoid catching his head on one of the clotheslines strung across the room. The dangling clothes represented Olivia and Yvonne's hours of hard work.

After changing back into her work dress, Jayne set about helping her sisters clean the house with the leftover soapy water. As Yvonne wiped the table with a wet rag, Jayne and Olivia scrubbed the floorboards. While they all worked, Jayne told her sisters what had unfolded in town.

As Jayne repeated Mrs. Sterling's words, she watched Olivia out of the corner of her eye. Twice her sister opened her mouth as if to say something. Then she shook her head. Remaining silent, Olivia rubbed the boards with more vigour.

With a start, Jayne realised her own hands moved violently enough to sand the floorboards. At this rate the floor would be cleaner than usual. As the thumping of Olivia's rag continued, Jayne changed the subject, determined not to let Mrs. Sterling ruin her sister's day. Before long Olivia's laughter rang around the room.

Yvonne clapped in delight when Jayne mentioned the quilt and only just stopped herself from rummaging through the piles of clothes with dirty hands. Merry laughter was still echoing from the house as the girls plopped their rags into the dirty water for the last time.

"It's jolly company I see I'm keeping," said a voice with an Irish brogue. Yvonne, who stood closest to the door, giggled. Both Jayne and Olivia spun around, the laughter dying on their lips.

Cass leaned his head past the partially-opened door. "I knocked, but you didn't seem to hear me."

Jayne shot a glance at their washing, which hung in plain sight from the ceiling, and exchanged a mortified look with Olivia.

Cass pushed the door open wider and stepped inside. "Thought perhaps you could do with a hand emptying those washtubs." With a grin, he flexed his arm. "Got to show Jed somehow that the Irish have some muscles."

Jayne decided there was nothing to do but ignore the clothing behind her. She ventured a laugh. "Sure enough, we would appreciate it." Bending over, she swept her hand through the water in the washtub nearest her, removing the rags they'd been using for cleaning.

At a nod from Jayne, Cass leaned down and heaved the tub off the ground. He glanced at her sideways. "From what Jed tells me, you're to have a few more of these to empty before the week is out."

Jayne nodded as she watched him effortlessly carry the tub that was a struggle for two of them to lift and empty.

"Where am I to dump the water?" he asked, pausing outside the doorway.

Jayne beckoned for him to follow her. As they walked to the Reids' vegetable garden, the silence grew long between them. Jayne tried to think of something to say, but everything she thought of felt lame.

Even the sound of trickling water did little to break the uncomfortable silence as Cass walked along the rows of plants, emptying the tub. As they started back towards the house, the distance seemed to stretch before them. To Jayne's relief, Cass began to whistle a lilting melody. Something about the tune sounded familiar. Finally she remembered. It was one her daddy had liked. She'd forgotten all about it.

While Cass re-entered the house to fetch the rinse tub, she hummed the first line a few times so as not to forget it. Though

Cass no longer whistled when he stepped back outside, the tune still danced in Jayne's memory.

She had no sooner latched the garden gate and opened her mouth to thank Cass for his help, when she saw Jed striding rapidly towards them. Jayne squinted, trying to see him better. Maybe something had happened to one of the animals, and he needed help. But as she continued to watch his approach, she realised his step was one of eagerness not alarm. His face confirmed she was right. Far from appearing disturbed, it wore a look of excitement.

As Jed drew near, he waved something white in the air. "I got a letter for you in town." He shook his head. "Don't know how I managed to forget."

"From Ireland?" Jayne barely waited for Jed's nod before turning and running to the door of the house. "Come quick. We've got a letter." A cry of delight reached her ears as she spun around and raced back to meet Jed. Just as her fingers touched the envelope, Olivia and Yvonne burst from the house behind her.

Her heart thumping and her fingers trembling, she tore at the letter. To Jayne it represented a tie to her parents. As her mind and fingers continued to race, she faltered. This could be a response to the news of her parents' deaths. All her excitement drained away, and instead of the treat she had anticipated, the letter seemed like poison.

Trying to delay the inevitable, she continued to fumble with the opening. At the same time, she glanced up to see if anyone had spotted her sudden change in behaviour, but Olivia and Yvonne clutched each other's hands, too full of anticipation to have noticed.

At last, she drew out the stiff pages. When she looked up again, Jed and Cass lingered a short distance away, as if torn between good manners and curiosity. She turned back to the pages in her hands and tried to lubricate her dry mouth. Still feeling everyone's gaze on her, Jayne began reading: "To my dear, dear son."

She paused. Her fear was unfounded. At the time of the letter, her grandparents had been unaware of the deaths of their son and daughter-in-law. But instead of the relief she expected, her throat ached, and she blinked back tears. Through the mist, she skimmed the page, partly to steel herself and partly to check the contents of the letter. When she reached the middle of the page, Jayne froze.

Yvonne grabbed at her arm, urging her to read aloud, but everything seemed to be coming from far away. The next thing she knew she was sitting on a stump, and Jed was calling her name. Two hands grasped her shoulders and gave her a gentle shake as her world spun. Jayne became aware of other voices, then something moved beside her and leaned against her legs. With great effort she looked down and saw Yvonne gazing up into her face. The terrified look in her sister's eyes jerked Jayne back to the present. She motioned to the letter and looked to Jed for help. "Read it."

Jed hesitated, searching her face.

"They need to hear." Her voice cracked, and she dropped her head. "I'm sorry. It brings back such horrid memories."

Jed fingered the pages for a moment longer. Then he began to read. "To my dear, dear son, I'm so sorry I did not write sooner. For weeks I tried to write but simply could not bring myself to do it. Your younger brother offered to do it for me, but I refused, saying it was news that had to come from a mother." Jed's strong voice stopped.

Jayne looked up and gave a little nod, grasping Yvonne's hand as he went on.

"My precious son, your dear father has passed from this earth. But rest in the assurance that he is a child of Almighty God. One day we will see him again in a land far better than any earthly kingdom. I beg you to draw comfort from this. Words on paper sound so hollow and cold. I only regret not being able to tell you in person, to be there and wrap my arms around you. How I wish I could hear your voice—even just once more. But I know not whether I shall ever look upon your face again. The distance between us is so great, son, that I sometimes loathe it. If only I could grow wings and fly! Know that though the physical distance be great, you are never far from me. Can a son ever be distant from a mother's heart? I think of you always and pray for you each day." Jed's voice had grown husky, and he stopped to clear his throat.

As the news sank in, Olivia's face went from rosy to white, and Yvonne buried her face in Jayne's skirt. Jayne couldn't tell if her youngest sister was crying or not, but she stroked Yvonne's head as Jed read the details of the funeral.

Jayne's eyes flickered up as a noise intruded upon the little group. As her overloaded brain processed what was happening, she found that Cass had been the cause of the muffled groan and cracking branches. As he stalked away, her gaze lingered on his back, and she shook her head, confused by his strange behaviour.

When she turned back, Jed had finished reading. She could only guess what was going on in each of her sisters' heads as they sought to process the new information and the memories it reopened.

Jed reached out to help Jayne rise. "I'll come back to the house and see to it that you all get some hot tea in you. Could do with some myself." He rubbed his hand over the top of his head, looking suddenly tired.

Jayne poked at the fire, making logs tumble and sparks fly. Then she plopped into a chair and traced patterns on the wooden tabletop, barely noticing either of her sisters' presence. She jumped up again. "I'm going for a walk. I've still got a little daylight left."

"Don't linger too long. It's so cold and—" Olivia sent Jayne a warning glance, making sure Yvonne didn't see.

Jayne nodded. "Even the cold couldn't keep me inside tonight. I need to be free."

Yvonne stayed silent during the exchange. Though her needle kept darting in and out of the fabric of the little quilt, she hadn't shifted positions since Jed drank his tea and left them. Her face worried Jayne. It was tight and unmoving. The sight made the ache in her own heart worse.

Jayne pulled her cloak off its nail. As she tucked herself into its folds, the warmth and softness instantly made her feel more secure. She had her hand on the door handle when Olivia marched towards her. "I think I might go check on the lambs in the barn."

Still expressionless, Yvonne's eyes shifted from one big sister to the other.

As her feet edged closer to the door, Olivia asked, "Will you be all right while we're gone?"

Yvonne stared at the quilt in her lap and nodded. "You both go on. I've got plenty to keep me occupied anyway." She continued to stare into her lap, not meeting their eyes.

Olivia looked satisfied, but Jayne hesitated, impulsively returning to give Yvonne a hug. Yvonne's lips quivered a bit at the sudden show of care, but she pushed gently at Jayne. "Go on."

Jayne headed for the door. "I'll try not to be too long." She turned and threw Yvonne a kiss before entering the twilight. Ahead of her, the trees swayed back and forth as wind swirled through their leaves, creating a rustling noise. As soon as she reached their cover, Jayne threw back her head and gazed at the treetops. The motion caused her hood to fall against her back, leaving her face exposed to the wind. As hair blurred her gaze, visions of the past drifted in. She no longer saw the leaves of Auchenblae but other leaves from another time and place. The rustling of the leaves became the sound of soft crooning, until there she was in her bed in Ireland with Mam singing her to sleep.

How many years had passed since those times of soft night songs and happy mornings? Yet still they felt so real. Barely would Mam's lullaby have drifted from her dreams, when she awakened to the feel of Mam's hand. After she was bundled up for the day, they stepped out, hand in hand before the sunrays warmed the soil of Ireland. Sometimes they ran through the paddocks, enjoying the breeze on their faces. At other times Mam threw back her head, just as Jayne did now, and spread her arms wide, laughing with sheer joy at God's beautiful creation.

Jayne remembered how Mam twirled her around and laughingly said, "How great is our God who made all this and so, so much more. If only we could see it all at once."

Jayne tasted salt and realised that silent tears trickled down her cheeks. She brushed at them with one hand and sniffed. Pretending she was once again enjoying a frolic with Mam, she spread out her hands and twirled slowly around. "All I can do is behold, but You, O God, created this unspeakable beauty." Her eyes slid shut. "If only I could see it all at once."

Propelled on, she rushed through the trees. Faster and faster she ran, her breath coming in little gasps, until her foot snagged on a fallen branch. Jayne sprawled on the ground, her head resting on the dirt and her foot throbbing. Crossing her hands beneath her forehead, she lay there a few moments, listening to the bush sounds. Her heart pounded patterns against the ground. Then the cold seeped into her body. She tried to sit up but yelped as the motion caused more pain in her foot. Moving with care, she propped herself against the thickest part of the unyielding branch and rubbed her foot until the ache subsided.

With a sigh, she ran both hands over the ground in a circular motion, as if by doing so she could wipe away all the confusion of the day. She looked up at the darkening sky through a gap in the trees. A lone star twinkled down at her as if encouraging her not to lose hope. As she continued to run her hands over the earth, Jayne felt something oddly familiar. She stopped and looked at her hands in the dim light, but all she could make out were smudges of dirt over the palms of her hands.

Somewhere in the bush, something rustled. Jayne half rose to her feet and looked all around. To her right some of the underbrush swayed. Fighting her rising feelings of terror, she looked up to see if the leaves above her still moved in the wind. To her relief they were being tossed back and forth in much the same way as the bushes. Breathing deeply to calm her nerves, she told herself to quit being so jumpy.

Resolved to head back to the house as soon as possible, Jayne hastened to finish investigating her discovery. She crouched, ready to flee at the smallest indication of danger, and rummaged around in the dirt and leaves until her fingers found what she was looking for. Beneath a layer of plant matter and earth sat a mound of coals. She laid a hand on the rough pile. The coals felt like they were still warm.

Desperately wanting to be wrong, Jayne pressed her other hand to the pile. To her cold fingers the warmth, though slight, was unmistakable. Unwilling to let on to whoever had lit the fire that it had been discovered, Jayne scooped up dirt and piled it back in place. Fingers trembling, she scattered leaves and twigs around to hide all signs of meddling. Unsatisfied with her attempts, she moved sideways, trying to get away from the soft dirt to a spot where a low-growing branch sheltered the ground from dampness. From this position, her feet didn't sink into the ground so much.

The toe of her shoe knocked against something, and it rolled away with a metallic ring. She drew in her breath as the sound pierced the silence. Her heart thumping, she crouched down, glad for the shelter of the leaves, and felt around in the hollow beneath the branches. She touched something cold and rough, and as she pulled away, another ting rang out. All her nerves screamed at her to flee, but she had to find out what lay in the shadows.

Her fingers inched their way along the ground until she located the object and yanked it out where she could see. In her hand she held a dinted pannikin. Whose lips had curled around its edges? Did their owner also hide in the shadows around her? Jayne thrust the cup back into its hiding place, hoisted her skirts, and ran. With each thud of her feet, her chest rose and fell in fear.

12
A Startling Discovery

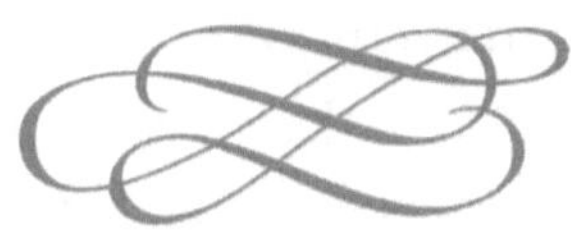

Jayne halted. She should have reached the beaten-down trail by now. With frantic glances she tried to get her bearings, but the gathering darkness made it difficult. Everywhere she looked, she was surrounded with branches and leaves. Jayne took a few more steps, then turned in a full circle. The trees and shrubs looked the same in every direction.

Off to the side, something rustled. Ahead she spotted the shadow of a man separating itself from a tree. As she stifled a scream, Jayne realised it was just a swaying sapling. Each shadow seemed to have come alive to taunt her, and she spun around, trying to look in every direction at once. Too terrified to move, but too terrified to stay where she was, she backed against a tree trunk.

"What time I am afraid, I will trust in Thee." Her whisper ended in a croak, but her lips continued to move as she mouthed the words over and over. Jayne crept forward, using all her willpower not to rush back and cling to the safety of the tree she had just left. A branch scraped across her legs. As she stooped to push it away, Jayne recognised a jagged tree stump to her left and was filled with relief. If she kept going, she would come out somewhere behind the stable.

A sound sifted through the trees, and Jayne strained to hear it again. Was her mind playing tricks, or had she really heard voices? Heart beating rapidly, she waited. An instant later the noise came again. This time the sound was unmistakable. Who was it—friend or foe? With no intention of finding out, Jayne prepared to run. But which way should she flee? All she could distinguish was a faint murmur every now and then. What if in her haste she ran straight into the arms of strangers?

Dropping low, Jayne looked around for a better hiding place. Locking her eyes on a thicket of brush a few yards away, she counted to three, then held her breath and dashed forward. Once she felt the prickle of shrubs on her hands, Jayne dropped to her knees and crawled beneath their cover.

Leaves and dirt stuck to her palms. As she inched forward, branches cracked, and Jayne froze, unwilling to make even one more sound. If she stayed silent, perhaps whoever prowled among the trees would pass on and leave her to depart in safety. But what if they didn't? Maybe she should scream to attract Jed's attention.

Before Jayne could decide, the murmur of voices came again. Did they sound louder? Or did she imagine it? Maybe they had spotted her. They spoke again, and this time Jayne could distinguish two different tones. One voice sounded high-pitched. When a second voice replied, Jayne stiffened. Without question it belonged to a male. As the lower voice droned on, a sliver of doubt crept into her mind. It didn't seem deep enough for a man, but neither did it sound exactly feminine. As Jayne continued to listen, she realised that the lower voice belonged to neither a man nor a woman. It was the voice of a child.

The more she listened, the more confident she became that both voices belonged to children. Where before there had been fear, now she felt indecision. What were children doing out at night? What were children doing on Auchenblae at all, for that matter? Feeling safe enough to abandon her shelter, she shuffled along until she could stand. Now that she had emerged from the bushes, perhaps she would hear or see something to indicate the intruders' whereabouts.

A pattern of light, crunching footsteps filled the night, and suddenly two forms appeared from around a cluster of saplings. Jayne jerked back, then lunged forward, covering the distance between herself and the two children before they could evade her. Just as the taller figure thrust out its arms, Jayne grabbed at it. The boy dived away like a night creature dodging an owl. After grasping at air, Jayne latched onto the boy's shirt.

The sound of whimpering distracted her, and she turned to find the source. Just behind her, a little girl cowered in shock. Jayne reached for her dress but felt the boy's shirt slipping from her fingertips as he twisted.

"Run!" Edged with fury, the word exploded into the air.

The girl whimpered again. Jayne felt like she could join in the whimpering as a foot connected with her shin. All her efforts became focused on dodging kicks and keeping the boy in her grip. He fought so fiercely that Jayne feared his shirt seams would rip at any moment. Again, he shouted a command to flee, but a glance over Jayne's shoulder assured her that the girl hadn't budged. Either she was too frightened to move, or she was unwilling to leave on her own.

Jayne's shoulder muscles seared as the boy lurched to the side. She'd have a myriad of bruises by morning if the throbbing in her legs was any indication. "Stop it!" Her voice rose in frustration. If she'd been stronger, she would've given the boy a good shaking, followed by a slap.

The struggle lessened, and Jayne thought he'd given in. But the lapse gave way to renewed force. If she didn't do something soon, she'd lose the fight. Already she felt her hold weakening as her fingers cramped. She had to act now, and she had to be daring. With a prayer on her lips, Jayne released her grip on his shirt. Surprise won over as she grabbed the lad around the neck and shoulders, squeezing as hard as she could. "Stop your struggling"—her breath came in gasps—"and we'll talk."

The boy lashed at her with his feet, giving no sign he'd even heard her plea. Then a small hand tugged the boy's sleeve. "Please stop." The voice called him by a name Jayne didn't catch. "They're nice. Maybe she'll help us."

"Be quiet." He shrugged her hand off, and the girl began to cry.

He struggled and twisted a minute longer, then stopped. "What do you want with us? Let us go. We won't cause you no more trouble."

Jayne let go of one of his arms and gripped his other arm with both hands. A scowl crossed his face as he positioned himself farther away and stuck his arm around the girl's shoulders.

In the semi-darkness, Jayne looked from one child to the other. "You're siblings?" There was no answer. "I've sisters of my own and wouldn't let anyone hurt them. I'd protect them with my life." She smiled as best as she could under the circumstances, hoping kindness would be conveyed in her tone. "Why don't you come back with me? My sister Yvonne makes nice tea. She's a good cook too."

The boy twisted his head down towards the little girl. Jayne couldn't see or hear what passed between them, but finally he said through clenched teeth, "We'll come."

Jayne loosened her grip a fraction. "My name's Jayne. What's yours?"

When the girl began to speak, the boy hushed her, and she fell silent.

Jayne chose what she hoped was the right way and started walking, still holding the boy's forearm. Forming a chain, the three wound their way through the darkness over branches and slippery leaves. Partway back home, as the pain in her legs continued testifying of the boy's sullenness and ferocity, it dawned on Jayne that she knew nothing about either child—nothing good anyway.

Worried, she stopped abruptly. A muffled grunt and groan, as of two people colliding, reminded her that both children still followed. She ought not to have been so thoughtless, but that was just it. How many times had she been cautioned to think before acting? Now she tried to think, but there wasn't much time and no one to consult with. She didn't want her rash decision bringing trouble upon her sisters. *God, give me wisdom,* she pleaded silently.

Overhead, the stars had appeared. As they twinkled down on them through the treetops, she stared at them, wishing they held some answer to her problem. She couldn't just turn her back now, could she? Maybe the children needed someone to show them a glimpse of love and listen to their story. If they would speak, that is. Her mind made up, Jayne marched forward. A cry from behind reminded her not everyone in tow had long legs.

It was with a feeling of intense relief that she spied the stable looming ahead. In a few more moments, they would reach the path leading to the house. As Jayne's own eagerness to reach home increased, the boy dragged his feet, as if sensing that the end of the track lay just ahead. The closer they got, the more he lagged until Jayne felt like she was pulling him along. She tensed, getting ready for another struggle, but none came.

Like a beacon of warmth and hope, light shone from the window of the house, but when Jayne reached the door, she hung back. What a shock her sisters would get when she brought two strangers inside. Wishing there was some way to warn them, she reached for the door handle.

The moment the door swung open, Yvonne threw herself at Jayne, Olivia right behind her. "I was so worried. I—" Yvonne's mouth hung open.

Olivia pushed forward. "What's the— Where did they come from?"

"It's all right." Jayne tried to look relaxed. "Let us in, and I'll explain."

Wordlessly her sisters stepped backwards, allowing Jayne to pull her night prowlers inside. For a moment, all five of them stood gaping at one another. When she felt less dazzled by the sudden light, Jayne released her hold on the boy and flexed her finger muscles. He stepped away, pulling the young girl with him. As she leaned against his side, the boy laid his arm across her shoulders.

Jayne gazed around at everyone. Each face held confusion, and all those faces were watching her. As she continued wondering what to do, a shiver ran through the little girl's body. That decided it. Stepping forward, Jayne nudged the children towards the fire. To her surprise, they submitted without resistance and drew close to the fire, holding out their hands.

Jayne used the children's distraction to huddle with her sisters and give them a short explanation. When the story was finished, Olivia whispered, "What are we going to do now?"

Jayne shook her head. What to do—the question sounded so simple, yet it set her brain reeling. "I don't know."

"Maybe someone will come for them."

"Maybe." Jayne couldn't mask the doubt in her voice.

Yvonne squeezed Jayne's hand. "They're such poor darlings."

Jayne smiled as she gazed down into her youngest sister's earnest eyes. "Darling" hadn't been how she felt like describing them earlier. Her legs still throbbed from where the boy's boot had connected with her shins. Jayne sighed. "At least one thing holds no question. They need food." Her words propelled all three of them to action.

As Jayne set pannikins on the table, she watched the boy out of the corner of her eye. His body was still, but his eyes flicked about the room. She stepped aside to let Yvonne through with the kettle of tea. As the brew streamed into the cups, Jayne's stomach growled, and she realised that she hadn't eaten since lunch. She wondered if her sisters had either. Beside her, Olivia peeled potatoes and Jayne set to slicing them, with one eye on the children in case they decided to make a dash.

In the glow of the firelight, there was no doubting that they were related. They looked as alike as two sheep. Both had the same blue eyes and sandy-coloured hair. Or at least Jayne thought their hair was light. Right now it looked like a mass of knots, dirt, and who knows what.

The girl wore an oversized coat on top of her dress. As Jayne's eyes moved to the hem of the dress itself, she wondered if it had once been a well-made garment. Whatever the case, it was now patched and threadbare, fit for use as a rag. Despite the winter weather, the boy wore only a shirt. Jayne surmised he'd given up his coat for his sister.

As she headed to the fire with the potatoes, both children moved back against the wall. The way they scuttled from her made Jayne feel like she had the plague. The potatoes sizzled and popped as they touched the fat-laden pan. Off to the side, the boy sniffed the air. When their eyes locked, he stiffened and flushed. Jayne bit her lip to keep from laughing. What a stubborn fellow he was.

Yvonne spooned extra sugar into two cups of tea and handed one to the boy. He took a mouthful, then handed the rest to his sister. His face registered surprise when Yvonne held out the other cup to him. As he reached to take it, she smiled. Her face was so laden with love and compassion that it should have been enough to make even the toughest heart melt.

He nodded in thanks, and, pressing his hands against the sides of the cup, he blew across its surface. The way he gulped the tea with such abandonment made Jayne decide that he must have forgotten where he was. Perhaps his hostility was starting to fade, and they would be able to get some answers.

How Jayne longed to talk more with her sisters, but the small abode offered little chance to talk without being over-heard. Both of her sisters' natural inclinations would be to pamper the children, treating them like old friends in the Irish tradition of hospitality. Jayne desired it too, but something held her back. Whatever it was, the weight felt stifling. She had been taught to always show compassion and hospitality, and not many months ago, it wouldn't have been an issue. Yet now, with the responsibility of her sisters on her shoulders, Jayne was tugged in two directions.

Yvonne set more water over the fire to boil. Humming as

she worked, she mixed up a batch of what was soon to become delicious round sinkers. She certainly seemed intent on pampering the children.

The smell of potatoes frying made Jayne's stomach growl again. Every time Olivia scraped them around the pan, the sizzle was almost too much to resist. Jayne went to the cupboard in the corner and found some golden syrup to pour over the sinkers once they'd boiled. After setting the table, she turned to the boy and pointed to a chair. "Sit down." It was more of a command than she had intended, and there was an awkward silence. Even Yvonne stopped her flittering to see what would happen. Then with stiff movements, the boy took the nearest chair, pushing out the one beside it for his sister.

As if sensing the delicateness of the situation, Olivia and Yvonne hurried to the table. Jayne bowed her head. "Almighty God, thank You for such a hearty meal. Please watch over these children You have brought to share our table." At these words Jayne couldn't resist peeking at the siblings through slitted eyes. She half expected to find them staring back at her, but to her amazement they sat with heads bowed and eyes closed—the picture of reverence.

Once the prayer ended, a silence filled the room. Jayne broke it as she dished out the food. "Have you ever heard such wind or felt such cold?"

Olivia shook her head.

Jayne tried again. "I sure am glad to have food on such a night."

Olivia laughed, this time catching the hint. "There's something about fried potatoes that warms you from the inside out."

Nodding, Jayne hurriedly tried to think of something else to brighten the dull clunk of cutlery. As the meal progressed, the little girl's head kept turning back and forth as Jayne and her sisters tried to keep the stream of words flowing. Whenever they laughed, her face lit up. The boy was another matter. He sat as expressionless as a stone wall, his face only moving to accommodate his constant shovelling of food. Jayne hoped the old saying—the shortest road to a man's heart is down his throat—proved correct. But before long the food would be gone. Then what? She stared at the boy's head, wishing she could see his thoughts.

He looked up. "We're much obliged for the meal."

Jayne fought back a smile and dipped her head. "You're very welcome."

"We won't cause you any more problems." His eyes fell on the leftover potato. Then he stood up and reached for his sister's hand.

Jayne stood up too and laid a hand on the girl's shoulder. Surely, the boy wouldn't leave without his younger sister. As if he were tugged in two directions, his eyes flicked from the door to his sister, then back to the door. Jayne was about to force him to stay when she thought of another tactic. "It's so cold outside. You really are both welcome to stay the night." She shrugged. "Your sister could have a soft bed to sleep on, with blankets."

Again he gazed at the door, then his sister. With a frown, he slumped back into his chair.

Olivia pushed the remaining food in his direction. "Someone has to eat the rest. Could you manage any more?"

The corners of his mouth moved ever so slightly as he nodded. Scooping up a spoonful, he moved to put it on his plate, but stopped, turned, and placed it on his sister's. He repeated the process with another heaping spoonful, then put the remainder on his own plate. His eyes went to Olivia. She nodded and pulled the empty dish back towards herself. "Good. Now I needn't worry about what to do with the leftovers."

Jayne felt grateful for Olivia's efforts to make the situation less awkward. She sighed and closed her eyes for a moment. The day had been physically and emotionally trying in every way. It felt like weeks ago when she had been in town going from house to house. And even longer since Jed had filled her in on the little he had found out about Lamberton. Then there was the letter. It all made her brain spin and her eyes heavy.

Jayne shifted her sore ankle and legs. Now she had brought two children home. Meanwhile, Jed sat in his hut none the wiser, enjoying a peaceful night by the fire. There would be time enough to tell him about the wanderers in the morning. That is, if they were still there to tell about.

Jayne rose to fetch the golden syrup and help carry the servings of dessert to the table. When the children saw the dessert placed before them, their faces lit up as if they had forgotten all their woes. Here was the opportunity she had been waiting for. So long as the children were occupied with the sweet dish, Jayne felt as certain as she could that they wouldn't go anywhere. Her foot found Olivia's leg underneath the table. Their eyes met, and Jayne indicated towards the bedroom with a tilt of her head. Together they slipped inside their room, leaving Yvonne with the children.

"What do you think?" Jayne asked the moment the door closed. "What should we do?"

Olivia looked pensive. "We can't turn them back out into the night, that's for certain."

Jayne focused her gaze on the floor. "It would be so different if Daddy and Mam were here. I wish—"

Olivia didn't let her go on. "Oh Jayne, they aren't. Now we must do what is right on our own."

Jayne bit her lip. It sounded so simple, but what was the right thing?

"Do you think it's safe to have them in the house with us?" Olivia fingered the edge of her sleeve, her voice no longer confident. "The boy is so surly looking."

Jayne shook her head. "I just don't know. I would fetch Jed, but I'm afraid it'll just frighten them off if I do. Then we'll never have the chance to discover who they are or what they were up to."

As she spoke, she thought of the missing candle and the bumping in the stable. "Do you think?" Jayne stopped. "Do you think maybe . . ." When their eyes met, she felt sure they were thinking the same thing.

13
NIGHT VIGIL

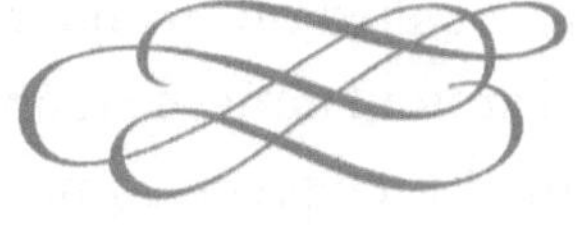

Jayne sat at the table, still dressed in her day clothes. The only sound was the tick of the clock and the occasional pop from the fire. Nearby, the children lay on a makeshift bed of straw and blankets. It would be a long time before Jayne forgot the contented look on the little girl's face as she snuggled up under a quilt. The girl now slept curled against her brother, who seemed to be asleep as well, though in the semi-darkness Jayne could not be sure.

When Olivia appeared in the bedroom doorway wearing her nightgown, Jayne got up and tiptoed over to her.

"Do you think we should take it in turns watching them?" Olivia whispered.

Jayne nodded. "It's nine-thirty now." She masked a yawn. "I'll wake you up in four or five hours, if I can keep my eyes open that long. I didn't know one day could be so exhausting."

Olivia leaned over to plant a kiss on Jayne's cheek. "All right, then. See you bright and early in the morning."

Jayne yawned again. The rustle as Olivia climbed into bed filled her with longing. She turned away, trying not to think how good it would feel to snuggle up under a blanket and close her eyes. Everything—the glow of firelight, the smell of straw, and the sound of steady breathing—urged her to give in to her exhaustion.

This would never do. She had to find something to keep herself from falling asleep standing up. But nothing seemed very appealing at this hour. Then Jayne remembered the embroidery she had begun. If she could manage to focus on making neat stitches, it would provide something to keep her mind off sleep. She crept to her bed and pulled off the quilt. Hugging it to her chest, Jayne rummaged around until she found the embroidered verse where she'd stuffed it between some scraps of material. Upon returning to the main room, she folded the quilt, placed it in front of the fire, and sat down with her back to the children, trying to get as much light as she could on her project.

She finished stitching the words, then began embroidering the first of a cluster of flowers. After the second flower, Jayne stopped. One petal was fatter than the rest and another stuck out at an odd angle. She pulled it out and started again, trying to get her tired brain and hand to cooperate.

As the flames dwindled, the light dimmed, and Jayne rose to put another piece of wood on the fire. Despite her best efforts, the piece of wood beneath it collapsed into the coals with a clunk. Her eyes flicked over to the sleeping forms, but the boy merely stirred and rolled over, mumbling something incoherent in his sleep.

As Jayne resumed her needlework, the new log caught alight and filled the house with a dancing glow. Squinting, she turned from its heat and watched the flickering patterns of the flames against the wall. Then her eyes wandered to the children. Maybe they were fatherless too. The thoughts became a dream, and her eyes slipped shut.

Jayne's body jerked, and she opened her eyes. After rubbing them to clear out the mist, she stood up to check the clock on the mantelshelf. It was only eleven o'clock. She groaned. Still a couple of hours to go before she could wake Olivia. Maybe there was leftover tea in the kettle. If she could just convince her body to move enough to fetch herself a cup, the tea might wake her up. Then she would write in her diary.

Before she sat down again, Jayne shifted her quilt farther away from the fire's edge. Then she flipped through the diary, noting that most of the entries were from months ago. Before her parents had died, she had written every day. Now when she tried to write, she often felt overwhelmed with memories, and memories brought pain. But today she had a fresh story to tell. She dipped her pen and began scratching it across the page, pouring forth the events of the previous hours and halting only to re-ink her pen. As she wrote, the words turned into a prayer for wisdom. Only when the ache in her back forced her to straighten up did she stop.

Jayne set aside her pen and stretched. The clock read quarter to twelve—still a while before it was time to fall into blissful rest. Pulling up a chair in front of the fire, she started humming ever so quietly to herself. When that tune finished, she began another, then another.

Her body jerked, and Jayne grabbed the air to stop herself from falling. This would never do. Jayne reached for the Bible on the mantelshelf and forced her eyes to focus on the words of a Psalm. As she read another chapter, the sentences started to blur together, and her eyelids drooped.

Jayne awoke and blinked a few times, trying to clear her sleepy mind. Shifting on the hard chair, she looked at the fire which had burned down to only a few coals, then down at the Bible in her lap. How long had she been asleep? As she remembered why she wasn't snuggled up in bed, her gaze flew to the corner where the children were supposed to be. But the room was so dim that she couldn't see if the dark shapes were empty blankets or the forms of children.

The cold nipped at her toes as she hurried across the room. Bending down, she made out two distinct shapes on the ground. They were still there. What would Olivia and Yvonne have said if she'd fallen asleep and let the children slip away? *Olivia.* She was meant to wake her to take over the night watch.

She tiptoed into her sisters' room, but the sound of sleep filled breathing stopped her as she reached for Olivia's arm. It might not be long before sunrise, and she didn't think she'd be able to get back to sleep now anyway. Going to the bedroom window, she pulled back the curtain. Stars still shone in the darkness, but some of them had begun to fade in the pre-dawn sky.

Returning to the main room, she placed another log on the fire. Allowing herself to become lost in thought, she prayed until a noise caused her to glance across the room. As she watched, the boy sat up and wiped the sleep from his eyes. When he noticed her, Jayne whispered, "Why don't you come and get warm?" She bent to put another log on the fire, hoping that the night's rest had made him more agreeable. When she turned around, the boy was standing just inside the radius of heat. She smiled at him. "I still don't know your name."

The boy cleared his throat. "Aiden."

Jayne nodded. "Your sister?"

Aiden looked at the sleeping girl. "Imogen."

Jayne felt like shouting with excitement. "Aiden, I think you and I have something in common." She waited to see if he was listening, and when he glanced at her, she went on. "Both of us have younger sisters who are our responsibility to protect."

Aiden nodded slightly but went on staring at the ground.

Jayne searched for the right words. "For as long as you choose to stay, have no fear that Imogen will come to harm. I will look out for her as if she were my own sister. You have my word."

Aiden's head rose, and their eyes met. "Imogen has no one but me to care for her. I'm all she has now. If anything happens to her . . ." He shook his head. "It'll be all my fault."

His last words were so hushed that Jayne almost missed them. She bit her lip. Acting on impulse, she laid a hand on his shoulder. "You and I have more in common than I thought." Her tone matched his in volume. A moment of awkward silence followed. Then Jayne said the first thing that popped into her head. "We share something else—our Irish heritage."

The words brought the first sign of a full grin Jayne had seen on Aiden's face. He said something in Irish so fast, Jayne missed it. But she laughed at the sound of his words. In the corner, Imogen stirred, and her eyes fluttered open.

Jayne clapped her hand over her mouth, hoping Imogen would roll over and go back to sleep. Instead, she sat up and stared at them.

Jayne smiled. "I'm sorry I woke you."

Imogen got to her feet and walked over to Aiden's side. At once, he pushed her nearer to the warmth of the fire. When clarity dawned on the little girl's face, Jayne asked how old she was. Imogen's eyes swung to her brother, and he nodded.

"Eight." Imogen smiled and twisted from side to side, so her tattered dress swung around her legs.

Jayne turned to Aiden. "And you are—?"

"Thirteen."

"Only a year younger than my sister, Yvonne."

As if on cue, Olivia and Yvonne walked into the room, dressed for a new day. Olivia rubbed her eyes and squinted at Jayne. "You should have woken me." She unplaited her hair and began brushing it. Imogen's eyes followed the movement of the brush. Olivia stopped mid-stroke and considered her a moment. "Would you like to brush my hair?"

Imogen looked at her brother, then back at the brush. A light came into her eyes, and she nodded. Olivia seated herself and let her hair fall down the back of the chair. She pressed the brush into Imogen's hand. The girl clasped it and fingered Olivia's hair before running the brush downwards in timid strokes.

Jayne turned to Aiden, who stood watching his sister. "Yvonne will cook us some breakfast while I milk the cow. You can come with me, if you like."

Aiden nodded. "Come on, Imogen."

Imogen skipped to her brother's side as Jayne suppressed a sigh. She'd hoped to keep Imogen inside. That way she'd have no fear of Aiden running off to resume his life in the bush. Two people were also much less conspicuous than three. She didn't want Jed or Cass to spot them until she had a chance to explain the children's presence out of their earshot. The last thing she wanted was to create a scene that might make the children feel like unwanted intruders.

Once outside, Jayne walked a few steps, then stopped and looked in all directions. A bit farther on, she did the same thing. Aiden stared, suspicion written all over his face, and Jayne began walking at a normal pace. She hadn't meant to appear so hesitant and on guard. One way or the other, it wouldn't be long before Jed or Cass discovered the children, but she just hoped it wasn't right now.

As the stable swallowed them, Jayne felt some of her tension disappear. She seated herself by Checkers's side and set to work. Imogen moved her hand up and down the cow's neck, feeling the stiff hairs. When Checkers turned around and gave a low moo in her direction, she giggled.

When milk half-filled the bucket, Aiden spoke in a rush, "Can I try?"

Jayne's head shot up, and she tried to keep the surprise out of her voice. "Of course." She moved aside and waited to see what Aiden would do. First, he crouched down and stared at the udder. Then he covered two teats with his hands and squeezed. Nothing came out. He squeezed again. Still no milk streamed into the bucket.

Jayne bent down and with slow movements showed him how to close his thumb and finger before squeezing. He tried again. This time a squirt of milk came out. He grinned at Imogen, who clapped her hands and smiled back.

Checkers peered around, as if to see what was going on. She let out another low moo. To Jayne's astonishment, Aiden laughed. "What's her name?"

"Checkers."

"Steady now, old Checkers. You just relax and give us lots of milk."

So he could say more than a few words at once. Jayne studied the boy. It was as if she was no longer there. After the milk had risen a few inches, Aiden stood up and flexed his hands. Jayne sat back down with a laugh. "You can try again tomorrow."

Imogen edged nearer to Jayne. When Jayne felt her brush against her arm, she looked up. "Would you like a turn?"

Imogen's eyes lit up, and she nodded. Jayne reached over and placed one of Imogen's hands on the teats. The teat was so large and the hand so small that the sight brought a smile to Jayne's face. When prompted, Imogen tried to copy what Aiden had done, but nothing happened. Jayne placed her own hand over Imogen's little one and squeezed downwards. A stream of milk hit the white surface. Imogen laughed and eyed the bucket of milk with satisfaction. "Wait till I tell—"

"Won't the milk taste good, Imogen?" Aiden's voice was louder than necessary. "It'll be so creamy and fresh."

Jayne stopped milking and stared at him. What was he hiding?

Aiden's eyes flickered from her face to the bucket of milk. As his face flushed, he stared down at his feet.

Seeing his embarrassment, Jayne nodded. "That's right. Today we'll have fresh warm milk—a whole cupful for you both."

Aiden's eyes widened, and Imogen rubbed her stomach in anticipation.

Jayne finished the milking and put Checkers out to graze, before leading the children to the house once more. It took more work than she had realised to keep an eye on two children. Respect for her own mother grew as it dawned on her how much time Mam had invested in her and her siblings.

After washing their hands, she and the children joined her sisters at the table. Without waiting for it to cool, Jayne scoffed down her buttermilk porridge, burning her tongue in the process. It still smarted as she pushed back her chair. "You all finish off here. I need to go do something outside." She stood up and backed away, trying to catch Olivia's eye. When no one else was looking, Jayne mouthed Jed's name. Olivia inclined her head, then went back to eating as if nothing had occurred.

As Jayne escaped the confines of the house, the thud of an axe resounded through the clearing, and she strode towards the noise. Her steps led her towards the usual path, but she ignored it. Picking one's own trail was much more invigorating than sticking to a well-worn path. Allowing the noise to be her guide, she tramped through the underbrush until she came out at Jed's bark hut.

Again the axe cracked the silence. Jayne circled around to back of the hut, intent on telling Jed everything. Her steps halted when she spotted the bent-over figure. It was not Jed but Cass who leaned over a log, trying to pull the axe head loose. Beside him sat a mound of freshly split wood for Jed's fire.

Jayne shrank backwards, placing her feet carefully to remain unheard. When she had made it to the front of the hut again, she tapped on the door. No welcoming call came from inside. She rapped again, hoping Jed had somehow missed her knock. Nothing happened. With a sigh she turned and trudged back towards the woodpile—and Cass. Before she could speak, a twig snapped beneath her foot.

Cass swung around. "Hello there." He stretched his back and grinned. "How are things this morning?"

Jayne ignored his question. "I was after Jed. Do you know where he is?"

Cass shook his head, looking forlorn. "Not even a greeting. And I thought you came to see me."

Jayne flushed. She ought to have been more polite.

With a chuckle, Cass turned back to his work. "I believe you'll find him headed that way." He pointed in the direction she had come. "Don't know how you missed him."

Feeling she ought to make up for her rudeness, Jayne stopped to explain. "I didn't stick to the path."

"A wanderer like your mam, then."

Jayne raised her eyebrows and said nothing.

Cass shrugged. "Or so it seems. Jed has mentioned your love of the outdoors. Just like Mrs. Reid, he told me." His axe swung through the air and landed with a thud in the middle of a log.

Jayne threw her thanks over her shoulder and hurried away. When the hut sheltered her, she broke into a run. She had to find Jed before he had time to reach their house. If she didn't, her sisters would be faced with explaining everything in front of the children. Worried that such an encounter would shatter the tiny bit of trust Aiden had showed, she ran faster.

By the time the stable flashed into view, Jayne's breath tore at her chest. She shot a glance towards the building and saw that the door was open. Without slowing down, she changed directions. One last stretch of her legs brought her to the stable doorway. Too late, she saw Jed coming towards her. The air left her lungs as she thumped into his chest.

"Jayne! Watch out." Jed threw up his hands and called a late warning. "You and Wattle make a good pair, always rushing about."

"I'm sorry." Jayne drew a shuddery breath. "I was looking for you."

Jed grinned. "Well, you found me all right." He sank down on an upturned crate. "So, what's the problem? Must be something worrying you."

Jayne turned away and kicked a dry bit of horse manure with her foot. She had so much to tell and yet so little information.

Jed cleared his throat. "You'd better come out with it, or I won't be able to help."

"We had a thirteen-year-old boy and his sister stay with us last night." Jayne slumped down on another crate near Jed.

Jed shook his head. "That sounds like your mam, all right."

When Jayne told him about how she had found the fire and pannikin, his eyebrows rose even higher. "What were the children up to?"

Jayne shrugged. "Your guess is as good as mine." She sighed. "They wouldn't even tell me their names last night. This morning Aiden told me that they had no living family. He's all Imogen has."

"And that's all you know?"

"Apart from that they're Irish, and Aiden's mighty protective of his sister, Imogen." Jayne rubbed one of the bruises she had received last night. "I tried to stay up to keep an eye on them last night. I was afraid they'd take off. I want so much to help them. I know what it's like"—her voice cracked—"to have no parents."

"You'd seen no other sign of them before last night?"

Jayne started to shake her head, then changed her mind and nodded, before shaking it again. Her hands flew up in dismay. "I can't be sure." Everything tumbled out—the noises in the barn, the slippery carrot tops, and finally the disappearing candle. "Do you think they're all connected?"

"Makes sense. That candle didn't walk off on its own. How long would it mean they've been here?"

Jayne's skin tingled as she thought about it. How long could someone have been living on their property without them even knowing? She shook her head and motioned helplessly with her hands. "I'm not sure. With everything going on, I've lost track of time. It must be almost a week since I heard those noises in the barn. Who knows how long they could have been here before that, though."

Jed stretched out his legs. "Well, I suppose you can't just turn them out. What do you plan to do?"

"Give them a home for as long as they need it." At his

prolonged silence, Jayne spoke again. "How could I do any less?" The passion in her own voice startled her.

Jed nodded. "Have you thought of the implications? How long it could mean?" His voice was steady and gentle. "The responsibility?"

Jayne studied the ruts in the dirt floor. At thirteen, it would only be a couple of years before Aiden could go out and fend for himself. But Imogen, she was so young. She might need a home for at least another eight years. The thought was over-whelming. But if they really had nowhere else to go—no friends or relatives—Jayne couldn't just turn them out, could she? After all, it could have been her dear sisters.

"Perhaps they could do with a little love." Jayne's throat ached, and she struggled to talk as she faced Jed again. "I know what it's like to lose father and mother. For that reason alone, I am bound to help them all I can, whether that be for a day or the rest of my life."

Jayne thought again of what her words meant. Aiden and Imogen would always be there. It would never just be her and her sisters sitting down for a meal or taking part in their Sunday evening routine. She thought of the extra money it would take to clothe them and provide for their needs. Would it mean depriving her sisters? What would happen if she got married? She shrugged away the questions and doubts. "How can I do any less?" The words were meant to be a statement, but somehow they came out as a question.

"Jayne." Jed's voice was firm but kind. When she met his eyes, he went on. "Your parents would expect no less of you. God will provide and give you strength as you need it. Ask Him for wisdom. Delight yourself in Him, and He will give you strength and joy in every situation." He placed his hands on his knees and pushed himself to his feet. "It's a heavy task to take on." He laid a hand on her shoulder. "Perhaps your experiences of the past months are for such a time as this."

Startled by his final comment, Jayne pondered the possibility as Jed left to go about his work. After a time, she followed him out the door, intending to go straight back to the house. Somehow, she just couldn't do it. Everyone would look to her for guidance—everyone.

14
Visitors

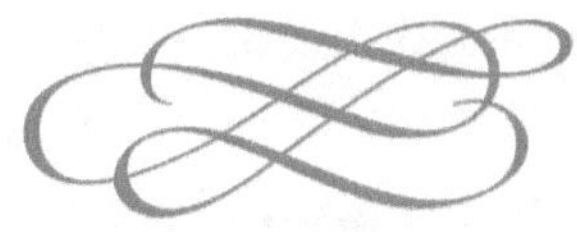

As Jayne walked into the bush, it seemed as if every verse she had ever read about caring for the fatherless tumbled around in her head, so that she was unable to focus on any of them. She covered her head with her hands, and her pent-up emotions tumbled out in a prayer. "Please God, give me strength." A response echoed in her heart. *The joy of the Lord is your strength. Delight in the Lord, for God is always gracious.* The words were from Mam's story. Jayne pulled her hands from her head and looked around.

Unwittingly, she had retraced her steps of last night. About ten yards in front of her lay the fallen limb she had tripped on. Jayne leaned down to press her ankle as the sight brought back memories. Now that she was so close to where she had discovered the children, she might as well look around to see if she had missed anything.

Scanning the ground as she walked, Jayne skirted the branch and stopped. A mound of dirt still covered most of the coals, though she hadn't done as thorough a job in the dark as she thought. With her foot she pushed the remaining dirt aside. There was nothing unusual about the coals underneath—just ordinary black charcoal.

Jayne strode over to where she had stuffed the pannikin. It still lay beneath the leaves where she had shoved it in her haste. The cup was rusty and dinted but still useable. Jayne decided to take it to Aiden. It might be one of the only things he owned.

Overhead, a bird chirped, and another answered it. Funny how things didn't seem so scary by daylight. She hunted around a bit more but found nothing—not a single thing to shed light on what the children had been doing or why they were here.

Jayne shoved a branch out of her way, ready to give up. Once more her eyes flicked to the ground, and this time her breath caught in her throat. There were a man's footprints mingled with her own and those of the children. None were very obvious, except in a few places farther away from the fire and one or two prints beside the charcoal. Her brow creased with thought. Perhaps they were Jed's. Had he come to have a look at what she told him about? Or was it worse? Had someone else been with the children? Someone that still lingered nearby?

Jayne felt a chill creep down her neck. Maybe the children were part of a bigger plan. Perhaps they had wanted to get caught and were only acting. She looked about her, then leaned down to inspect the prints closer. It looked like a couple of footprints were over top of her own from last night. If that were the case, then perhaps they were Jed's or Cass's. Surely they couldn't be Jed's, though. There hadn't been enough time for him to have come and gone between their conversation and her arrival at the spot. That left Cass. Why did everything always have to involve Cass?

Jayne stood up and shook her head, thinking that she would be very old before she had the wisdom to make sense of everything. But she did know one thing. Despite anything else, she felt bound to care for Aiden and Imogen, no matter the cost to herself. She just hoped she was not digging herself into a dangerous hole.

A giggle sounded from the corner of the room as Olivia walked past Imogen and tickled her. It was refreshing to see the little girl looking so full of life. A few days ago, Jayne had insisted the children take a bath. It made a world of difference. Once they were clean and their hair brushed, they seemed to carry themselves with more dignity and confidence.

Jayne smiled at Imogen's slightly odd appearance. Once the little girl had washed, she owned nothing fresh to wear. Because Jayne couldn't stand the thought of making Imogen put her dirty clothes back on, she found an old dress for her to borrow. Though it had been worn by all three girls and was faded, Imogen moved around as if she were clothed in a priceless gown. She had been reluctant to do anything, lest she damage the dress. Finally, Olivia had coaxed her not to worry about it, and the little girl ran off to frolic outside in the winter sunshine.

Jayne picked up the bowl of vegetable scraps and considered asking Imogen to take them out for her. Imagining the little girl trying to hold her dress up daintily with one hand while juggling the scraps in the other, she dismissed the idea.

The newness of the day refreshed her as she stepped outside. Already the addition of the two children had made a difference to their routines. Now every morning Aiden accompanied her when she milked Checkers. The new arrangement caused her a tiny bit of regret. Always she had valued the task as a time to think and prepare for the day. Still, she felt glad for a way to build some sort of a relationship with Aiden.

Jayne flung the scraps to the group of chickens scratching in the clearing behind their pen. With excited clucks, they rushed for the food, and their cries alerted the few that had strayed. With necks outstretched, the wanderers ran towards the group, scattering a few feeding sparrows. Jayne heard a loud rustling as a kangaroo bounded away in the bush beyond the chickens. "You girls are disturbing the morning peace." Jayne laughed and continued to talk to her flock until she heard the children's voices.

Aiden marched along carrying an axe while Imogen skipped along behind him. To any onlooker they appeared a carefree pair, but Jayne knew that up close, their faces held shadows and the burden of untold secrets. It disturbed her that neither Aiden or Imogen ever mentioned their father or mother. If only they would speak of their past. It was unhealthy to shut off a whole portion of life like it didn't exist. But then, she had no idea how raw their loss might be. Would she be open with her innermost feelings to someone she barely knew?

As she watched Imogen doing her best to help Aiden move a log, Jayne resolved to talk more about her own past. Perhaps if she mentioned Mam or life in Ireland, it would trigger some comment from Imogen. From now on, she would be on the watch for an opportunity to do so, and Olivia and Yvonne could help too. Between the three of them, they might be able to discover some information. But as she walked back towards the house, it dawned on her that Imogen might not be old enough to even remember much of her past.

"Look, I'm helping Aiden." Imogen waved at Jayne. The split-second distraction made Imogen trip on the hem of her dress. She wobbled, her arms waving about and a cry escaping her lips. Aiden caught her as she tumbled downwards. Imogen covered her mouth with her hands and giggled.

Jayne smiled and waved back. For their sakes, she would not give up.

The nicker of a horse and the mingled sound of a man's voice and a woman's laugh reached her ears. She hurried around the corner of the house to see who approached. Though it was still at a distance, she saw a wagon pulled by a Clydesdale she recognised as the O'Donnell's. She smiled, overjoyed at the realisation that Mrs. O'Donnell must be significantly better.

But how would she explain the presence of the children? As dear as Mrs. O'Donnell was, she could not be counted on to think before she spoke, and Jayne didn't want any awkward scenes. She ran the rest of the way to the door to alert her sisters and remove the children's makeshift bed. Together she and Yvonne rolled up the blankets and deposited them out of sight, while Olivia grabbed up the straw.

Jayne stepped outside with her sisters as the wagon rolled to a stop. She hoped Imogen would not choose to run around the corner just yet. Olivia apparently felt the same way, for she stood near the corner of the house like a sentinel. Mr. O'Donnell lifted his wide-brimmed hat in greeting, while Mrs. O'Donnell laughingly held out her hands to the three sisters. "You're all looking chirpier than ever. How are you all, my dears?"

Mr. O'Donnell secured the reins and jumped down from the high seat. "My Aileen's been beggin' me to visit ye for some time now, and I thought ye could do with some company." Reaching up, he grasped Mrs. O'Donnell by the waist and swung her gently down. As soon as her feet touched the ground, she hugged first one girl, then the next.

Mr. O'Donnell lowered his voice when Jayne approached him. "I feel mighty ashamed-like that I haven't been around to check on Brian's lassies much. Not been half the neighbour I ought've been." He nodded towards his wife. "Now that Aileen's a bit more perky, I'll try to stop by more often. See if I can't find something to help with." He shook his head. "When I think of how much the Reids have done for us . . ."

Jayne shook her head. "You don't owe us a thing. Your friendship means so much to us already."

Yvonne stepped up beside Jayne, and Mr. O'Donnell swept off his hat and bowed low. "How's the youngest Miss Reid?" His hand went to his pocket and brought forth a crinkled paper bag. He held it out to Yvonne, whose eyes lit up.

"Ye didn't think I'd have forgotten ye like lemon drops, did ye now?"

Yvonne took one and curtsied playfully. When she went to give the bag back to him, he shook his head. "Ye keep them, lassie."

Her face full of delight, Yvonne thanked him again. When Mr. O'Donnell walked away to adjust a strap on his horse, she turned to Jayne. "The rest of the bag." Her lowered voice was full of awe. "I can't wait to give some to Aiden and Imogen. The expressions on—" She clapped her hand over her mouth and looked over at Mrs. O'Donnell, as if the words could somehow have reached her hearing.

Mr. O'Donnell climbed back into the wagon. "I'm on my way to help Mr. Anderson fell some trees in exchange for help with fencin' my boundaries. I need to get them fence lines done before I run out of time and the land selector's office gets me farm. I'll stop by when I done finished up there this afternoon." With a wave of his hat and a flick of the reins, he drove away.

Mrs. O'Donnell turned to Jayne. "I do hope you don't mind my intrusion, dear."

Jayne opened her mouth. It wasn't that she had intruded. Only—

Olivia laughed and draped a hand over Mrs. O'Donnell's shoulders. "You could never intrude. You ought not to be outside in the cold, though. Come in and sit by the fire."

Mrs. O'Donnell let herself be led towards the house, commenting on how they were just like her husband, always fussing over her so.

Yvonne dropped behind and whispered to Jayne. "Can I go give Imogen a lolly?"

Jayne nodded. "Try to keep them outside for as long as you can. I'll explain the moment Mrs. O'Donnell is seated."

But they were too late. As soon as Jayne stopped speaking, the two children appeared with armloads of wood. Their faces aglow, they chattered back and forth, oblivious to the newcomer's presence.

Mrs. O'Donnell turned to the sound of voices at the same instant that Aiden noticed her. Fear flickered across his face, and his whole body tensed. Almost fiercely, he gave a command to his sister, and Imogen stepped backwards to hide behind him. The look on Aiden's face as he stood ready to flee made Jayne feel like she'd betrayed him.

Jayne moved towards them with all the composure she could muster. If she could just reach them before they ran. She stretched out her hand and rested it upon Imogen's head. As she did, the little girl smiled up at her, as if trusting that Jayne's presence would make everything all right.

As Jayne looked between Aiden's scowling face and Mrs. O'Donnell's questioning one, any relief she had felt faded. "I think we should all come inside and introduce everyone." As she passed Aiden, Jayne leaned close and whispered, "It's all right. Mrs. O'Donnell is like family."

While Olivia seated Mrs. O'Donnell by the fire, Jayne directed the children to deposit their armloads of wood and then turned to her guest. "This is Aiden and his sister Imogen. They've been staying with us for the last few days"—she motioned to the split wood—"and helping with things around the place to earn their keep."

Aiden drew himself up and laid his arm across Imogen's shoulders. She responded by resting her head against her older brother. Mrs. O'Donnell nodded approvingly, and then came the torrent of words Jayne had been expecting. "What of their parents? They mustn't have family, for if they did, they would not approve of sending their children off to be cared for by others."

Aiden scowled again. Jayne tried to signal Mrs. O'Donnell to stop this line of questioning, but Aiden pulled himself together and took over the situation for himself. "Excuse us, ma'am. We'll be going"—he backed towards the door—"to finish off out there." He didn't wait for an answer before hurrying his sister outside.

Although Jayne longed to make sure they were not disappearing, never to return, she forced herself to trust Aiden a little and resisted the urge to follow them. Instead, she poured Mrs. O'Donnell a cup of tea. "I'm sorry I didn't get a chance to tell you about the children before they happened upon you. In a way, they just happened upon us and took us all by surprise too."

Yvonne nodded. "One day there were only three of us, and now there are five people to feed and take care of. But we don't mind, do we?" She looked at Jayne.

Jayne shook her head. "Of course not." Though there were times she wondered what they'd gotten themselves into—like now.

Mrs. O'Donnell threw her hands up. "I'm afraid I still feel confused, dears. Before my curiosity can be satisfied, you'll have to explain some more. Why are the children here, why do you have to feed them, and"—her brow furrowed—"where did they come from?"

Jayne took a deep breath and started from the beginning. To her surprise, it was a relief to share the story with Mrs. O'Donnell. When she finished the tale of the children's discovery, Aiden's protectiveness, their dirty, hungry state, and the lack of family to look after them, their neighbour looked like she would burst if she didn't voice her opinion.

"Of course you must keep them, the poor lost dears, but it's a big responsibility. One not to be shirked." Mrs. O'Donnell handed her cup to Olivia and folded her hands in her lap. "I would do it myself, but you know my health hasn't been good of late. It's all I can do to keep the house for myself and my husband, let alone two children." She sighed and turned pensive for a moment. "I know I'm not as fit as I once was, but surely there must still be some way I can help."

Jayne nodded, not wanting to make her friend feel useless, but at the same time not knowing what she would be able to do.

Mrs. O'Donnell chuckled. "As my dear mother always used to say, there is work to be found for whoever is willing to look. I might just have to look extra hard." Lowering her voice, she added, "Mind you, Mr. O'Donnell might have something to say about my helping. He's mighty protective of me. Very particular of what I can and can't do, you know."

She turned a curious gaze on the piles of folded clothes and unfinished mending that sat beside the bedroom door. "Now, what's all this, dears?"

Jayne stammered over her reply, embarrassed to let on more

than necessary about their financial situation. To her surprise, Mrs. O'Donnell relaxed back into her chair with a huge smile on her face. Had she even been listening? Jayne certainly didn't think the announcement that they'd taken on washing work merited such a pleased response.

As she started to re-explain, Mrs. O'Donnell clapped her hands and laughed. "What did my mother used to say? Yvonne, get me a needle and thread, dear." She laughed again. "And Olivia, fetch me a pile of that mending." An eruption of coughs silenced her outward enthusiasm, but as soon as she was able, Mrs. O'Donnell chuckled again. "Finally something useful to do."

As their visitor settled back to repair a torn petticoat, Aiden slid the door open and poked his head in. It disappeared a moment later, but not before Mrs. O'Donnell had spotted him. Her face lit up. "There you are, dears. Come right in. I've been hoping you would reappear soon. I have a story to tell you."

Aiden stepped inside, dragging his feet. He stopped near the doorway and would go no further, but Imogen seemed drawn to the woman. With lowered eyes, she smiled and walked closer as Mrs. O'Donnell beckoned to them. "Come gather around. It's warmer here by the fire." Imogen glanced back at her brother. He shrugged, and it was all the permission she needed. She sat down at Mrs. O'Donnell's feet with her over-sized dress spread around her and looked up into the older woman's face.

Jayne brought another pile of mending to the table. There had been so many distractions over the past few days that they'd been unable to apply themselves to getting the mending done. Perhaps with Mrs. O'Donnell helping, they would be able to finish the rest before it needed to be delivered. Olivia sat down opposite Jayne, and Yvonne fetched the quilt she had nearly finished binding.

As Jayne began stitching, Mrs. O'Donnell wove a tale in which every memory triggered another. She told of her years as a Scottish tenant, the Highland Potato Famine, and her forced voyage to Australia at the age of thirty-eight. So skilful was she as a storyteller that Jayne had to remind herself to keep working.

Mrs. O'Donnell fell silent. Her hands, which had been deftly fixing item after item and never resting for a moment, finally lay quiet in her lap. She seemed to be pondering the span of years that lay between her and Scotland. Imogen watched Mrs. O'Donnell's face expectantly. Even Aiden leaned forward, eager to hear more.

"I'm afraid that will have to be all, dears."

When Mrs. O'Donnell spoke, Jayne realised she had been holding her breath in anticipation.

The frail woman leaned back and closed her eyes for a moment. "I've talked far too much already for a person in my condition. What would Mr. O'Donnell say if he knew?" She clucked her tongue.

Disappointment was reflected on every face. Jayne rose to her feet and gazed out the window, picturing the scenes of Scotland that Mrs. O'Donnell had painted so vibrantly. For some reason the stories had left her feeling melancholy and drove her to reflect on her own childhood with her parents in Ireland. She turned back towards the silent group. Apparently the stories had had the same effect on Imogen, who sat staring at Mrs. O'Donnell with a range of expressions crossing her little face.

Finally the young girl spoke, her face a picture of concentration, "I remember when we were in Ireland still. We were very hungry and—"

Aiden coughed and sputtered with sudden violence.

Jayne bit her lower lip. She stared at Imogen, willing her to continue.

Mrs. O'Donnell smiled. "Go on, dear."

Imogen shook her head and kept her lips pressed shut, watching her brother with wide eyes.

15
Unanswered Questions

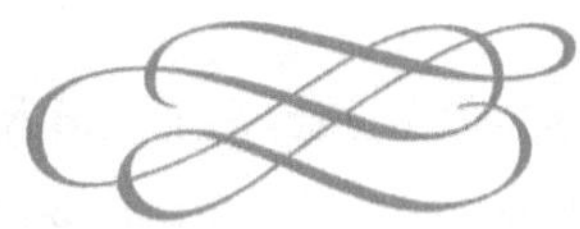

As she crouched down to inspect the soil, Jayne took a deep breath of fresh air mingled with the smell of dirt. She looked over at Aiden to find that he was trickling a handful of soil between his fingers to the ground below. Though the wind was chilly, the sun shone, providing a bit of warmth. Jayne felt that the last day of winter was a fitting day to begin work on their spring garden. In her mind, she went over what they needed to plant— potatoes, pumpkins, corn, peas, beans, cabbage, and carrots. The list felt daunting, but they had to eat.

Standing up, she surveyed the area within the garden fence, noticing how grass had grown over parts of the previously cultivated ground. With the toe of her shoe, she toyed with a lump of dirt. "We'll start with this area first, then dig up some fresh ground over there." She motioned to one of the undug patches nearby.

Armed with shovels, Jayne and Aiden began attacking the ground. Jayne welcomed the exhilarating work. Before long, she was wiping sweat from her face. Aiden noticed her and laughed. Jayne joined in, glad to see him with a happy face.

At the cries of birds overhead, she stopped and looked up, pointing to a flock of galahs that flew past. As the birds dodged between tree branches, she saw flashes of pink.

"What are they called?" asked Aiden, staring after them.

Reminded of how little she knew about Aiden and Imogen, Jayne realised that she didn't even know how long they had been in Australia, and already, she was forming a question of her own. "How long were you and Imogen on our property before I caught you?" She cringed at her hastily-chosen words, but it was too late to take them back.

Aiden's foot slipped off his shovel, and he frowned. "Don't know." His frown disappeared as he shrugged. "We saw you leave for church twice."

Jayne thrust her own shovel into the dirt, disturbed by the eerie thought of someone watching unbeknown to her and her sisters. How many other times had the children spied on them in the past weeks? She didn't like to think about it.

As Aiden's shovel bit into the ground again, his head jerked up. "Are you going to church tomorrow?"

Jayne nodded, caught off guard by his question. They almost always went to church, though they hadn't gone last week. It had felt like the worst place to take the children given their skittishness. Now a whole week had passed, and here it was upon them again. She could only guess how Aiden would respond to such an outing. Whatever his past, he appeared frightened of being seen. At least if the way he'd reacted to Mrs. O'Donnell's presence was anything to go by. Why this was the case, Jayne couldn't guess, but she didn't think he would welcome the idea of attending church, where people were sure to stare and ask questions.

An idea occurred to Jayne, and she pondered how she might get Aiden to agree. It would mean leaving Imogen for a few hours. But perhaps if she gradually exposed Aiden to people, giving him the chance to overcome his fear, it might be easier for him to attend church. It would also give her more time to build a relationship with him.

In the meantime, however, she ought to be using the time she had with him now. "Do you like working in the garden?" Jayne already guessed the answer from the enthusiasm he showed in ripping through the grass and weeds.

Aiden nodded. "I used to love working in our garden in Ireland"—he flexed his arm half-heartedly—"using my muscles." A smile flickered across his face. "I used to race with—" He shook his head and changed his words. "We used to have so much fun." He sniffed loudly and turned away, attacking a weed with his shovel.

Jayne wanted desperately to ask whom he had raced with, but she resolved to give him time. She jumped on her shovel blade, trying to sever a thick root. After slamming her shovel on the root a few times to no avail, she fell to her knees and used her hands to try to dislodge it. She looked up to see Aiden grinning at her again. "What's funny?" she asked, puzzled at his sudden mood change.

"You." Aiden pointed to her dress. "How'd you get so dirty?"

Though Aiden's pants were dirt-smeared, her dress had little clumps of dirt all over it and large patches of dirt around the hem. She had managed to get far dirtier than necessary, and the job was only a quarter done at the most. Jayne lifted her hands and shrugged.

Aiden grinned again, and for a long time, the only noise to be heard was the cutting of their shovels in the soil and the plopping of dirt as they tossed it. Then the chooks roamed nearer, clucking at them through the fence. Jayne flapped her skirt at them, trying to discourage the fowl from flying over the fence and scratching among the precious vegetables.

Imogen ran out of the house and came to lean on the fence near her brother. "Guess what?" Her eyes sparkled.

Aiden paused his work. "Go on, tell me."

"Olivia and Yvonne have been teaching me to write more letters. Look!" She bent over and ever so carefully drew letters on the dirt with a stick. His face full of interest, Aiden went over to peer at the ground. Jayne followed at his heels, wondering what her sisters had been up to.

"See, it's my name," Imogen said, smiling and standing straight as a soldier, with her stick resting over her shoulder. "I want to tell Mother. She'd be so pleased, wouldn't she, Aiden?"

Aiden shook his head. "You can't tell her. You know that." His tone brightened. "But I'm pleased with you." He rubbed her head, getting dirt in her hair. "Why don't you go see if you can find any eggs for Jayne." He pointed to where the chooks had wandered and gave her a push. "Go on."

Imogen walked from the garden with her shoulders slumped.

Jayne looked from Imogen to Aiden, but he turned away, refusing to meet her gaze. This exchange between brother and sister left her feeling even more baffled. She sighed. Had life been so confusing before her parents passed away? Her throat ached as she tried in vain to remember. Even though it was less than six months ago, she had to resign herself to being unable to recall what life had been like before their deaths.

Jayne shivered and glanced up at the sky, letting out a gasp as rain drops fell onto her upturned face. The hens ran to the cover of their shed, flapping their wings and squawking in protest, but Aiden worked on steadily, not seeming to mind the rain.

Then the skies opened and torrents of rain descended upon them. Jayne let out a yell. "Hurry!" Shovels in hand, she and Aiden dashed to the gate, only just remembering to close it behind them. With shouts and laughter, they raced to the house.

Aiden reached the door first and pushed it open for Jayne to enter. Despite his show of manners, he crowded at her heels as they scurried to get inside. Once their shovels lay against the wall, they turned to stare at each other with laughter dancing in their eyes. Their mad dash left Jayne feeling exhilarated and glad to be alive.

Olivia, Yvonne, and Imogen eyed the puddles that formed around them with a mixture of amusement and dismay. "Looks like you two brought the rain inside." Olivia placed her hands on her hips. "You'll turn the house into a mud hole if you stand there much longer."

With a comical expression, Imogen studied Jayne from head to toe. "You're dirty all over—even your face."

Olivia and Yvonne burst into laughter, and Imogen giggled. Jayne pretended to give the little girl a hug, but she backed away, holding out her hands. "No, thank you. I'm clean." Imogen took refuge behind Olivia, and when Jayne didn't follow, she peeked out and laughed.

While Aiden and Jayne mopped themselves up a bit, Olivia went back to the dough she was shaping, then lifted the lid of the camp oven to check its contents. The smell that wafted out made Jayne's mouth water.

"Sounds like the rain has stopped." Aiden pointed to the roof. "Should we go back and get some more done before lunch?"

Jayne thought for a moment. "All right, but lunch sounds nicer to me right now."

Yvonne handed Jayne a cup of tea. "Here, drink this before you go." She handed another one to Aiden.

Jayne waited only long enough for the drink to cool sufficiently for her to gulp it down, the heat of the liquid running all the way to her stomach. After Aiden finished sculling his tea, they returned to the garden and surveyed what they had done.

"I don't think we'll get much new ground dug up today, but let's make a start." Jayne hesitated, wondering if it was wise to tell Aiden her idea. Feeling too unsure, she said, "Let's start over here and work our way back towards the fence."

Aiden set to work in a way that made Jayne admire his grit. Even though the going was harder now that they were working unbroken ground, the sound of his shovel was relentless. Jayne paused to inspect the land around her. Here and there little saplings had sprung up in defiance of Daddy's efforts to clear the garden plot and the land surrounding their house. Patches of bracken fern also joined the protest. It would be a constant battle, one that could only be won by persistence and hard work.

Jayne bent down and gathered up some branches that had blown to the ground during a winter gale. The fresh smell of rain made her senses tingle, and she inhaled the sweetness. Faint sun rays warmed her back and made the patches of grass near the house glisten. Jayne felt an overwhelming desire to praise God, and the feeling erupted into a song of rejoicing. With amusement she noticed that Aiden kept glancing in her direction. When he discovered her watching, he lowered his eyes and concentrated on the spot he was clearing.

Left to her own thoughts, Jayne hummed another hymn. As the tune filled the silence, Jayne could hear Reverend Hastie's deep voice in her head. She pictured him at the pulpit with his face uplifted and etched with a sense of awe as he sang with all his might. The image reminded her of her plan. A quick prayer sprang from her heart, asking God's guidance upon her words. She spoke before she could talk herself out of it. "Aiden."

At the sound of his name, Aiden's head jerked up.

"Maybe you could come with me this afternoon to Buninyong."

Aiden froze, his face expressionless as Jayne said, "I'll be delivering the wash and collecting the money. It would be helpful having you along to carry things, and in truth, I would appreciate your company."

She didn't at all relish the thought of facing everyone on her own again—especially Mrs. Sterling. Also, it was the perfect opportunity to make known Aiden and Imogen's presence, because a few of the women to whom she had to return clothes attended their church. The more people those women told, the fewer awkward explanations would be necessary at church tomorrow. It was the one time Jayne felt grateful for hurrying tongues.

As she waited for his response, she tried not to make Aiden feel pressured, but she knew her eyes were imploring him to say yes.

Aiden avoided her gaze, scuffing his feet in the dirt. After a long moment, he lifted his head. "I don't know."

Jayne felt like rejoicing. She had had little hope he would even consider it. At least he hadn't flatly refused.

"What about Imogen?"

Jayne barely heard the question as she wondered if he didn't mind going out in public after all. She sighed. There were so many things she didn't know about these strangers who had plunged into her life.

Then she saw that Aiden was still waiting for her to reply. "I thought it might be best if Imogen stayed home. Olivia and

Vonnie can watch out for her. She'll be perfectly safe." Again, Jayne held her breath and waited.

Aiden nodded. "Imogen likes Olivia."

Jayne's heart leapt.

"I'll think about it," Aiden said, his face serious.

Jayne went back to work feeling more sober than before. At least she had gardening to focus her efforts on while she tried to be patient. The cutting of their shovels sounded again and again as the two worked on without talking, and the sun crept ever higher in the sky.

Jayne stopped to scoop up a worm and watched as it wiggled through her fingers to the dirt. It disappeared under a pile of weeds, and Jayne resumed her work, glad to have been able to straighten up for a moment. She glanced over at Aiden as his shovel stopped moving for the first time since their conversation.

Leaning the shovel handle against his shoulder, he locked eyes with her. "All right. I'll go as long as you think it will be fine."

"Thank you." Silently, Jayne thanked God for His answer to her prayer. "It'll be so much more pleasant with you along."

Aiden could not keep from smiling at Jayne's words, though she could tell he tried to suppress it.

"We need to leave straight after we've eaten," Jayne said, trying not to sound overly excited. "I want to drop in on a friend to see how she is going. You'll like Mrs. Eddington. She does lots of baking. If we hurry, we'll be back before dark so we can haul water for our baths."

Aiden made a face, but Jayne ignored it. "We've made good progress," she said, surveying what they had laboured over all morning. "I should've started digging it up earlier, but hopefully it'll still be ready in time for planting." She started towards the garden gate as she spoke. "I won't be able to get back to it until at least Tuesday if we are able to get more washing when we're in town. If so, we'll be doing the extra washing on Monday along with our own." She latched the gate securely behind them before facing Aiden. "It'll be a long, hard day of work."

Aiden nodded. "But Imogen and I will help." He shrugged. "We could even dig up more of the garden for you on Monday after we help with hauling water for the wash."

Jayne laid a hand on Aiden's shoulder. "I'd appreciate that." She gave herself a shake. "Well, I guess I'd best focus on one day at a time. Let's go get cleaned up."

"I'll take your shovel." Aiden headed for the stable without another word.

Feeling mystified, Jayne gazed after him. Perhaps these children were God's provision for them. Aiden certainly seemed keen to pull his share of the load.

16
"Mark My Words"

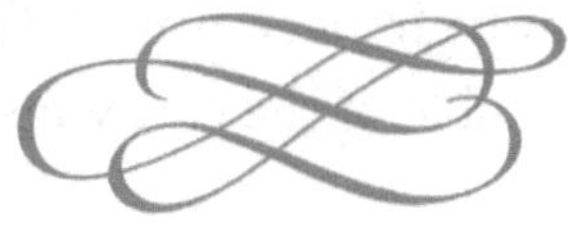

"I'm going to drop in on Mrs. Eddington," Jayne said to Olivia and Yvonne as they ate lunch. "Is there something I can take her?"

Olivia nodded. "You can give her one of the soda loaves Imogen helped us bake this morning. They're a lovely golden colour. The best we've made for a while."

At Olivia's direction, Imogen went to wrap one in a cloth. She skipped back over to the table. "Here you are."

With a word of thanks, Jayne rose from her chair. "Ready, Aiden?"

As she hitched Betsie to the cart, Jayne explained the process to him. He followed close beside her, helping whenever he was able. Jayne let him lead the mare up to the house, and together they worked at stacking the bundles of clothes in the cart so they wouldn't get dirty or rumpled on the trip to town.

When they'd done the best they could, Jayne climbed up to the cart's seat, and Aiden leapt in beside her. Imogen, who had been helping carry things from the house, ran around to Aiden's side of the cart. Standing on tiptoes, she reached as high as she could. Aiden stretched down and squeezed her hand. "You'll be all right. Keep helping Olivia with the baking while I'm gone."

Imogen nodded. "I will." She locked eyes with her brother. "You'll come back, won't you?"

Aiden nodded. "Of course. You know I wouldn't leave you. When I get back, I'll have lots of stories to tell." He tugged one of her sandy-coloured plaits, then straightened back up. "Go on now."

Imogen ran to where Olivia and Yvonne stood and slipped her hand inside Olivia's. Jayne clucked to Betsie and slapped the reins. As they rolled away, Imogen waved. Her little voice rose to be heard over the rumble of the cart wheels. "Bye Aiden. I'll miss you."

Aiden swivelled on the wooden seat and waved until she was out of sight. Then he slumped in his seat and said nothing. Barely turning her head, Jayne saw a mixture of despair and sadness roll over his features, then disappear.

Jayne bit her lip. It would never do for it to be a silent ride to town, nor did she want Aiden to dwell on his sorrow. As the cart jolted along, Jayne turned to him. "Have you been in towns much?"

Aiden shrugged and went on staring at the passing scenery. "Now and then."

Jayne rolled her eyes. That certainly gave her a lot of information. She began talking about anything she could think of, determined to cheer him up. Aiden nodded every so often and answered any questions with the fewest words possible, until a group of kangaroos bounded in front of the cart. Aiden leaned forward to watch them disappear into the bush, then turned to Jayne, full of questions.

Before she knew it, they had covered the distance to town and were ready to deliver to their first customer. While Jayne climbed down from the cart, Aiden grabbed the bundle she had indicated. The woman who answered the door inspected the clean clothes and disappeared into the house, returning a moment later with some coins. After Jayne and the woman exchanged some pleasantries, they were off to deliver the next lot.

When Jayne pulled Betsie to a standstill after several successful deliveries and Aiden jumped down with the next bundle, she could tell that his step had grown more relaxed. He looked all around him, taking everything in. She hurried to catch up with him as he started down the path without her. This was one of the stops she had been waiting for. Now to find out if this part of her plan would work.

"Good afternoon, Jayne." The middle-aged woman greeted her with a pleasant smile. "Will we see you and your sisters at church in the morning?" As Jayne nodded, the woman looked Aiden up and down. "Well now, who is this well-built young fellow?"

Jayne's eyes flicked to Aiden, and she smiled at him. "Aiden and his sister are staying at our place to help us out a bit."

The woman looked Aiden over again. She shook her head, but her face remained pleasant. "The world's full of surprises. I can't wait to tell Mrs. Daley." She disappeared into the house, then returned with the money and some more garments to be mended, full of praise for the neat work. As they prepared to leave, she held out a piece of shortbread to Aiden.

He stared at it in surprise until Jayne nudged him, compelling him to reach for the treat. "Thank you, ma'am."

Jayne could barely contain her happiness as she walked back to Betsie and the cart. They had more work, Aiden was letting down his guard, and the woman from church would spread the news, hopefully sparing the children from too many questions. Everything around her took on a cheery quality. The sun peeked out from behind a cloud, birds sang overhead, and the grass and bushes danced in the breeze. Smiling, Jayne turned to Aiden. "Isn't it a beautiful spring day?"

Aiden pointed to a flock of clucking hens that were pecking about in a nearby front yard. "They seem to think so too."

When Jayne twisted on the seat to point out the next lot to be delivered, the sun disappeared behind a cloud, and she shivered. The next house was Mrs. Sterling's. As she wondered if she could just leave the items by the front door without knocking, her shoulders slumped. There was one undeniable problem with that option. If she didn't knock, she wouldn't be able to collect the money they'd worked so hard to earn. A bird flitted past her head, singing. She glared at it. What was there to sing about?

As they drew up in front of Mrs. Sterling's gate, Jayne considered sending Aiden to the door. She shook her head. She wouldn't send one of her sisters in her place, and though Aiden was a boy, she still felt that it would be mean and cowardly of her. In fact, it might be best to leave Aiden at the cart. If Mrs. Sterling didn't see him, Jayne wouldn't have to explain his presence and endure another lecture on how irresponsible and incapable she was. She had just convinced herself to leave him when she noticed that Aiden had already filled his arms and started towards the gate.

He looked back at her. "What's the matter? Aren't you coming?"

Jayne sighed and climbed down.

"Don't you like the people who live here?" Aiden studied her face.

Jayne hadn't realised it was that obvious, but there was no use denying it. She shook her head.

"Don't worry," Aiden said. "It won't take long, and we'll be off to the next one."

Jayne tried to smile at him, but she just couldn't.

Without giving Jayne the opportunity to delay further, Aiden passed through the gate. She had no choice but to follow him, though she did so with slow steps. Her heart beat harder as she rapped on the door. She started to advise Aiden not to take what Mrs. Sterling said to heart, but before she had a chance to finish, the door handle moved. It was as if the woman had been waiting to pounce on her. But when the door opened, it revealed a man.

"Why, Mr. Sterling, how do you do?" Jayne stammered.

The man inclined his head. "Jayne." He gave Aiden a long, hard look.

Aiden squirmed and edged sideways in an effort to avoid the inspection.

Hoping to rescue Aiden from his discomfort, Jayne took the bundle and held it out to the man. "Here are your clothes, sir. I hope you find them to your satisfaction."

Mr. Sterling took them but continued to stare at Aiden. "Indeed." Without another word, he stepped backwards and closed the door. Jayne had no idea if he intended on coming back. But right then and there, she decided she was not going to knock on the door again—even if it meant not getting paid. She exchanged a look with Aiden.

"Reckon he's going to come back?" he asked.

When Jayne opened her hands in a helpless gesture, Aiden bent forward with his ear near the door. As Jayne copied him, she could hear voices inside, but they seemed far away. She stepped back. "Maybe we should just leave."

Aiden shook his head. "What about your payment? You worked hard."

Jayne nodded. They had worked hard. Those clothes had been filthy.

"You should ask for it."

Jayne looked at Aiden with a feeling of wonder. He must be braver than she felt. Trapped in indecision, she caught the sound of footsteps, and before she could think, the door flew open. Mrs. Sterling stood before her.

Jayne stepped backwards, prepared to flee down the path without waiting for any payment, but as she turned, her breath caught in her throat. Mr. Lamberton was ambling past on his horse.

To leave meant being seen by Lamberton and a possible confrontation with him. To stay meant talking with Mrs. Sterling. Neither were pleasant options. Fighting her desire to press as close to the house as she could, Jayne clutched Aiden's arm and drew herself back to face Mrs. Sterling.

The woman sniffed. "I must pay you I suppose, whether or not the job meets my satisfaction." She thrust the money at Jayne, while at the same time turning on Aiden. "Who is this?" She looked down her nose at him. "Young man, what's your name?"

He stood taller. "Aiden."

"What are you doing here?"

Aiden braced his feet and clenched his hands. "We're living with Miss Reid and helping her out," he said, not bothering to explain who the "we" he referred to was.

Despite the tense situation, Jayne felt her heart fill with gladness at the words, "We're living with Miss Reid." They sounded very definite.

Mrs. Sterling shook her head in disgust. "You seem mighty big for your boots, Master Aiden. In fact, the both of you do." She glared at Jayne. "Mark my words. This latest rash decision will end in your destruction."

Jayne's face heated with frustration, and she opened her mouth, ready to vent her anger. But a verse of Scripture restrained her: *When a man's ways please the LORD, he maketh even his enemies to be at peace with him.* Jayne nearly choked in her effort to hold back her angry words. How she wanted to teach Mrs. Sterling a lesson!

But Mrs. Sterling hadn't finished. Her eyes narrowed. "You'll get no more work from me and no charity either. When you fail to make ends meet, don't come begging to me." The door banged shut, and Jayne flinched.

She was afraid that Aiden would take Mrs. Sterling's words to heart, thinking he and Imogen were an unwanted burden. She watched Aiden kick something invisible with his toe and wished it wasn't unladylike for her to do the same. People had no business to go ranting about things that didn't concern them.

Before she moved off the front porch, Jayne scanned the laneway. She ventured down the steps, stopped, and looked again. To her intense relief, Mr. Lamberton and his horse were no longer in view.

Aiden scowled. "If I were older, I wouldn't let that woman talk to you like that."

"It's all right," Jayne said, but the words sounded forced.

Aiden shook his head in disagreement and spat. "It's distasteful."

She stared at him in horror.

"I'm sorry, it's just . . ." He shook his head and gritted his teeth.

"Don't let her spoil your day," Jayne said as she climbed back into the cart. The only response she got was a sigh. She knew how he felt. Looking back at the door of Mrs. Sterling's house, she clenched the reins and fumed. "What she said was her opinion." Jayne slapped the reins on Betsie's rump. "An opinion I don't share."

It wasn't easy to avoid letting Mrs. Sterling ruin the day. Somehow the woman had created a sour twist upon everything. When they finally pulled up in front of Mrs. Eddington's house, Jayne felt a new dread rising in the pit of her stomach. What if her friend no longer occupied the house? What if the infamous Mr. Lamberton now had it in his possession? She ought to have asked Jed about it. "Stay here." She passed the reins to Aiden. "I want to see if Mrs. Eddington is at home." She climbed down, looking all around her for signs of life. Then she slipped towards the house, hoping no one watched from the window.

A rooster crowed. Jayne jumped and clutched her chest. Already she had spun around, ready to flee. Feeling foolish, she met Aiden's eyes. He was grinning at her. Jayne turned back to the house and crept forward again. Instead of going to the front door, she walked around the house and looked in the back yard. Nothing suggested Lamberton's presence.

Jayne marched back to the front of the house, determined to push aside her fear. With a trembling hand, she rapped twice. When the door opened to reveal Mrs. Eddington, Jayne rushed forward. "I'm so glad you're still here." She wrapped her arms around her friend and squeezed her tight.

When Jayne let go, Mrs. Eddington chuckled and held her at arm's length. "You certainly took me by surprise, Jayne, rushing at me like that. But who's waiting in the cart? Tell him he's welcome to the warmth of my home."

Jayne beckoned to Aiden. "Come on. Everything is all right." She turned back to the elderly woman. "Aiden and his sister are staying at our house."

Mrs. Eddington looked enquiringly at Jayne, then turned to hold out her arm in welcome to Aiden. "Come in, both of you, and make yourselves at home." When they stepped inside, Jayne saw that everything Mrs. Eddington owned seemed to be strewn about the room. But the older woman pointed to the table as if everything was normal. "Help yourselves to a piece of fruit bun."

While Jayne found a seat amongst the mess and bit into a mouthful of sticky goodness, Mrs. Eddington dodged around the piles of clutter and the upended crates all over the floor, getting out the tea things and putting water on to boil. She waved her hand. "Do excuse the mess, won't you? It's surely a sad job packing up to leave the house your husband built with his own hands." She wiped at the tears that formed in her eyes. "I don't know quite what I'll do now that I've sold."

Jayne rose. "Why did you sell?" As Mrs. Eddington's face tightened, Jayne half-wished she could take back the question. But she had to know.

17
A WIDOW'S TROUBLE

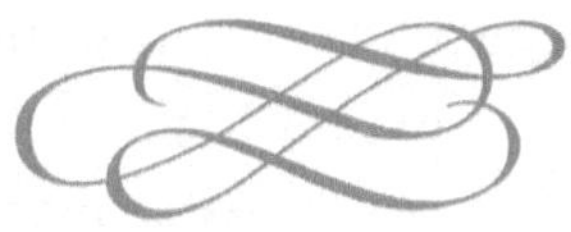

"Let me get some tea to quiet my nerves." Mrs. Eddington drew a shuddery breath and rubbed her temples. "Then I'll tell you all about it." She waved Jayne back to her seat. Then she set the sugar pot on the table and scooped a spoonful into her empty cup.

Jayne watched with growing surprise as Mrs. Eddington spooned not two, but three spoonfuls into her empty teacup. As if that wasn't enough, she went back for more. Jayne reached out and laid a hand on her friend's wrist.

The gentle restraint jolted the older woman back to reality. "Now look what I've done. This mess of events has set my brain all a-muddle. Always forgetting what I'm doing and where I've put things. I'm just not myself since that man came." Sadness filled her face as she motioned again to the mess. "I'm glad you've come. You're an answer to my prayers. I was getting beside myself with everything that's gone on." She collapsed into a chair and laid her hands in her lap. They only lay still a moment before she reached up restlessly to finger the tea-spoon's handle.

Jayne stood. "Why don't you have something to eat? It'll make you feel stronger." She pushed the plate towards Mrs. Eddington, wondering if the sweet woman had been eating properly. Her fidgeting hands seemed frail and her frame more drawn than the last time Jayne visited.

The older woman shook her head. "No, I really couldn't eat."

Wanting to help her friend somehow, Jayne tipped the sugar back into the bowl and went to get the kettle from the stovetop. Her eyes lingered on the woodstove's lettering before her fingers ran lightly over the edge of the cast iron stovetop. Daddy had spoken of getting such a stove for Mam someday. Now it was a dream that had floated away, just like so many other things. But she wouldn't let Lamberton wrench away their plan of owning land as he had the home of her elderly friend.

After she had poured Mrs. Eddington a steaming cupful, Jayne stirred in one teaspoon of sugar. A smile flickered across her face at the thought of drinking a cup sweetened by three heaping spoonfuls. "There now, drink some of this." She poured a cup for Aiden and another for herself. "I'm only sorry I didn't visit you sooner. If you'd like, I'll send Olivia around to help on Monday."

Mrs. Eddington nodded and took a sip of tea. "Yes, that might be best."

Unwilling to press her friend further, Jayne sat down and waited to see if she would begin her tale.

Her hostess looked at Aiden and managed a smile. "Have another portion of bun. I know how young ones can eat." As he thanked her and took another slice, she continued, "You seem like a good boy. Did Jayne say you had a sister?"

"Yes, ma'am. Imogen. She's eight."

"Eight. I remember when my daughters were that old. Such a lovely, carefree age. But they've all grown up and moved to England. I wouldn't even know what they look like now." She sighed. "I'm sure you watch out for your sister."

Aiden nodded.

Mrs. Eddington fiddled with her cup, running her fingers around and around the rim. "It all happened a week ago today."

Jayne set aside her tea and leaned forward.

"The man knocked on the door and barged in without waiting to be invited. Once inside, he introduced himself with such pomp, acting like he was doing me an honour by coming to my house. But his display of importance lacked any real manners. I disliked him from the start."

Jayne tilted her head in acknowledgement, almost afraid to move lest she interrupt. That sounded like Lamberton all right.

Mrs. Eddington shrugged. "Mr. Lamberton, as he called himself, entered alone. Although I do recall someone lingering behind him on the road. Someone I didn't recognise. But from the way he hovered in the background, I thought he might've been with Mr. Lamberton. I heard him speak to a passerby just before Mr. Lamberton intruded, and the words had an Irish brogue to them. But that's all I noticed before other things crowded my mind."

Mrs. Eddington picked up her cup, then set it back down again. "It all seems like such a faraway memory that I find myself wondering if it even happened." She shook her head. "The truth is I don't exactly know how it all occurred. But before he left, Mr. Lamberton had me signing a piece of paper."

Jayne half rose from her seat in amazement. "You . . . you mean you didn't know he was purchasing your house?"

Mrs. Eddington waved her back down. "No, no. He explained

all that. Said he had to have it signed right then. Jayne, you know I never wanted to sell this place. It feels like the only real home I have, now that Mr. Eddington is dead and my daughters are all in England. How I miss them." Her face grew wistful, and she wiped her eyes with a lace-edged handkerchief. As she refolded the cloth in a precise triangle, her look changed to one of indignation.

"Did you know he wanted me out the next day? God gave me the presence of mind to speak wisdom on that. For which I'm inexpressibly grateful. I told that man I needed at least two and a half weeks to clear my belongings." She took a shuddery breath. "He got quite agitated then, pacing around my house and turning dark red." Her face full of shadows, Mrs. Eddington lifted a trembling hand to smooth her hair.

Jayne wished it could be that easy to smooth away the whole horrible situation. But it wasn't. The man's audacity made her skin crawl, yet there was nothing she could do.

The distressed woman clasped her hands, seeming unable to relax. "All of a sudden Mr. Lamberton went quite mannerly again. It was exhausting and confusing. One minute he acted like he would break all my things and maybe me. And then he said that of course he understood I must have the extra time. Regrettably, he would not be able to pay as much, though, due to my lack of compliance."

At that Jayne jumped to her feet, her face hot. This time Lamberton had gone too far. Imagine having the gall to pay a widow less because of "lack of compliance." In reality, all Mrs. Eddington desired was a barely adequate amount of time to get organised. No human being ought to act so monstrously. Jayne was about to vent her disgust when she happened a glance at Mrs. Eddington's face. Misery and despair were written on every feature. Voicing her anger would do her friend little good, and it might stop the flow of the story.

The noise of someone shifting positions alerted Jayne to Aiden's presence, and she shot him an apologetic look. Poor Aiden. When he stepped inside Mrs. Eddington's home, he'd had no clue what he was plunging into. If only Lamberton's name could have stayed unfamiliar to his ears, for knowing the man was no pleasure. At any rate, the boy had probably heard enough.

Pointing at the back door, she suggested in a whisper that Aiden might split some of the wood she had seen. At first he frowned in confusion, but after a few more whispered words, Aiden understood. The look on his face changed to one of relief, and he slipped quietly out the door.

Again, Jayne sat and waited, giving Mrs. Eddington the opportunity to continue when she deemed fit. But when the older woman went on staring at her hands in silence, Jayne's impatience got the better of her. "There's something I don't understand."

Looking up, Mrs. Eddington laughed, though without her usual merriness. "By the time you reach my age, you'll learn that there are many things in life you'll never understand." She shook her head. "But what is it?"

Jayne hesitated, not wanting to cause Mrs. Eddington to return to her sad thoughts. "How did Mr. Lamberton get you to sign the paper?"

The elderly woman closed her eyes and moaned softly, but she answered with surprising strength and calmness. "He caught me by surprise and made me confused by using words I didn't understand. I was intimidated and flustered. He didn't give me time to think, just kept pressuring me, always talking. Over and over Mr. Lamberton said what a great deal he was offering me.

How I might not have another opportunity like this again. Then he started mentioning my age, as if I couldn't possibly manage the upkeep. He told me to imagine how displeased my husband would be if I let it get run down. He wouldn't accept no for an answer. When I requested time to consider what he'd said, he threatened me. All I wanted was to ask someone I trusted. But he said bad things might happen to me if I didn't sell right away. I can hear his cruel voice saying, 'Don't be sure you'll stay safe, Widow Eddington. It's well known you live by yourself with no one to aid you.' "

She lowered her voice. "I wondered if he meant that he, or someone he knew, would do something horrible if I did not comply with his wishes." She shuddered. "I've never been afraid at nights, but since his visit I've been scared. Always jumping at the least noise." Mrs. Eddington frowned. "I've gone over his conversation so many times I'm no longer sure what else he told me. But I remember his body language well. It haunts me at night. Indeed the mind is a powerful thing. If I didn't work to tame it, it would ruin me."

Jayne nodded, knowing well the truth of her words. Her own mind had taunted her often.

"Jayne, something else plagues me when I think about his visit. I can't place it, but I know it's important somehow."

When Mrs. Eddington continued to stare at the tabletop, Jayne wanted to say something to help her. But what was there to say?

The elderly woman lifted her eyes to Jayne's. "A few times he seemed to imply there were others beside himself. But no." She bit her lip. "No, that can't be what bothers me so much. There's something else." She searched Jayne's face as if it held the clue to her bafflement. "It's almost like I've seen him before—in a photograph or something."

Mrs. Eddington got up and paced to the front window. As Jayne stared at her companion's back, she wondered if her friend was trying to reconstruct the bully's visit. Mam had always valued Mrs. Eddington for her sound wisdom and gentle ways. What was it that evaded her now?

The tapestry of Jayne's own life seemed a confusion of knots and tangles. If Lamberton hindered them from reaching their payments, he could take over their home. Would he get their property, just as he had managed to get Mrs. Eddington's?

Running her hand nervously up and down her arm, Mrs. Eddington turned back to Jayne. "I wish I hadn't signed. Every time I replay it in my mind, I wish I could go back and refuse. But he made me feel like I didn't have any choice." She threw up her hands. "I don't know what I'll do once Tuesday comes or where I'll go."

"You're welcome at our house for as long as you need. Though I'm afraid it won't be very private. Aiden and Imogen sleep in the main room, and there's only the other room where we have our beds. I'm afraid it's not much to offer you."

"Nonsense." Mrs. Eddington managed a smile. "Your home has always been the most welcoming one around. I don't know what I'll do, but at least I can feel like there's some place for me to go."

Jayne nodded, wondering whether she should mention her own confrontation with Lamberton. She didn't want to add to Mrs. Eddington's worry, but perhaps it would help her friend grasp what else was amiss with the man.

Fixing her eyes on her hostess, Jayne decided to take the plunge. "I've met this Mr. Lamberton. He paid us a visit a couple of weeks ago too."

Mrs. Eddington gasped. Jayne cringed, but tried to keep her outward appearance as calm as possible. "I was all alone apart from Olivia, and she was out checking the sheep and their lambs. Lamberton wanted to buy our farm, but God gave me the courage to resist."

Mrs. Eddington walked over and grasped Jayne's hands. "Don't let him do to you and your sisters what he did to me. I couldn't stand to see him take your parents' home from you. There may not seem any way he could, but I don't trust him. He might stop at nothing to get what he wants. Be careful, won't you?"

Jayne rose and gave her friend a hug. "We'll be on our guard. I promise." There was a certain sweetness that came from mutual trials, and she felt a closeness lingering between the two of them as she stepped away from the embrace. "We'd best be going. I don't want to be out while it's dark."

Mrs. Eddington nodded. "Where's that young man gone? I didn't notice him leave."

Jayne motioned outside. "I believe he's splitting your wood."

Mrs. Eddington listened for a moment, and a dull thud came through the walls of the house. "Such a good boy."

As if sensing their approach, Aiden halted his attempts at splitting a hefty piece of wood and looked up. Upon spotting them, he piled his arms with split wood. Jayne met Aiden when he was halfway across the yard. As he glanced at her over the top of his precarious load, she shot him a smile. "Thanks for your help. I'll explain later."

As Jayne filled her own arms with wood, she heard the older woman praising Aiden for his work and grinned. You could always count on Mrs. Eddington to make someone feel worthwhile.

Leaving the woodbox filled, the two young people adjusted Betsie's harness while Mrs. Eddington stroked the mare's neck, telling her to trot along faithfully with her passengers. When Aiden unwound the reins, Betsie yanked her head away, trying to munch on the grass previously out of reach. Aiden shouted and grabbed for the reins, his eyes full of laughter as he gave the mare a stern warning.

Mrs. Eddington turned to fold Jayne in another hug. "Take care." Her hands lingered on Jayne's a moment before she stepped aside, calling her thanks to Aiden.

Jayne waved, thinking Mrs. Eddington had never looked so alone and defenceless. She blinked back tears. This injustice couldn't go on forever; righteousness would prevail. "I'll keep you in my prayers."

"And I you."

Jayne clucked and Betsie started forward, for once seeming eager to be off. As the stores with their bold lettering and wooden verandas flowed by, Jayne turned to Aiden. She owed him an apology as well as an explanation. The question was, how much should she say? He already had far too much weighing on his young shoulders without her adding more. Perhaps she would err on the side of telling only the necessities and wait for his reaction.

Aiden listened silently to Jayne's account of her own confrontation with Lamberton. When she finished, he shook his head. "Don't like the sound of him. I sure wouldn't like to meet him anyhow."

Jayne decided to leave it at that. As she watched, he leaned back into the seat with his hands resting on his legs, casually taking in the surroundings. It was the most laid-back she'd ever seen him.

Perhaps this was the moment she'd been hoping for. While

part of her hated to encroach upon his serenity, she couldn't miss the opportunity. Yet even the thought of asking about his past made her nervous. She'd been desperate for such a chance, and she didn't want to mess it up. She drew a deep breath. "I'm curious. Where were you and Imogen before you came to Buninyong?" Jayne hoped it sounded like a casual question, a way of making conversation. In reality her pulse raced, and beneath her trembling hand, the reins shook noticeably. She reached out to steady her grip, afraid he would notice.

Aiden stretched, then yawned what appeared to be an artificial yawn. When he stopped shifting around, he gazed nonchalantly at the road ahead, but his back was stiff. "Just here and there, can't really say exactly. Been travelling for the last few months." He squinted into the fading sunlight. "You know, we would've been all right if you hadn't found us. I could've taken care of Imogen fine."

Jayne felt a rush of indignation. Already she had sacrificed time, privacy, and food to look after him and his sister. To her ears his comment didn't sound very appreciative. She tried to shake off her offense as another question demanded to be asked. "Why did you stay so long on our property and not keep going?"

Aiden ran his hand through his hair and tapped his boots together. The look on his face told Jayne there were a great many places he'd rather be than here with her questions, and she feared she had pushed him too much.

Finally, the boy shrugged. "Guess you all looked kind. And in the stable one time we heard you talking about helping people."

Jayne felt goose bumps form on her skin as she realised that the children had been eavesdropping on her as she worked.

"We didn't think you'd mind if we stayed on your property temporarily." He cleared his throat. "Imogen was tired of being cold and your stable was warm. I didn't know what else to do." The last words belied his earlier statement, and the flush that rose on Aiden's cheeks told Jayne he knew it. "Imogen didn't want to leave."

Jayne nodded. "Thanks for being honest with me." Aiden turned to face away from her. As she saw his stiff posture, Jayne knew the conversation was over. She hoped fervently that she hadn't made a wrong decision. Earlier he had appeared to be growing more relaxed. It would be almost unbearable if all the progress made today was ruined by a few unwelcome questions.

Behind them, the town had long faded into the distance. Left to her own thoughts, Jayne pondered what Mrs. Eddington had said about something else plaguing her concerning Lamberton and his visit. Was it something real that bothered her friend? Or did the elderly woman's uneasiness flow from restless nights and hours of worry?

Jayne sighed aloud, then let her mind wander to church the next day. Suddenly she sat up straighter. What would Imogen wear? Certainly not what they had found her in, and the hand-me-down dress was hardly presentable either. That left one option—a late night dress alteration. She didn't know why they hadn't done something sooner.

While the others settled into bed fresh and clean for the service tomorrow, Jayne had set out the sewing supplies. Now she sat feeling quite alone, though she shared the room with two worn-out children. The dress she planned to alter lay untouched in her lap while the conversation she'd had with Imogen earlier still captured her attention.

She had stood enraptured by the night sky when the little girl waltzed up beside her in a nightgown. They smiled at each other in the windowpane, the moon's glow reflecting on their faces. Together they gazed into the starry night until Imogen tilted her head to look at Jayne.

"I'm glad you found us." Imogen slipped her fingers inside Jayne's hand. "It feels safe."

Instantly alert, Jayne turned the little girl to face her. "Safe from what?" Her hand rested on Imogen's smooth hair.

Imogen shrugged. "Just safe."

Before she could ask anything else, Aiden came up behind them and wrapped his arms around Imogen's shoulders. "Time for you to get some sleep, little sister."

To mask her disappointment, Jayne had turned back to the window. The night sky seemed like a cavern of mystery, dotted with sparks of hope. Only the sparks were all too distant to grasp hold of.

With a shake of her head, Jayne picked up the dress in her lap. This time she'd been so close to finding a clue to the children's past. If only they could be convinced to trust her with their story. Sighing, she took hold of the scissors and made the first snip.

18
A Frightening Morning

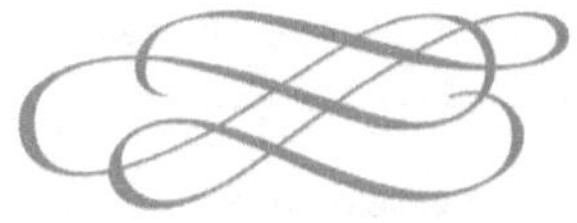

Olivia sank into a chair. "Well, I helped Mrs. Eddington pack the last of her belongings. Did you get much washing done after I left?"

Jayne nodded. "I finished ours, plus most of the clothing we collected in town. There wasn't as much extra this time. How was Mrs. Eddington?" Without giving time for a response, she went on. "Surely there's some way we can keep her from losing her house. It's all so unfair. That horrible man."

Olivia sighed. "I spent every minute on the way home praying for Mrs. Eddington and for us. The situation has me worried that Mr. Lamberton will find a way to obtain our house and land. He's so"—she searched for the right word with a frown—"so cunning."

Jayne laughed, trying to make the situation feel less tense. But her laughter sounded empty.

Olivia went on frowning as she scuffed her foot back and forth along the boards, making thuds with each swing. "Mrs.

Eddington told me she has to be out by four o'clock tomorrow afternoon."

"Has she decided what she's going to do or where she's going to go?"

Olivia shook her head. "I don't think it's sunk in that tomorrow is it." She pulled her braid over her shoulder and fiddled with it. "When I asked her about it, she just brushed the question aside. It seemed like she couldn't bear to think of it."

"Poor thing. That was about her response to me as well. I feel so sorry for her." As Jayne rested her face in her hands, the fatty smell of soap assaulted her nose, testifying of the day's labour. After a few moments of gloomy silence, she straightened up. "Well, there's nothing more we can do tonight. I already explained everything to Jed and asked him to consider visiting Mrs. Eddington tomorrow. Maybe that way he'll be present when Mr. Lamberton takes possession of the house. I don't know whether he'll go or not. He didn't say, only nodded and went back to his work. He seemed preoccupied."

Olivia squeezed Jayne's hand. "I don't see that there's anything he can do anyway. We'll have to keep praying."

Jayne smiled in acknowledgement, then sighed. "Tea's ready. Guess I'd better call the others inside."

The late morning sun sent its warmth over the earth, bringing the fragrance of spring to life as Jayne headed back to the house. All was well with their flock of ewes and lambs. As she followed the path, her own step matched the lightness of the lambs she had seen at play.

Halfway back, Jayne lifted her head and listened. Her pleasant thoughts of breakfast vanished as the stillness was shattered by the noise of something bounding through the underbrush. Her first thought was that it might be a mob of kangaroos, but the crashing sounded more like the noise of a horse in flight. The rustling of leaves mixed with the breaking of branches as hoofbeats thumped towards her with increasing volume. Before she could do anything, Jayne caught sight of a horse through the underbrush about a tree's length away. Its nostrils flared as it crashed onwards in the direction of Jed's hut.

For a moment Jayne froze. Then she dashed forward, trying to get another glimpse. Horrified, she realised she'd been right. It was Spark, Jed's horse. Fully saddled, Spark careened through the bush—riderless.

As she sprinted forward, calling Jed's name, vivid images of his possible injuries flashed into her mind. Jayne shook her head and refused to let the thoughts surface. Even so, she felt dizzy with panic. Jayne breathed in a lungful of air, then slowly exhaled. She wanted to run in every direction at once, but first she must calm Jed's restless horse. "Easy, Spark."

At the sound of her voice, the gelding snorted and slowed to a trot. Jayne inched towards him. "Steady there, boy. Where did you leave Jed?"

Spark shook his neck and faced her, dancing in place before trotting around her in a semi-circle. As Jayne's calm tone continued, he dropped to a hurried walk. She edged nearer, hoping he wouldn't spin and hightail it away. The gap between them closed until only an arm's length separated them. Desperate, Jayne lunged for the draping reins. Spark lifted his neck and backed away with a snort, but it was too late. Jayne's fingers had reached their goal. Never had the weight of leather straps in her palms felt so comforting.

Jayne ran her hand down the gelding's sweaty neck as he

jerked at the reins. "Easy does it now. What would Jed think if he saw you all worked up?"

Spark snorted. His sides heaved, but he stood still.

Jayne scanned the trees and fallen branches around them. Nothing presented itself as a step-up, and every lost moment meant increased risk for Jed. Her eyes fell on the base of a tree. Its protruding root would give her the extra height she needed—if Spark cooperated.

Pressing herself against the tree trunk, Jayne clutched a handful of mane and swung her body nimbly upwards. Spark skittered beneath her, but Jayne landed with precision and felt around for the other stirrup. Now to find Cass in the hope he knew what direction to search.

She turned Spark in a full circle but saw nothing more than peaceful surroundings. Loosening the reins, she started towards Jed's hut. Though the saddle felt much too large and the stirrups too long, she kept herself in rhythm with Spark's trot while she scanned the bush on both sides and called for Jed. Even now he could be strolling through the bush looking for his horse. But the more ground they covered, the more her heart sank. By the time Jayne reached the hut, a dark cloud of fear had settled over her heart.

"Cass, where are you? I think Jed's hurt." The words disappeared into the emptiness around her. After a pause she called again. "Jed!" When no answering shout came from either man, tears welled in Jayne's eyes. Brushing them away, she spun Spark around and dug in her heels.

The moment they skidded to a stop by the house, Jayne shouted again. When Olivia appeared, her mouth dropped open at the sight of her older sister sitting astride Jed's horse.

"Get the others." Jayne's command set Olivia back in motion.

Through the open doorway, Jayne heard the sound of hurried words, and a moment later the younger children came filing outside. Feeling like a commander with soldiers lined up to receive their orders, Jayne didn't wait for questions. "I found Spark tearing through the bush. Jed must've had an accident. Do any of you know where he was going?" Jayne looked at them in turn, but each one shook their head. "All right. All of you spread out. Try to find Jed or Cass. I'm going to try the road."

"What should we do if we find him?" Olivia's voice was resolute. Beside her, Yvonne stared up at Jayne with frightened eyes, obviously wanting answers.

Jayne hesitated. "If you don't know what to do, don't move him. Try to find Cass or me." At the touch of her heels, Spark bounded forward. "Steady, steady." Jayne's own nerves needed the reminder as much as the horse did. "Almighty God, please show me where to go. Be my guiding light."

As Spark cantered towards the road, Jayne kept a close watch on both sides of the track. Calling voices echoed through the air as the others tramped around the bush between their house and the road. Though the sounds faded as she rode onwards, she drew comfort from the knowledge that others now searched with her.

As she watched for Jed's form along the road, Jayne realised that at any moment she could ride past him and not know it. With just one misplaced shrub or mound of dirt, he'd be left without help while she looked elsewhere. The thought terrified her. As she tried to see farther into the trees, she slowed Spark down as best she could. Her eyes stung as she tried to focus on both sides at once. "Please God, help me find Jed. Preserve his life."

She yelled Jed's name again. Though she listened with all her might, no answer came. She felt like she was in a dream. A dream that she hoped wouldn't turn into a nightmare. "Jed, answer me." Tears choked her voice. Whatever would they do if he—

Up ahead on the edge of the road, something captured her attention. As Jayne stood in her stirrups and leaned forward Spark took it as his cue to go faster—and there on the ground lay Jed, still and silent. Jayne cried out, but he didn't stir.

She covered the last few yards in a matter of seconds, then reined up sharply. In an instant she was kneeling by Jed's side. His face was bloodied, and his eyes lay shut. Jayne closed her eyes to fight a wave of nausea.

"Courage." The word slipped from her lips, barely audible, and from the depths of her soul, she uttered a heartfelt prayer for mercy. "Please, not Jed too."

She opened her eyes and laid a hand on Jed's chest. A moment of relief replaced her terror when she felt the rise and fall of life. With trembling hands, she tenderly grasped his shoulders and shook his body, but his eyes remained shut. Jayne's gaze lingered for a moment on his dear face. She wanted to do something to make Jed more comfortable, but she feared injuring him further.

She stood and took a step backwards, unwilling to leave, but unable to stay. Help was needed and fast. It had to be done, but as she rode away from Jed's helpless form, Jayne felt she had betrayed him.

She found Olivia first. "Jed's hurt bad. Unconscious, bloody. Where's Cass?"

Olivia shrugged helplessly. "I can't find him. I've looked everywhere."

"Did you check the stable to see if Wattle's saddle was there?"

Olivia shook her head and started in that direction at a run. "Wait."

Olivia spun around, and Jayne locked eyes with her. "Find

Yvonne. Tell her to get blankets. We'll need water and a damp cloth. See if there's anything we can use to revive Jed, and if you need to, take Betsie. I'm going to look for Cass. Don't wait for me." Jayne started off, only to swivel in the saddle for a last instruction. "Aiden knows how to hitch up Betsie. Get him to do it while you gather the other things." She prodded Spark on, already feeling like she'd taken too long.

"Jayne!"

Impatiently, Jayne swung Jed's horse to face Olivia once more. Time was precious.

"Where'd you find him?"

"Down the road." Jayne pointed. "Near the second bend."

With a nod, Olivia raced towards the house.

Free to find Cass, Jayne gritted her teeth. Where was that man when they needed him? She felt like screaming his name.

Just then, she heard Yvonne still calling for Jed, and her youngest sister appeared through a gap in the trees. Her face was flushed, and her breath came in gasps. Using as few words as possible, Jayne filled her in, adding, "When you find Olivia, tell her to hurry. If Jed revives, one of us should be there."

Jayne dismounted and ran into the stable. One glance told her all she needed to know. Her father's saddle, the one used on Wattle, was gone.

"What's the matter?"

Aiden's voice made Jayne jump. She pointed to the rack where Wattle's saddle belonged. "It's gone and so is Cass. We're on our own."

Aiden didn't stop to reply. Already Betsie's harness dangled from his hand, and he moved to position the mare between the cart shafts. Jayne ran out to remount Spark, then urged him back towards the house.

As Jayne approached, Yvonne hurried out of the house with an armload of blankets, barely glancing at her sister. Nearby, Imogen stood holding a bucket of water. The little girl pointed towards the road. "Olivia ran that way."

Jayne nodded and nudged Spark to a canter in the direction of the road. She would waste no more time looking for Cass—Jed needed her. Halfway to where Jed lay, she spotted Olivia. Bending low over Spark's neck, she drove the horse on until she overtook her running sister and reached Jed. With a leap, she dismounted and crouched beside him. He lay unmoved, his eyes still shut.

Time ticked by agonizingly until Olivia arrived, panting hard. She knelt down by Jayne and touched Jed's hand. "He's so cold. I don't like him being on the ground like this." Then she pointed to Jed's leg. "Even if he comes to, we won't be able to move him."

Jayne stared at the warped angle of Jed's left leg in dismay. "I can't believe I never saw it." Her voice shook as she inspected the rest of Jed's body. To her touch, nothing else felt broken, but Olivia was right. Jed's skin felt cold—very cold. The sensation triggered terrible memories. Again Jayne ran her hands over his body, wanting to be sure she hadn't missed anything else. Other than a rip on his sleeve and the dirt on his clothes, nothing more seemed obviously wrong.

Olivia rubbed Jayne's arm gently. "We need the doctor."

Jayne bit her lip. "I know, but I don't like to leave him again."

"Someone has to go, and you're the best rider."

Jayne racked her mind for another option. "Mr. O'Donnell could fetch the doctor." Even as she spoke the words, she knew it made no sense. The O'Donnell's farm lay in the opposite direction to town and the doctor.

Jayne's quandary was interrupted by the welcome sight of Betsie trotting towards them. Before the cart stopped completely,

Yvonne jumped down. After one look at Jed's crumpled form, tears filled her eyes and trickled down her cheeks. She wiped Jed's face with a damp cloth while Aiden and Imogen stood hand in hand, a little distance away.

"Jayne you need to—" Olivia began.

"I know. Be quiet. Let me think." The moment the words left her mouth, Jayne regretted them. "I'm sorry."

As Olivia squeezed Jayne's hand, Yvonne let out a cry. Every eye followed her pointing finger. Beneath their alert gazes, Jed's eyelids flickered.

"Jed, we're here. It'll be all right. I'll get the doctor." The words sounded so helpless, and Jayne didn't even know if he'd heard them.

Jed opened his eyes and looked straight at Jayne. "Watch . . . Lamberton." A tremor ran through his body as the shaky words filled the air.

"Don't worry." Tears choked Jayne's voice. "We'll get help."

Jed's eyes flickered shut, then opened once more. "Find . . ." He drifted back into unconsciousness, leaving them to wonder what he'd been about to say.

"That's it." Jayne sprang to her feet. "I'm going for the doctor. I've wasted too much time already." As Aiden handed her Spark's reins, she turned to Olivia. "Get him covered with blankets. If he wakes before I'm back, keep him quiet."

Using Olivia's cupped hands as a springboard, Jayne swung hurriedly into the saddle.

19
A FATHER TO THE FATHERLESS

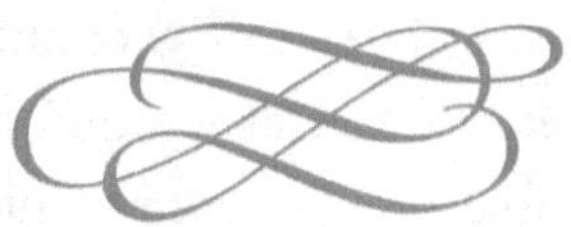

Jayne rode at a canter towards town. As she swayed with the horse's motion, she prayed she would be able to find the doctor quickly. If he wasn't at home, who knew where he would be. The trees flashed by as Spark's hooves ate up the ground, but still she bent lower, urging Spark on. Guessing from the landmarks that she was about halfway to town, she kicked her heels into Spark's flanks once more.

As she plunged around a bend, a rider appeared in the distance. Hope surged up in Jayne's heart. If the approaching rider was Cass, she could send him for the doctor and go back to Jed. Her desire was so strong that she felt sure it must be him, but as the still-distant horse and rider came into focus, she groaned. The horse was not Wattle, and the rider was not Cass. Thomas Lamberton stood between her and the help Jed needed.

Jayne yanked Spark to a stop, leaning back to keep from

falling. What should she do? She thought of making a run for it, but where would she go? If she went forward, she would be abandoning her sisters. And if she went back, she would only be leading Lamberton to them sooner. As long as she kept him here, Jayne at least knew the others were safe.

There was nowhere to hide, and in a few seconds, Lamberton would be upon her. His arrival would force her to make a decision—either to continue forward or to turn back. Both meant sacrifices.

In that moment Jayne craved the safety of her father's arms more than ever before. Eleven years ago he'd sheltered her from the angry dog on Ireland's shores. Why couldn't he be here with her now? A wave of fear and grief washed over her. What she longed for was impossible. Never again would she be safe in the arms of her father—not now, not ever.

A Father to the fatherless. The words seemed to float before her eyes. What had eluded her since the night Jed read that verse seemed clear in this moment of terror. Though her father was dead, she would never be fatherless. Even now, with Lamberton blocking her way, she was not alone. Nor was she unprotected. Though faced with an impossible decision, she had an Almighty, all-powerful Father who was present. He would be her guide even unto death.

Peace filled her heart, and as she lifted her bent head, Jayne noticed that Mr. Lamberton had dropped to a walk. Why, she couldn't guess. She only felt grateful for the extra time it had given her. But that time had nearly expired. Now was the moment to face her fears head on.

Mr. Lamberton smiled, but his eyes were mocking. "Why, Miss Reid, how pleasant to meet you. I was on my way to your place, would you believe? You must let me accompany you the rest of the way back." Despite his smile, there was no mistaking the fact that he expected her to obey.

Jayne drew a deep breath and met his eyes without flinching. "No."

"No?" he asked, his eyebrows rising as he feigned a hurt look. "You would refuse the escort of a gentleman?" With a yank at the bit, he brought his mount to a standstill.

Jayne was surprised to hear herself laugh. "An escort maybe, but one thing is sure—you are no gentleman. It's a fine gentleman that defrauds an elderly widow of her house. You refused to give her a reasonable amount of time to move out, then didn't have the decency to pay a fair price." Jayne knew she should stop, but the words kept coming. "Nor does a gentleman threaten any woman."

Mr. Lamberton flushed, and the muscles in his jaw began to work up and down as he nudged his horse closer to Jayne, pushing her to the side of the road. "That's big talk from someone in such a helpless position. Did you not realise that you are alone on this road with no one to come to your aid? It would be a pity if, as you say, I am not a gentleman."

Jayne straightened in her saddle, trying to look unafraid. Why had she been so foolish? If only she would learn to look before she leapt. Her eyes flicked for a moment to Mr. Lamberton's right hand, where it rested on his gun.

"What?" He leaned closer. "Have you nothing to say after such childish accusations? I feel that I may be more of a gentleman than you are a lady."

Jayne remained silent, refusing to respond to his comments. She had no idea what he would do if she continued to oppose him, but she was determined not to budge from the spot where her horse now stood.

"As long as we are having this conversation, I may as well settle the whole business. I am growing tired of your insolence and don't know how much more of it I will choose to tolerate." He pulled his gun from its holster and deliberately inspected it, before putting it away with a chuckle. "Oh, don't worry. It would be ungentlemanly of me to even think of threatening a woman."

Jayne clenched her teeth and tried to breathe easily. She couldn't let on how afraid she was. *Father in heaven, please help me.* Her back stiffened as hoof beats signalled the approach of another horseman. Who was it: friend or foe? A glance at Lamberton revealed nothing. He appeared unmoved, only turning sightly in the saddle with an air of disinterest.

How Jayne wished she could see whatever he could see, but she didn't have the nerve to lean sideways in her saddle, and Lamberton's looming form blocked her view. In the few seconds given her, Jayne prayed again for protection. Then as the second horse and rider skidded to a stop, she rose in her stirrups and peered over Lamberton's shoulder. Confusion flooded her already panicked head. "Cass?"

He barely acknowledged her, focusing his gaze on Lamberton.

Mentally, Jayne dared Cass to betray her. He hadn't been there to help when Jed needed a doctor, and from his unwillingness to meet her gaze, she had little hope that he would help now. Her one assurance was that she rested under the shadow of the Almighty. Come what may, He at least would never betray her.

Jayne noticed Cass's hand move towards his pistol. Lamberton appeared to notice too, for his fingers moved to his own gun.

Cass shifted in his saddle and shrugged cheerfully. "Caught me by surprise finding you both here." He grinned and brought his horse alongside Lamberton. Now Wattle's head rested between Jayne's horse and Lamberton's fine steed. In this position, Jayne could see both men clearly. She stiffened, then looked in surprise at Cass. Was she imagining things, or had he just signalled for her to move?

"Headed my way?" Cass addressed Lamberton with an easy tone.

Jayne peered closer at Cass. There it was again: that little tilt of his head. Since no other option presented itself, she decided to believe he was going to help her.

Trying to avoid being seen by Lamberton, she gently applied pressure on the reins, and Spark moved backwards a few steps. Jayne held her breath, gazing at Cass to see if he would give her any other indication. He was looking at Lamberton with a grin stretched across his face, but his head moved as if in approval. As Lamberton let his hand fall below his gun, Jayne backed away another step.

"Just out for a leisurely ride, when I ran into the charming Miss Reid." Lamberton motioned towards her with a sweep of his hand, and Jayne froze. But Lamberton didn't even look in her direction. All his attention was fixed on Cass. "Such a woman you are privileged to work for." Lamberton laughed, giving her another opportunity to edge farther away.

When Cass said nothing, Lamberton coughed. "You seemed in a hurry. Don't let me keep you."

Jayne's heart beat faster. At the very least, she thought Cass to be more of a gentleman than Lamberton ever would be, and she hoped he would not leave. As she opened her mouth to protest, Cass finally met her eyes. He tilted his head off to the side, and this time there was no mistaking his signal.

Cass moved his hand as if to clap Lamberton on the back. Jayne didn't wait to see what happened next. She drove her heels into Spark's flanks, and with a leap he darted into the vegetation. Behind her, she heard a commotion of voices. As she dodged the branches that grabbed at her face, Jayne heard a gunshot and tried to turn in the saddle to see if anyone pursued her. But a large branch swatted her on the side, scraping her cheek. She ducked, forced to watch her path.

Finally she reined in her horse, her cheek smarting and her heart pounding. What was going on back at the road? Was Cass's interference all just a trick? Mrs. Eddington had said she heard an Irish voice outside the day of Lamberton's visit. Could that voice have been Cass's? Perhaps Cass and Lamberton were in this together, and even now they were scheming some cruel plan.

Spark's head jerked up. Something had caught his attention, and by now Jayne knew enough to take notice of a horse's body language. She listened and waited, every muscle tense and every nerve alert. Spark's ears flickered, then Jayne heard it too. In a voice muffled by distance, someone shouted her name. Was it Cass? And if so, could she trust him?

Jayne nudged Spark to a walk and guided him hesitantly in the direction she had come from. After covering ten yards, she paused to listen. The voice sounded again, and she strained to make out the words.

"Don't be afraid. You can come back. All is well." This time the voice was unmistakably Irish.

Though Cass had spoken comfort and assurance, apprehension made Jayne's stomach hurt as she reluctantly directed Spark to continue retracing his steps. In a few minutes, the road lay just ahead. Peering through the branches, she saw that both horses' saddles were empty, and Cass knelt on the ground with his back to her. She stayed under the shelter of the trees, but the shuffle of Spark's hooves in the bark and leaves gave her away.

Cass turned towards her. "I'm going to need some help making sure this man receives justice."

Jayne stared in surprise, still unsure if she could trust Cass.

"Miss Reid, please. Don't listen to him." Lamberton's voice sounded strained, almost desperate. "He doesn't care about you. He's only trying—"

Lamberton's words ended abruptly as if Cass had silenced him.

Urging her horse on, she covered the last few yards and emerged into the open, where Cass had Lamberton pinned face-down on the ground with his hands behind his back. She felt relieved to see Lamberton in such a position. At least he wouldn't be endangering her sisters for the moment.

Cass kept his gun levelled on Lamberton's back and motioned to Wattle. "Unbuckle my stirrup leather so I can fasten his hands."

When Jayne dismounted, she kept her eyes on the two men, unwilling to turn her back. This sudden turn of events was hard for her to grasp. No doubt Lamberton hadn't expected it either. Her shaky fingers struggled with the buckle for a moment, then she stepped forward, holding the strap out to Cass.

As he reached for it, Jayne saw blood soaking through his sleeve. He noticed her looking and shrugged. "It isn't much. A bullet nicked my arm is all." He grinned. "It's good Irish blood." He handed his gun to Jayne and crouched down to tie Lamberton's hands behind his back. "There now, that should keep them secure enough."

Jayne handed the gun back with relief as Cass shook his head. "A regular criminal he is. I dare say Mrs. Eddington can keep her home now. Thought he could go around picking on the weak and innocent and dodge the law, he did."

Jayne glanced at Lamberton, but he gave no indication of having heard Cass's words. Cass nudged him with the toe of his boot. "Well, we shall see. There's a notice out for him. The police will be glad to get him into their grip."

Lamberton's whole body tensed as if to try to free himself. But he seemed to think better of it. "You lying scoundrel. You won't get away with this—either of you."

Jayne's eyes flew from Lamberton to Cass. She half expected to find Cass angered by Lamberton's words. Instead he appeared as calm as if he hadn't heard a thing.

"I thought it would be best to get the police rather than trying to haul him through town," Cass said. "Lamberton can wait, I'm sure. It'll give him some much-needed time to think about his actions."

Lamberton's hands clenched into fists as his arms strained against the leather that bound his wrists. "You're wasting your time. They'll never believe you."

When Cass ignored him, Lamberton tried again, his cockiness fading. "Let me go, and I'll leave you all alone. I'll even let that old widow keep her worthless home."

Cass shook his head, almost appearing sorry for his captive. He turned his gaze on Jayne. "You can go for Jed if you like. Then he can watch Lamberton while I go to the police station and convince them we've got this man in our grip."

The image of Jed's motionless body still lying on the ground filled Jayne's mind, and she shook her head. "I was on my way for the doctor."

Cass looked startled. "What's happened?"

"Jed fell from his horse. I found him unconscious. He revived only for a moment and tried to warn me. But I didn't realise what he was saying." Jayne bit her lip to stop a sob. "His leg's broken."

Cass nodded. "Ride straight to town. Find the doctor first. As I said, it won't do Lamberton any harm to lie here. Then I need you to find the police and tell them I'm holding a criminal by the name of Bert Lamon. That'll be all you need to tell them. Hurry now."

He stuck his gun in its holster and cupped his hands to help Jayne into the saddle. Jayne saw him smile as he looked up at her sitting astride. "Your father's daughter." He chuckled. "Full of spunk."

20
An Urgent Mission

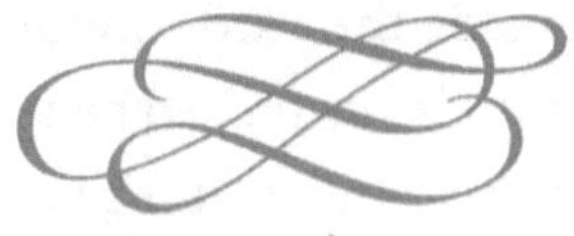

The time had come to complete the ride for Jed. Prodding Spark into a canter, Jayne rode for town. Even though they were keeping up a good speed, she felt like they were crawling along. How much time had already elapsed since she found Jed? Jayne shuddered. Though she'd tried her best, what if it wasn't good enough?

"Dear Lord, help me find the doctor. Make him be at home." Even if she found the doctor at his house, he still wouldn't be at Jed's side for longer than Jayne cared to acknowledge.

Finally the first signs of the township appeared, and the houses grew more frequent. As Jayne trotted past a cluster of buggies, she became aware that everyone was pointing at her as she rode astride. She heard one man laugh and call to his friend. A woman put a hand to her chest in shock. Though Jayne tried to ignore it, their reactions stung. All they seemed concerned about was convention. They didn't even stop to consider that perhaps there was a good reason, before pointing and mocking.

Jayne flicked her hair out of her face and kept her eyes straight ahead. As she trotted up a road lined on both sides with shops, she refused to meet anyone's gaze. Ahead loomed the imposing two-storey bank, and outside it, a group of men in bowler hats and fine suits stood talking to one another. As she neared the group, she overheard the name Reid mentioned and flushed. Her back straight and tall, Jayne gave no sign of hearing anything, but their chuckles followed her up the hill.

There it was—Dr. Sparling's house. Jayne dismounted and flung the reins around the fence. The neat lawns and canopy of surrounding trees beckoned her into their haven. She unlatched the gate and stepped inside the yard—away from the mocking eyes and whispers. The stones crunched beneath her shoes as she followed the wide path up to the doctor's house. Banging on the door, Jayne wiped a hand over her damp face. Her hand came back covered with grime. She wiped it on the back of her dress and looked at the elegant veranda. It would be a nice place to relax, but there was no time for that now. What was taking them so long to answer the door? Taking a deep breath, she raised her hand to pound on the door again. Just as her hand connected with the wooden panel, it opened. Jayne gasped and stepped backwards.

Dr. Sparling himself stood in the doorway, his eyes immediately changing from friendly welcome to concern as he took in her appearance. "What's happened? Whatever it is, it looks as if I'd better come right away."

Now that she was standing face to face with the doctor, Jayne's throat constricted, and tears came into her eyes. She blinked them away.

Dr. Sparling reached out and laid a hand on her shoulder. "Perhaps you'd better come inside yourself. You've had a bit of a shock by the look. Come get a good cup of tea into you."

Jayne shook her head. "I can't."

"Don't worry. Just tell me who and where my patient is, and I'll be off. My housekeeper will see to it that you get what you need. Doctor's orders, or you'll end up my patient too."

His calm manner helped clear her mind, but she refused to budge. "Jed's hurt bad. He fell off his horse." Jayne motioned back towards Spark.

"Where is Jed now? Is he well enough to walk?"

Jayne shook her head. "He was unconscious when I left him on the road near our place. His leg is broken. I don't know what else might be wrong."

"Is anyone with him?"

"My sisters."

"Right then, you leave it to me. And I want you to have some tea."

"I have to—"

"Don't argue." Dr. Sparling frowned, but he couldn't mask his underlying kindness. He disappeared into a side room, and Jayne heard the murmur of voices.

When Dr. Sparling reappeared, he held a leather bag. "I'm off now. Look after yourself, young woman." With a nod, he turned and strode down a passageway towards the back of the house, leaving her to listen to the echo of his steps.

Jayne stared into the spacious entry hall. Maybe she should just shut the door and walk away. She was fine. It was Jed who was in trouble. Just as she turned to go, she heard footsteps pattering down the hallway and saw a woman in a starched apron approaching.

The housekeeper greeted Jayne with a smile. "The doctor said you needed a bit of mothering after your shock. With five children to my name, I'm a well-practised listener. Come back into the kitchen and rest awhile."

Jayne shook her head. "Thank you, but I can't come inside. I have to hurry along."

The housekeeper made a disapproving sound with her tongue. Despite Jayne's refusal, she had a determined set to her face. She disappeared for a moment and reappeared with a cup of tea. "Drink this up." Her eyes followed the movement of the cup to Jayne's mouth, and when Jayne took a sip, she nodded approvingly. Then began a battering of well-intended questions.

Jayne struggled to answer. She kept wondering if Jed would be all right. Dr. Sparling had tried and failed when her parents had been sick. Would it end the same way? Suddenly, Jayne knew she couldn't stomach any more tea. She handed the teacup back.

The housekeeper shook her head and sighed. "I can't force you to drink it, but you mind the doctor's orders and take it easy."

Jayne thanked her and turned away. As her steps took her past the doctor's fine gardens, her heart beat faster. Now she had to call at the police station. Never had she been up to its door, let alone inside it. She wondered how the officer would react to her story. The tale did sound a little far-fetched, and she had no idea how Cass had gotten his information. What if they wanted to know more details than she had? If she was unable to answer, perhaps they would think she was only tricking them. Well, there was nothing she could do about it. Lamberton awaited justice, and she would not leave him free to cause her sisters more distress.

Without wasting another moment, Jayne managed to remount and started off towards the police station. At least it was only a short ride this time, and she could dodge the main streets. She passed the Buninyong gardens and pulled up in front of the courthouse. Just beyond it stood the police station with its red brick chimney pointing to the sky. Dismounting, Jayne smoothed her hair and shook her creased and dirty skirts.

Swallowing hard, she walked past the sandstone courthouse. All too soon, her faltering steps brought her to the door of the station. For a full minute, she gazed at the door as if she'd never seen one before. Was she supposed to knock or walk straight in? After another moment of quandary, she put her hand on the door handle. It didn't budge. Maybe no one was on duty. She gave it one last try. This time the handle squeaked and moved in her grasp. When she peered inside, a police officer stared back at her. Now Jayne had no choice but to go straight in.

"Good afternoon." His eyebrows rose a fraction as he stood up. "What can I do for you?" He ran his eyes over her face, then inspected her attire. When he met her eyes again, his face held a frown, and the sideways tilt of his head gave him an air of impatience.

Jayne felt like squirming but managed to hold herself together. "I've come to inform you that my farmhand has captured a man named Bert Lamon."

At her mention of that name, the officer stood erect. No longer did his face hold annoyance but sharp attention. "Here in Buninyong?"

Jayne nodded. "Yes, sir, out of town a bit."

Jayne heard him mutter the name under his breath. Then he yelled, "Pierson, come out here a minute." Another officer appeared almost instantly. This man was older than the first, with a grey beard and a hardened face. The first officer repeated what Jayne had told him.

After listening, the older officer turned to Jayne with his hands on his hips. "And you think that your farmhand—" He squinted, appearing to have seen Jayne for the first time. "That's right, is it? Your farmhand?"

Jayne nodded, wondering what hope she had of being believed.

Pierson grunted and cocked his eyebrow, exchanging a glance with the younger man. "This farmhand of yours has the supposed criminal, correct?"

Jayne nodded again.

"And you're confident the man will still be there?" The officer narrowed his eyes as if warning her not to waste his time.

"Yes, sir. He won't be going anywhere. My farmhand has him on the ground with his hands secured. He's guarding him with a gun in case he tries to escape."

The officers turned to each other, murmuring back and forth.

Jayne felt unsure how else to convince them. Before she could say anything, Pierson rubbed his grey whiskers and said, "Bert Lamon, eh? May I ask how you can identify this man?"

Jayne felt like running far away. But she bravely met the police officer's eyes. "I know him as Thomas Lamberton. When he confronted me this second time, my farmhand happened to come along. There was a bit of a struggle. Lamberton shot at Cass and nicked him on the arm. Then Cass got him on the ground. He told me to fetch the police and tell them he had Bert Lamon." When the officer continued to stare at her, she said, "He told me that's all I would need to say."

Pierson crossed his arms. "You said when he confronted you 'this second time.' If you had trouble with him before, why didn't you alert us then?"

Under the officer's keen gaze, Jayne felt like she was the criminal. She took a few steadying breaths and pondered her words carefully. "He came once to my property, wanting to purchase it.

Lamberton—I mean Bert Lamon—was quite threatening. But I didn't know who he was, nor did anyone else." Jayne lifted her hands helplessly. "I don't know how Cass recognised him."

"If this man is who you say he is—and we'll be able to tell soon enough—then you're dealing with a wanted criminal. He's a fraud and a thief, among other things. He's been on several rampages farther up in Victoria, and things must have gotten too hot for him. Looks like he may have been trying to stay low, farther away from his usual activities." Pierson rubbed his chin again. "Under a false name too. Won't he get a surprise." He looked at Jayne. "What name did you say he's been going under?"

"Thomas Lamberton."

"Write that down." He motioned to the younger police officer, who seated himself at the desk. "Do you know anything else that might be of use?"

Jayne bit her lip. "I'm not sure. He's riding a very fine horse." She shrugged. "It might be stolen. He has also been staying at Mrs. Young's Hotel. Or at least that's where I saw him in town one day."

The police officer nodded. "Anything else?"

"Yes. He went to a widow and bullied her into selling her home. In fact, he was due to take it over this afternoon. The widow's name is Mrs. Catherine Eddington. She lives on Eyre Street."

"Right, then. This has been most informative. Now, what was your name, and where did you say this Cass was keeping Lamon?"

"I'm Jayne Reid. Head down Learmonth Street towards Geelong." Jayne took a deep breath and tried to picture the familiar roads she always travelled. As the two men waited, she gave the rest of the directions as best as she could.

Pierson nodded. "Thank you again. Mrs. Reid, is it?"

Jayne shook her head. "Miss."

"I beg your pardon, Miss Reid. Some men will ride out at once." He inclined his head to her and turned to the other officer, who sat with his pen still poised above the paper.

Jayne felt she had been dismissed. Relieved, she sought to escape the building's confines, but before she stepped through the doorway, she cast one last glance at the officers. They were huddled over the desk in conversation.

21
EXPLANATIONS

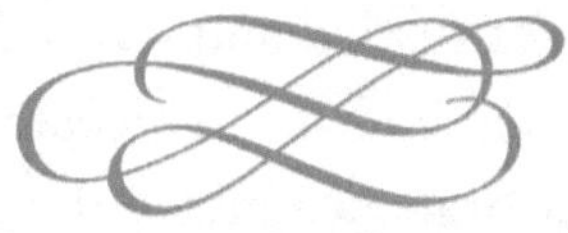

The wind on Jayne's face felt like a balm. Taking a deep breath, she leaned against the side of the police station. Now that she'd fetched the doctor and alerted the police, her tasks were complete. As the image of Jed's crumpled body appeared before her eyes, she straightened back up. There wasn't time for exhaustion yet. She needed to be with her sisters and Jed.

She trudged over to Spark and led him along the road for thirty yards, then down the short bank to the Gong. As she slackened her hold on the reins, Spark began drinking at once. Jayne swallowed, her own throat feeling parched.

Though trees blocked her view, she heard the clamour of a group of passing riders. With a sense of satisfaction, she realised that the police must have taken her seriously enough to send multiple men. And they were going fast.

When she thought Spark had had enough to drink, Jayne mounted for what seemed like the hundredth time that day. It felt as if days had passed since she'd blended her own voice with that of the birds celebrating the morning sunshine. How many different turns the day had taken since its happy beginning. Now she had one thing left to do—check if Jed was all right. In all the trouble with Lamberton, had he been well taken care of? What if the doctor had been too late? Again, she committed him to the care of her heavenly Father.

Beneath her, Spark stumbled. His usual spring had given way to a sense of heaviness, and Jayne felt his growing lack of enthusiasm with each stride. Feeling compassion for the worn-out horse, Jayne allowed him to drop to a walk.

Overhead, the leaves rustled and swayed as the chill of the approaching evening descended. A screeching cloud of white swooped down into the branches, and with a ruckus of squawks and flaps, a flock of cockatoos prepared their night perches. If only she had wings to soar home above the treetops.

Jayne had just sped up again when the rhythm of horse hooves reached her ears, and around the bend appeared a group of four oncoming horsemen. They rushed past her without slowing down. Pulling on the reins, Jayne turned to have a better look. Three of the riders were police officers. Behind the leading officer trailed Lamberton's mount with Lamberton securely on board, while the other two officers flanked him on either side. As the distance swallowed them up, Jayne fixed her eyes homeward again.

When she neared the spot where Jed had lain, Jayne looked all around but could see no clue as to what had gone on. How she yearned to be surrounded by her dear ones. The piece of road that still stretched between her and all that she longed for seemed longer than the rest of that day's rides combined. As if sensing he was almost home, Spark lunged into a canter.

There was no one near the house when Jayne drew close, so she rode on to Jed's hut, her stomach churning with apprehension. The first sign of life she saw was Olivia, Yvonne, Aiden, and Imogen huddled near the hut. Before she even finished dismounting, the others swarmed her.

"What happened? What took you so long?" Olivia asked.

As she started to reply, Yvonne's arms wrapped around her waist. Jayne squeezed back, looking over Yvonne's blonde head to Olivia. "It's a long story. How's Jed? Has Cass returned?" She turned to Spark and unbuckled the girth strap, yanking the saddle off his back.

Olivia nodded. "Cass got back a couple of minutes ago. He stuck his head in to see how Jed was and spoke to the doctor. Then he went to see to Wattle."

"And Jed? Did the doctor say anything? Is he still unconscious? Have you spoken to him?"

Olivia shook her head. "He was in and out of consciousness while you were gone. The doctor said it was from a knock on the head, plus the pain from his leg. There's a good-sized bump on the back of his head."

"Are you sure it was safe to move him?"

Olivia shrugged. "Dr. Sparling seemed to think it was all right. He put a makeshift splint on his leg, then we eased a blanket under him. We had to carry him all the way back, because he was too heavy for us to lift into the cart without damaging his leg. It wouldn't have been big enough for him to lie flat anyway. It took a while for us to get him back, but we kept him as still as we could. We haven't been back for long."

Jayne nodded. "What happened to Betsie?"

"Imogen led her, while the rest of us carried Jed. One on each corner of the blanket."

A groan came from inside the hut, followed by a yell of pain, and everyone spun towards the sound. Jayne bit her lip. "You'd better go wait inside the house. It's getting chilly anyway."

Olivia nodded and took Imogen by the hand. When the others left, Jayne lingered behind, unable to leave Jed again. She found a stump nearby and sat down. Resting her head in her hands, she closed her eyes and waited.

Someone cleared his throat, and Jayne looked up, half-expecting to see the doctor. Instead she saw Cass. He crouched down beside her. "I thought you might like to know some of the circumstances surrounding Jed's fall and how I came to know about Bert Lamon."

Jayne sighed. "I could certainly do with something to keep my mind off wondering how Jed is."

His eyes kind, Cass nodded. "I thought so. It'll take some telling, so you'll have to bear with me while I get all the details sorted out."

He sat down on the ground with his feet stretched out in front of him, his back resting against a tree. "The first time I came across Lamberton was in town, not long after you hired me. Somehow he knew I was working for you. He asked all sorts of questions about you and your sisters' situation. But I refused to tell him anything." Cass shrugged. "You could say he got a bit worked up about the matter. So I decided to keep my eyes open and learn what I could. From the little I had already witnessed, I thought him unsavoury at best."

Cass picked up a handful of dirt and leaves and watched it sift through his fingers before going on. "I began doing a bit of asking around myself." He chuckled. "I think people got suspicious of me, I asked so many questions. But all I managed to turn up was the same useless information that got me nowhere.

"Then this morning Jed asked me to go with him to town. On the way, he told me about Mrs. Eddington, and I began to think I might be getting closer to the answer."

Cass stood up and leaned against the tree trunk. "When we got to Mrs. Eddington's, she was all worked up. Her first words were, 'Praise God you've come. Please, oh please help me!'

"When we went into the house, she showed us a piece of rumpled newspaper. Apparently something she bought a while back had come wrapped in it. On that paper was a wanted advertisement with a small sketch that held remarkable resemblance to Lamberton. The man in the picture had a full beard, which made him look older. But under the circumstances, it would be natural to try to change your appearance. It had to be him. I was sure of it."

Cass crouched down beside Jayne again. "You can imagine our horror upon finding out Lamberton was a dangerous criminal. Jed regretted even more not being there when you needed him last time and had a strong urge to ride home at once. And knowing Jed, he didn't dawdle."

"So that's why Jed fell." Jayne felt pain at the realisation that protecting them was what had gotten Jed hurt.

"He told the doctor that a couple of kangaroos darted from the underbrush and spooked the horse." Cass shrugged. "Even though Jed's a good rider, with the speed he was going, it all must have happened so suddenly."

Jayne shook her head. "Jed tried to warn me about Lamberton when he came back to consciousness, but I didn't think he knew what he was saying. He also mumbled the word 'find.' Perhaps he was going to tell me to find you, so we would know about Lamberton."

"Likely so. Instead of going to the police station, I decided to see if I could locate Lamberton myself. I rode down the main street and spotted a shop assistant sweeping around the store's doorway. He told me he'd seen Lamberton not too long ago. You can guess my alarm when the young man pointed out the direction in which Lamberton was riding. I decided to follow him straightaway, hoping to be of assistance to you and Jed. I'm glad I did. If I'd gone for the police, I wouldn't have been there in time to help you. It was God's provision."

Surprised to hear Cass acknowledging God's goodness, Jayne was unable to voice a reply, but she nodded. God had protected her for sure.

Cass chuckled. "A while after you left to fetch the doctor and police, three officers rode up and at once identified our captive. Lamberton, or should I say Mr. Lamon, launched into a story about a look-alike cousin. I've never heard such nonsense from a grown man. When the police wouldn't believe a word of it, Lamon threw himself into a fit of rage.

"Once the officers dealt with Lamon, they asked me to go back with them. But I said I couldn't on account of Jed. I have to head to the station tomorrow, though, and I'll stop by Mrs. Eddington's to let her know what happened. I would go tonight, but I hate to leave under the circumstances. Perhaps I can send a message with the doctor to set her mind at ease."

He shook his head. "Poor Jed. This accident will put him out of action for quite some time. I don't know how he'll stand it."

The door of the hut creaked, and Jayne was on her feet in an instant with Cass beside her. In her eagerness, she nearly threw herself at the doctor. "How is he? Can I see him?"

"Easy!" The doctor held his hands out to ward off Jayne's enthusiasm. "I didn't expect to be stampeded." When she backed off a bit, he smiled. "Jed will be all right with time, but he won't be moving from his bed for some weeks. His leg was a clean break and should mend well. In the meantime, I know you and your sisters will take good care of him." He looked around. "Where are the others?"

"I sent them back to the house to wait."

"Right, I'll stop by on my way. I want to commend them for their efforts. They've been through a lot this past year." Dr. Sparling looked away for a moment, his shoulders slumped. When he looked back, he smiled, but sadness hovered in his eyes. "I'll see what I can do to put their minds at ease."

He stepped away from the door and lowered his voice. "Jed took a serious bang to his head, and you'll need to keep an eye on him, both of you. Someone will need to be with him the whole night. Don't let him sleep for over an hour without waking him. That leg is going to give him quite a bit of pain too. I've already given him a little bit of laudanum. You'll find the bottle on the table with instructions. He'll need more in three or four hours."

"Can I go and see him now?"

The doctor nodded. "He wanted to know if you were all safe. Said something about a fellow called Lamberton a few times, but I didn't know what he meant. Keep him warm and feed him broth when he can manage it. I'll call around again in a day or so to check how he's going. Take care now."

Jayne thanked him over her shoulder as she rushed through the doorway. When her eyes had adjusted to the dimness, she saw Jed lying beneath a blanket with his leg propped up. His eyes were closed, so Jayne picked up a chair and tiptoed forward. She'd only moved a few steps before the chair, her body, and the table collided with a thud. She cringed and waited. In the silence that followed, Jed lifted his head off the pillow.

Jayne set aside the chair and rushed forward to kneel by his side. "I'm sorry I woke you."

Jed tried to shake his head. "Needed to see you. I was worried."

Jayne smiled. "We're all fine. It was you who gave us all such a scare. I was so worried we were going to lose you, Jed." She laid a hand on his arm.

A small grin settled over Jed's lips. "I'm alive. Won't be doing any kicking for a while though." He groaned. "It was stupid of me." His eyes slipped shut. "Cass," he murmured. "Be careful of—"

"I know," Jayne said, stopping him from using more energy. "Lamberton's in the police officers' grasp now."

Jed opened his eyes and looked into Jayne's. "Good. I can rest easy."

"When you're feeling more like yourself, I'll tell you the details of his capture."

Jed nodded. "Can't keep my eyes open."

"Don't mind that. Get some rest. We're all praying for you."

Jed's head moved almost imperceptibly.

Her hand clasping Jed's rough one, Jayne listened to his breathing become more even. Sleep overcame Jed quickly, but she lingered by his bedside, her eyes locked to the motion of his chest. With a heart overladen with gratitude, she thanked God for preserving Jed's life.

When Jayne left the hut, she was surprised to see Cass still standing there. In her concern for Jed, she had forgotten all about him.

Cass was gazing into the twilight, looking as if he'd forgotten anyone else existed. But as Jayne approached, he turned. "I gave the doctor a message for Mrs. Eddington."

"Thank you. I'm so glad she can stay in her house." Jayne couldn't stop the happiness from spreading across her face.

Cass nodded but didn't return her smile. "Jayne, there's something else I need to tell you."

Jayne's smile faded as she waited for him to go on, but he said nothing.

Finally, he shook his head. "I'm afraid it will come as a shock to you no matter how I tell it. I've been trying to think of some way to break it to you, but . . ." He shrugged. "The time has come for you to know."

22
A REVELATION

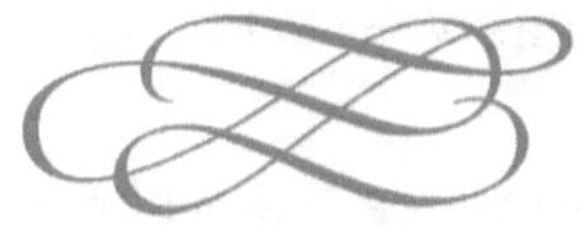

Jayne's heart thundered in her chest. She didn't know if she could take much more.

"Jayne"—Cass looked her straight in the eyes—"I'm your uncle."

Jayne laughed. At eighteen years of age, she felt old enough to know how many uncles she had. And this man wasn't one of them.

"I'm telling you the truth." Cass smiled and shook his head. "I know it sounds unlikely, but I am your father's brother— Uncle Casey."

Startled at the mention of her uncle's name, she looked at him intently. It sounded ridiculous. But she tried to picture the Uncle Casey she'd known in Ireland.

Cass cleared his throat. "I know it's hard for you to believe, but you'll have to trust me."

Trust him? Again Jayne felt like laughing, only she didn't

think it was funny. Oh sure, trust a stranger who's telling you that he's your dead father's brother. Her uncle was in Ireland, not here in Buninyong.

Jayne took a deep breath, then exhaled as she tried to remember her first meeting with Cass. In a flash it came back to her. From the back, she had mistaken him for her father, even though Daddy had been dead for five months. What if Cass was telling the truth after all?

She looked him up and down. Surely this man couldn't be her uncle. On the other hand, hadn't Mrs. O'Donnell said his name wasn't really Cass? Try as she might, she couldn't remember what her friend had called him. None of this made sense. Maybe Cass was crazy.

She took a step backwards. "I don't know what to say."

A look of pain crossed Cass's face, but he nodded. "Perhaps if I were to explain from the start, it would be easier for you."

Jayne stared at him, wondering whether to listen. The day had been long enough already, but what harm could it do? She sighed. "All right." Folding her arms, she waited for him to start explaining.

Instead, Cass walked a few yards away and reached for the reins of Jed's horse. "It's getting cold, and Spark needs looking after. Let's talk in the stable."

Jayne hefted the saddle from where she'd left it by the hut and stared at Cass's back. Finally, she made herself follow him, hanging back as much as she could without being obvious.

When they entered the stable, Cass picked up a bucket of water and offered it to Spark. "Here boy, good thing Wattle left some for you." He got some feed and placed it in a trough. When he'd put Spark in a pen and rubbed him all over, Cass plopped down on an upturned crate. He nudged another one towards Jayne.

As much as she wanted to stay erect and firm, her legs felt like they would collapse if she didn't comply. Jayne pulled the crate farther away from Cass and sat on it.

"I'll try to start from the beginning. Ask as many questions as you like." Cass stretched his legs out in front of him and stared at the ground. "When my father—your grandfather—died, he left me a small portion of money. He wanted me to use it to visit his absent son and check up on his wellbeing. How I longed to see my older brother again." Cass stopped, struggling to keep his voice steady.

"After some of the longest months of my life sailing across the sea, I landed on the shores of Australia with high hopes. But as I finally approached Buninyong, I spotted a man heading to town with a loaded wagon and asked if he knew where Brian Reid lived. He told me that he did, but both Brian and Abigail were dead. Only his daughters remained." Cass's voice broke, and he ran a hand over his face. "I was too late."

This show of emotion made Jayne's own throat tighten. She looked away, her thoughts swinging between belief and disbelief. When she sneaked another look in his direction, Cass's mouth looked firm and resolute.

He continued, "When you received the letter from your grandmother, it caught me by surprise. I had no idea you didn't know about the death of your grandfather, and I couldn't bear to see you suffering more. All the heartaches of life suddenly seemed like too much, and my resolve to be strong almost crumbled."

He shook his head. "In a strange land with all my dreams turned into nightmares, I better understood my father's deep grief that his oldest boy wasn't nearby. He didn't resent Brian for seeking a good life for his family, just wished he hadn't sought it so far away." Cass sighed heavily.

On impulse, Jayne got up and laid her hand on his shoulder, sympathy overcoming her doubts. "Daddy would've been grateful his brother was here to protect us when he couldn't be."

Cass nodded, a smile chasing some of his sorrow away. "I'm thankful God gave me the opportunity to help Brian in that way. I desperately wanted to help you and your sisters through your pain. But at times I think I only added to your grief." He looked Jayne straight in the eyes. "The strain between us was evident, but I didn't know how to remedy it without giving away my identity. I could see very clearly that you, at least, didn't trust me."

Jayne felt ashamed and embarrassed. "I'm so sorry."

"No." Cass shook his head. "Don't apologise. You had no way of knowing I was honest. I guess it was understandable."

"Thank you, Uncle Casey." Jayne smiled at how strange it felt to call Cass that.

He grinned. "I didn't think it would feel so good to hear you call me Uncle."

Jayne sat back down. "There's something I still don't understand. Why didn't you let on you were our uncle right from the start? Why did you hide it from us, if you really wanted to help?"

Cass looked grim. "When I found out your parents were dead, I made up my mind to make you come back with me." He held out his hand as Jayne jumped to her feet. "During my walk to your house, I changed my mind. I decided to wait until I saw how you were faring."

Jayne sank back down as her alarm faded. It was here that her father had brought them. And this was where she would stay.

"I know Reids can be of an independent spirit, and I didn't want my presence to appear as a threat to your already fragile circumstances. I thought if you were anything like my brother, you might be prone to pretend that everything was all right, even if it wasn't, and I felt my duty was to see who you really were, and how you were truly coping. At the time, it seemed the best way to achieve this was to observe you in secret—without your feeling the need to appear in control." He bowed his head a moment, resting his forehead on his clasped hands. "Perhaps I was wrong."

Jayne felt herself smiling. "If I'd have known you had any intention of making us return to Ireland, I would have done my best to make things seem like we were managing." She laughed. "I am, as you say, my father's daughter."

"Then perhaps I was wise." Cass shook his head with a rueful smile. "My first dilemma upon deciding to keep my identity hidden was how to observe you closely while masquerading as a stranger. I decided the best solution was to get a job with you. That way I would be able to interact with you and maybe even live on the property. It would be less suspicious, or so I thought." Cass sighed, then chuckled. "I should have known better. I could never hide anything from Brian." He sighed again. "My brother was a good man. How I miss him."

Jayne found herself blinking to keep her tears at bay as Cass went on.

"I didn't know what the likelihood of getting a job with you was. Knowing your upbringing, I thought maybe you wouldn't turn me away, even if you couldn't afford to hire me." He shrugged. "God answered my prayers. But I won't be taking money off my brother's daughters. Except for a few necessary expenses, I've kept what I earned. You must take it back."

He sounded so final that Jayne knew arguing would be wasted breath.

"There was one other thing that prompted me to observe my nieces from a distance." Cass dug around in his coat pocket and held up a small parcel. "My father gave this to me while he was on his deathbed. 'Your older brother must have this package,' he said. 'Promise me . . . give it to Brian.' "

"I knew my father wouldn't have asked such a thing without reason, so I agreed after only a moment and asked if there was anything else I needed to know. But he shook his head. 'Brian will understand. He will tell you.' His breathing was getting weaker, so I told him to rest. When he'd been asleep for an hour or more, he half-sat up and grabbed my arm with startling strength. 'If you cannot get it to Brian, one of his children must have it.' "

Jayne felt her chest tighten with apprehension. What did the package contain, and what had her father known about it? Would she also understand?

"My father gripped my arm more tightly. 'My whole life I tried—' His eyes closed, and I thought he was asleep again, but he continued, 'The box must return to its . . . embittered . . . owner. Should have shared the story with . . . with you. But you were too young. The story too painful to speak of. Brian alone is able to fulfil my wish. Or his children . . . might know. You must find out if they be prudent—wise and discerning—else they come to harm through this box. Observe your way well, son. Learn . . . learn the lesson of the box.'

"Feeling dazed, I nodded, still not quite knowing what it all meant. Then Dad lifted his head off the pillow until he was staring directly into my eyes, seeming to question my earnestness. I felt like a young lad again as he said, 'Give me your word.' "

Cass passed the rectangular package to Jayne. "I have fulfilled this duty to my father."

With clammy fingers, Jayne worked to untie the string that held the rough cloth in place. When she finally had the string loose, she held her breath and glanced for an instant at Cass. He nodded, prompting her to go ahead. Still hesitating, she closed her eyes, trying to imagine Cass and her grandfather in a dimly-lit room as Grandfather passed the bundle to his son.

Cass cleared his throat, and Jayne's eyes flickered open. Bracing herself, she drew back the cloth to reveal a box, its exterior worn and unimpressive. She turned it over, but it triggered no remembrance of anything her father had ever mentioned. Hoping that everything would be clearer when she opened the box, she carefully slid back the lid. Nestled against the navy velvet interior was an oval piece of wood about a quarter of an inch thick. When she flipped it over, an intricate carving of a woman's face stared back at her. She looked up at Cass. "It's such beautiful workmanship."

Cass nodded. "You know nothing about it?"

Jayne bit her lip, then shook her head. "I'm afraid it holds no meaning to me at all. Not even a slight recollection. Nothing."

Cass sighed. "I hoped it might have been different, but it's as I feared it would be."

Jayne's gaze dropped back to the carving in her hand. Would they ever find out what importance it held?

Cass stood, and Jayne rose with him. After embracing her briefly, he asked, "Do you know what I've seen during my time here?"

Jayne shook her head.

"Three tight-knit sisters who are plucky and determined despite the struggles within and without. More than once I saw you doubting yourself, but I had confidence knowing you have been taught where to look for answers. God is faithful to His children, always faithful."

Jayne felt her throat tightening.

"You're a fine sister to them."

"Thank you." Her eyes brimmed with tears. Wiping them with the edge of her sleeve, she said, "There's so much to tell. Won't you come back with me? We can tell them together."

Cass nodded. "That sounds good, but first I'll stick my head in on Jed to see how he's doing."

Jayne nodded, feeling sober. "I'll go with you."

When the two reached the hut, they found Jed lying on his back, sound asleep. Cass put his hand gently on Jed's shoulder. "I hate to wake him." He gave the injured man a shake, but Jed went right on sleeping, unaware of his disturbers. "Must be the laudanum." Cass looked grim as he shook Jed harder, this time calling his name.

Jed's eyes flickered open, and he grunted. "Can't a man get some sleep?"

"Doctor's orders," Cass said apologetically. "How are you doing?"

As he spoke, Jayne studied her uncle. Every movement was intriguing. She hadn't laid eyes on any family members, save her parents and sisters, since she was seven. Now to have a relative within arm's reach was almost beyond her comprehension.

As they walked back to the house, Jayne imagined telling her sisters and felt a tingle run along her spine. Yvonne would not remember her uncle at all. In fact, the youngest Reid had no memories of any other family members. All she knew were names, stories, and words on a page.

Even Olivia had been only five when they left Ireland. It was old enough, perhaps, to have some recollections, but Jayne herself had only faint memories of her grandparents and other relatives. It was little wonder that Cass had been able to masquerade as someone else without them realising.

Cass and Jayne exchanged a smile as he pushed open the door. The first thing she saw when she entered was Olivia sitting at the table with her head in her hand.

Olivia jumped up. "How's Jed? The doctor came and said he was fine. Is he really?"

Jayne felt a pang of guilt for being so thoughtless. While she sat in the stable chatting with Cass, her sisters had been longing to know what was going on. "Jed is sleeping peacefully. We just checked him again before we came here."

Olivia frowned. "Where have you been? I thought you must have been with Jed the whole time."

Jayne shook her head. "There's so much to tell you. So much has happened since I found Jed's horse this morning. I want to hear your stories too." She looked at Aiden and Imogen as they huddled near the fire with solemn expressions, and Yvonne, who still sat at the table. Then she glanced at Cass again. Despite the gloomy mood in the house, there was a twinkle in his eyes. As much as she wanted to tell the others about Uncle Casey right away, she supposed she should save the best news until last. She looked at Cass to see if he would say anything. When he didn't, Jayne decided to dive in.

"Everyone sit down, and I'll go from the start." Jayne sank into the nearest chair and waited for the others to seat themselves. "First of all, I had trouble fetching the doctor."

Olivia nodded. "We figured the doctor must've been out when you took so long, but we just kept praying."

Jayne shook her head. "The doctor was at his house. It was Lamberton that caused me trouble."

Olivia's eyebrows shot up.

Before her sister could say anything, Jayne went on. "He stopped me halfway to town."

Yvonne shuddered, her face mirroring the terror Jayne had felt. "I would've run away screaming."

Jayne smiled, something she hadn't been able to do at the time. "I was extremely alarmed but knew I had to get the doctor. And I also didn't want to lead him straight back to you. Just when I thought I wouldn't be able to cope, a verse leapt before my eyes." Jayne stood. "I'll be right back."

She left the others staring after her and went into the bedroom to fetch her now-precious piece of cloth. When she came back, she held it up for everyone to see the embroidered words. "Jed read this verse one night to us, but I could never understand it. The words just didn't seem real to me. But when I was confronted by Mr. Lamberton, I desperately wished for a father's protection and presence. That's when I finally understood what this verse meant." She paused a moment before reading the verse aloud. " 'A father to the fatherless, and a judge of the widows is God in His holy habitation.' "

Jayne gazed at the embroidery. While its dainty blue flowers and swirling leaves were beautiful, it was the verse that captivated her heart. "I knew I was safe in the arms of my heavenly Father, and I had courage to face whatever danger came." She locked eyes with her sisters. "No matter what happens to any of us, we are never out of our Father's care."

Silence filled the room as Jayne placed the embroidery on the table and ran her hand over its soft patterns. Then she took her seat and set her thoughts back on the tale waiting to be heard. "This encounter was far worse than the time Lamberton came here. He had less restraint and even threatened me with his gun." Feeling embarrassed about her next words, Jayne looked over at her uncle. As he met her gaze, his relaxed features gave her confidence that he would understand. "When Cass rode up, I didn't

It was then that Jayne noticed Aiden and Imogen still sitting on the floor by the fire. They appeared left out and unsure what to do. Jayne wondered again what their past held and what their future would bring. Would they always feel so alone? Her musings were interrupted by Yvonne's laughter. Jayne turned back in time to see Yvonne hugging her new-found uncle.

"Won't you have tea with us, Uncle Casey?" Olivia's eyes shone with happiness.

Cass shook his head, the regret clear on his face. "I don't believe there's anything I'd rather do, but I don't like leaving Jed any longer."

Olivia nodded. "You're right. Someone ought to be with him."

Jayne's mind raced. "How about we have a special meal tomorrow evening? If Jed is up to it, we can eat it with him in his hut. We have so much to rejoice about."

Yvonne nodded, spinning on her tiptoes. "It'll be a family celebration. We'll have time to cook something extra nice."

"And we'll be able to tell Jed our secret about Cass, I mean Uncle Casey." Olivia corrected herself with a laugh that made the whole room ring with merriness.

Cass looked at all three of his nieces and nodded. "It sounds like a wonderful idea. I'll look forward to seeing you all then." He crouched down to tousle Imogen's hair, then turned to go.

Jayne followed. "Thank you for sitting with Jed. Some of us will come out later to take a turn."

As Cass stepped out the door, Yvonne skipped up behind him, with Olivia on her heels. "Bye, Uncle Casey. I can't wait for tomorrow."

A Father of the fatherless,
and a judge of the widows, is
God in His holy habitation.

Psalm 68:5

 GLOSSARY

Billy/Billycan: a lightweight cooking pot made out of tin. Commonly used for boiling water or making tea over a campfire.

Lolly: a sweet treat or candy

Pannikin: a small metal drinking cup with a handle

The Bush: a term used to describe native Australian forest

Chook: an Australian name for a chicken

Mam: an Irish name for mother

Auchenblae: an Irish house name meaning 'home'

Land Selection: the selection of crown land in Australian colonies by settlers. The Victorian *1869 Land Act* required settlers to pay half of the price of an allotment of land at £1 per acre upfront. The settlers then had to continue to pay rent and make specific improvements to obtain full ownership. If they failed, they lost everything.

AUSTRALIAN AND WORLD EVENTS

1851 Gold found in Buninyong and Ballarat, starting the Victorian gold rush.

1854 The Battle of the Eureka Stockade takes place between miners and troopers in Ballarat (10km or 6 miles from Buninyong).

1859 Rabbits successfully released in Australia by Thomas Austin of Geelong, leading to widespread rabbit plagues.

1859 Charles Darwin publishes his book, *Origin of the Species*.

1860 Burke and Wills expedition leaves Melbourne to cross the continent from south to north.

1861 American Civil War begins

1867 Laura Ingalls Wilder is born.

1868 Last convict ship, the *Hougoumont*, arrives at Fremantle, Western Australia, ending convict transportation to Australia.

1868 Granny Smith apples first propagated by Maria Ann Smith in New South Wales.

1869 World's largest gold nugget found in Victoria. The *Welcome Stranger* weighed 72 kilograms or 159 pounds.

1872 The year *Jayne's Endeavour* is set in.

1872 Australian Overland Telegraph Line (3,200km or 1,990 miles of line) connects Darwin to Port Augusta in South Australia, allowing fast communication between Australia and the rest of the world.

1872 In Victoria a "free, compulsory, and secular" education act is passed. All children over six must go to school.

1873 Horatio Spafford pens the hymn "It is Well with My Soul."

1876 Alexander Graham Bell makes the first successful telephone call.

1878 "Advance Australia Fair" is written by Scottish composer, Peter Dodds McCormick.

1880 First telephone exchange opens in Melbourne.

1880 Capture of bushranger Ned Kelly

"For the kingdom is the LORD's: and He is the governor among the nations."

Psalm 22:28

$\mathcal{A}$CKNOWLEDGEMENTS

With God all things truly are possible.

I started the process of writing *Jayne's Endeavour* amidst a major physical struggle—a back injury that made sitting almost impossible. The fact that you hold this book in your hands is a testament to God's faithfulness.

I'm so grateful for my parents (David and Maree) and my siblings (Robert, Johanna, Caitlin, Timothy, and Jonathan). Their support, prayers, and encouragement meant so much to me during this trial.

I want to proclaim that God's strength is made perfect in weakness!

* * *

I'm in awe of the way God helped me with every twist and turn of the writing process. He blessed me with so many ideas and caused the plot to come together far better than I ever could have! May God be glorified through this book. Without Him, it would not exist!

Mum, thank you so much for all the times you listened to my dead-ends and helped me come up with the next scene. You read my first attempts and encouraged me, while at the same time being honest! You've spent *hours* reading the entire manuscript multiple times and giving me valuable feedback. My novel is much better because of you. Thank you for your endless encouragement!

Dad, thank you for your enthusiastic response when you finished pre-reading *Jayne's Endeavour* and for being interested when I first told you my story idea so many years ago.

A big thank you to my sister, **Johanna**, for the hours she spent carefully going over my book. Her edits were invaluable. I'm so grateful for her encouraging nature.

Thank you also to my youngest sister, **Caitlin**. I appreciate the many times you stopped what you were doing to answer my questions (before I went crazy). You must have heard me say, *"Hey Caitlin, what sentence sounds better?"* way too many times!

Jessica, you became my sister-in-law during the writing of *Jayne's Endeavour*. But even before that you were excited about my novel. Thanks for all your encouragement and enthusiasm!

Pa and Nana, thank you for your interest not just in my book but in me. Your input in my life means a lot. I love you both heaps!

I'm truly grateful to my whole family. They've put up with me prattling on about Jayne's story and given heaps of their time. I love you all!

Mrs. Buijs, it's finally done! You must have thought you'd never hear those words. Now you won't have to keep asking if it's finished yet. Although there is book two . . . Thank you so much for spurring me on!

Elisabeth Adams, thank you for your skill as an editor! I learned a lot during the process of working with you and am grateful for your perception and ability to tweak scenes until they shine!

Amanda Tero, it's been a blessing to have a fellow author to talk writing with! Thanks for being the first non-family member to read my manuscript and for encouraging me forward when I was at a standstill.

Be on the lookout for book two of the JOY series—*The Orphans' Secret!*

"They're hiding something, and I don't like to think what it might be."

Jayne sighed and fixed her gaze on the sky. Fluffy clouds glared back at her. "Or what it might make them do."

Secrets linger in the shadows of Aiden and Imogen's eyes. But they can't hide their past forever—or can they? What will it take to cause the children to open up? And will these discoveries be the Reid sisters' undoing?

Find out in book two of the JOY Series!

Be the first to hear about new books by Lauren Compton. Sign up for exciting announcements at **www.NovelsThatEncourage.com.au/subscribe**

About the Author

Lauren Compton writes books not just to entertain but to encourage. Her desire is to write books that point readers to her heavenly Father while at the same time being a whole lot of fun!

She values you, her readers, and would love to have you stop by at **www.NovelsThatEncourage.com.au**